Behind You

Behind You

a novel

Catherine Hernandez

HARPER**AVENUE**

An imprint of HarperCollins*PublishersLtd*

Published by Harper Avenue, an imprint of HarperCollins Publishers Ltd

First Canadian edition

HarperCollins books may be purchased for educational, business,
or sales promotional use through our Special Markets Department.

HarperCollins Publishers Ltd
Bay Adelaide Centre, East Tower
22 Adelaide Street West, 41st Floor
Toronto, Ontario, Canada
M5H 4E3

www.harpercollins.ca

Library and Archives Canada Cataloguing in Publication

Title: Behind you : a novel / Catherine Hernandez.
Names: Hernandez, Catherine, 1977- author.
Identifiers: Canadiana (print) 20240291808 | Canadiana (ebook) 20240291816
ISBN 9781443469289 (softcover) | ISBN 9781443469296 (ebook)
Subjects: LCGFT: Novels.
Classification: LCC PS8615.E75 B44 2024 | DDC C813/.6—dc23

Printed and bound in the United States of America
24 25 26 27 28 LBC 5 4 3 2 1

To those lost and found

This is a work of fiction loosely based on true events.
It's not about him, it's about us.

Behind You

Chapter 1

Let me use the language I'm most accustomed to: film editing. Imagine I'm editing a scene of two people talking and the director wants me to omit something one of the characters says. When I make that cut from one clip to another, one of my many tasks is to ensure there aren't any audio blips. Personally, I like calling them "apples" instead, because these minute bits of audio from the last clip that you have to trim down for the transition to be seamless are like the peel you shave off an apple. Carefully, bit by bit, not wanting to waste the flesh of the fruit. The audience feels none of this. *Shouldn't* feel any of this. Not if I do my job right. Instead, they focus on the story itself. Like an impeccable sentence, everyone from the director and cast to the creative team pitch in the words to that sentence, but I'm the one who gives that sentence its grammar.

The order of these clips moves your eye towards a particular message, or sensation, or emotion. Change the order, and you change the message.

Maybe that's why I had to edit out the memory of you. To edit the story I have in my head about those days long gone, and pretend that it never changed me. You and I both know that is a lie. Although I imagined your death a thousand times when I was younger, I managed to forget about you. That is ... until last night.

I was in the dark of the video editing suite pulling another twelve-hour shift. The day before, I had received the thumbs-up for my final cut of episode nine of *Infamous*. It's this new True Crime series exploring the most notorious serial killers of the twentieth century. Nothing terribly inventive as far as docuseries go, other than the fact that it's hosted by heartthrob Max Woodruff. Although I'm not sure whose heart he's throbbing. Certainly not mine. Yes, I know I'm a queer woman and I am impervious to his supposed good looks, but the dude has the nerve to call himself a journalist when he's not much more than a celebrity with a podcast. Can you tell by my tone that I've spent one too many hours splicing footage of his Zoolander-like gaze towards the camera? By the time I began cutting episode six, I kept looking up at the ceiling, wondering where I could loop a rope around my neck and end my suffering.

To make things worse, I had Eduardo to contend with. He's one of the producers of this shit show, and I have a sneaking suspicion that, given his surname is Reilly, his original first name was just plain Ed and he changed it to Eduardo to give himself a sense of mystery, because there's not much to him. He's pretending he's all auteur and stuff when he's just vanilla Ed Reilly from Windsor, Ontario, who wears designer spectacles and likes to bark orders at me. That's my take on things, anyway.

I'll let you in on something: I actually love notes. I love getting them, because having the eyes of the story editor or the director on my cuts gives me a different perspective. After staring at the screen piecing things together like a puzzle all day, I definitely run low on perspective. Hearing other people's takes on what can go where, what can stay and what can be nixed always helps me get to the finish line.

But an hour or even fifteen minutes of notes with Eduardo? Yeah. Not so much. During the final screenings with the producers, Eduardo loves to sit on the leather couch directly behind my editing console and breathe down my neck. He's close enough that I can hear his skeleton fingers pensively rubbing the stubble on his chin, like he's the Scorsese of True Crime television. Sometimes he asks me for adjustments, like, "Can you trim a few frames off this clip here?" and I'm like, *Really, dude? Really? Are you frame-fucking me right now?* Jesus Christ. At first, I would bend over backwards for him, trying to realize whatever vision he had. But now what I do is pretend to press buttons and move things around. Then, when I replay a transition for him, he congratulates himself by saying things like "Brilliant! That's exactly what it needed," when in fact I haven't changed anything. It's my little secret. It's horrible, I know. But it helps me get through the day.

Anyway . . . I finally got the thumbs-up for episode nine and was eager to move on to the last episode of the season.

To be honest with you, I didn't even look at who the last killer was for the series. It was later in the day and I was downloading all the materials for episode ten onto my hard drive.

That night, the office was perfectly quiet after my co-workers went home, which meant I could open the soundproofed door to let in some fresh air. The smell of my armpits didn't stink as much as the smell of the tuna fish sandwich my wife had packed me. Nira made me promise to eat better after my last physical determined that I was prediabetic. I've been fine with being fat all my life, but hearing this news was kind of devastating. I had an uncle who was diagnosed with diabetes and it's a major lifestyle change I didn't want for myself. That didn't stop the Chinese bakery beside the office from having a two-for-one special, though, and I was under the spell of my PMS. One thing led to another and I was left with this extra tuna fish sandwich I had to eat so that Nira wouldn't find out that I'd cheated on my diet. Again.

So there I was, stuffing my mouth with lukewarm seafood between two slices of gluten-free bread, when I was emailed the story editor's paper edit. It's sort of like the assembly instructions you get with your IKEA furniture. Only, instead of building a flimsy bookshelf, you're building a True Crime episode full of clichés. On a regular day, I'd look at the time signatures outlined in the paper edit and begin isolating clips of re-enactment footage, which would later be interspersed with newsreels, interviews and animated sequences to illustrate reports of the killer's wrongdoings. A typical sequence could be something like: A class photo with a slow zoom into the innocent face of the serial killer as an innocent child, with a voice-over of one of the killer's kindergarten teachers explaining how sadistic he was even then. This cuts to re-enactment of his mother finding his dead sister in the basement, followed by archival newsreels reporting the death. That sort of thing.

The document was named something innocuous like "Infamous.110.paperedit.stalker." I just opened it and began perusing it, trying to figure out the lay of the land. It wasn't until I started downloading the crime scene photos that I clued in.

One by one, the files filled my hard drive.
ScarboroughStalker.CrimeScene2
ScarboroughStalker.CrimeScene2b
ScarboroughStalker.CrimeScene2c
ScarboroughStalker.CrimeScene3
ScarboroughStalker.CrimeScene3b
ScarboroughStalker.CrimeScene4
ScarboroughStalker.CrimeScene5
ScarboroughStalker.CrimeScene6a
ScarboroughStalker.CrimeScene6b

The first batch was eighty-five photos in total. There were another sixteen folders to go through—one file for each of the Scarborough Stalker's victims. Just seeing his name gave me a sudden tickle in my throat. I coughed hard, lying to myself that I was gagging because the alfalfa sprouts in my sandwich tasted like straw. I picked them out and dumped them into the wastebasket next to my desk. I took a breath. *What the hell is wrong with you? Get to work, Alma,* I told myself as my cursor hovered over each image icon, willing myself to open the file. It's not like I haven't spent weeks looking at photos of dead kids or massacres. I'm not saying I'm this cold-hearted person who isn't affected by the gruesome nature of these atrocities. But work is work. How would an audience ever get to watch this show if I just sat there horrified all the time?

My eyes widened as I opened each one. I had never seen these photos before. Like the rest of the public, I had seen only a PG version of everything that happened. There were also dozens of photos of the five young women who survived his attacks. Ligature marks on their wrists. Wounds on their torsos. Their bruised eyes closed as the camera flashed. I had to remind myself to chew my food. Was I holding my breath? It was time to change gears, I promptly decided. Perhaps this was best viewed during the day, after I'd had some rest. Tomorrow. Tomorrow I would start the crime scene photos.

I began downloading the interview footage with the investigator who finally arrested the serial killer after more than a decade-long search. Usually, I'm a machine. I'm a favourite among producers because I'm efficient. But this time, I couldn't help but watch all two hours of the interview.

Was it the investigator's smug face? His stocky neck, which bulged out of his button-up shirt enough that the sound technician had to move the lav microphone down to the middle of his tie? No. It was the way he described his findings. So pleased with himself. As if stumbling upon clues was a fun game of sudoku or finally finding that missing six-letter word in a crossword puzzle. But he was talking about a serial killer who targeted women and girls.

My rage became real when the investigator described his conversation with his wife after he had successfully put the killer behind bars. "You don't have to worry now, dear," he said with a wry grin. "I took care of it." I isolated the clip so that I could repeat his sentence a few more times. *I took care of it. I took care of it. I took care of it.*

The last of the sandwich crust sat, jagged and sharp, in my throat. This gave me the excuse to make my way to the staff refrigerator and crack open a can of cola (which was not in my diet). The crust moved down my esophagus after three satisfying gulps of sugary liquid.

I raised my can in a mock toast to the empty office. "Don't worry, everyone! He took care of it!" I said at the top of my lungs in the direction of Lois's reception desk. "We're all safe now. He took care of it," I said, turning towards the boardroom.

I saw the clock hanging over the waiting area. Eleven fifteen. I downed a few more sips and dumped the rest of the soda into the sink. In that same sink, I rinsed my mouth out, partly because I had bad breath, partly because I didn't want Nira to smell the two pork buns I'd scarfed down earlier in the day under the aroma of tuna. If I rushed home fast enough, I could still watch an episode of *The Crown* with my wife, without her advancing through the series and using my overtime as an excuse to punish me with spoilers.

Suddenly, the hairs stood up on the back of my neck. I had this overwhelming feeling that someone was watching me. I looked quickly around the office, seeing nothing but my reflection in the darkened windows. Instead of calming me, it heightened the feeling, as though the inanimate objects in the room—the tape dispensers, the lamps, the paper clips—were all staring, frantically pointing at someone behind me that I couldn't see. What made things worse was the silence. I've edited my fair share of suspenseful scenes in the past, and silencing the soundtrack for a brief moment before something scary happens is Thriller Movie 101. I was obviously losing my mind. It was time to go home.

I hastily gathered my backpack and my lunch box and headed out into the warmth of that summer night. In the alleyway at the back entrance to the studio, I could hear crickets and grasshoppers singing their songs to one another. My hands were shaking as I turned the alarm system on. As the door swung closed, I realized I hadn't turned off the office lights but couldn't imagine going back into the building. I was too scared. Characters going back into haunted houses because they forgot something is also Thriller Movie 101. What if something happened? What if someone attacked me?

A figure rounded the corner of the building and I screamed. From the bottom of my belly button to the edges of my lips, I screamed. Eyes closed. Fists tight.

"Are you okay?" said the woman walking her miniature schnauzer.

"You scared the shit out of me!" I said a little too loudly. The woman looked back at me, confused. She was as short as me, standing at a very threatening five feet tall, her dog at a menacing ten inches. In one hand, she held her dog's leash. In the other, she carried a tied-up green bag of her dog's poop.

"Sorry?" she replied with this upward inflection that made me feel foolish.

She passed by me and I tried my best to change my tone and smile. "I thought you were . . . Sorry." The woman turned right, down another alleyway, but the spinning feeling remained, the feeling like I was escaping a house on fire.

I fumbled with my keys, trying to open my car door. I looked behind me. What was that sound? A cracking of a twig? Footsteps? Whispers? No. It was my own heartbeat in my ears. I clambered up into my car, my feet stumbling on the tread. I don't know why Nira insisted on getting an SUV. It's much too tall for my short legs. Shutting the door, I immediately locked it and looked towards the passenger seats. To be extra sure, I even climbed over the driver's armrest into the back and examined the hatchback trunk. Empty. My breath. I was breathing hard. And for what? I rushed home, constantly looking at the rear-view mirror as though I was being chased. I had exactly twenty-two minutes before I had to pull into my driveway and pretend everything was normal.

"You're late, Alma."

I removed my Birkenstocks in our foyer and looked up at Nira, standing at the top of the stairs.

"I'm already in my housecoat. I've had a nice bath. I am going to bed now and having a nice sleep without you. I have to be up early tomorrow."

"For what?" I asked, climbing up to join her, following her down the hall.

"To prep for my interview with the school board. I don't know why I'm even throwing my hat into the ring. There's a long list of other candidates for this vice-principal position." Nira took off her housecoat and hung it up in our walk-in closet, beside the tangle of belts that no longer fit me. She looked so damn cute in her kitten-pattern pyjamas, but I didn't want to distract from this opportunity to encourage her.

"Sure, but they're not you. You're a born leader. You always have been."

Nira made her way to our ensuite bathroom and looked in the mirror, determination in her eyes. "You're right. Ablenook deserves someone with vision. And that's me."

I pouted. "Come on! Don't go to bed yet. Watch the first half of the next episode with me. Just the first half?" I don't know why I was begging for her company—I didn't want to be around anyone. I guess it's what I always did, and I didn't want her to suspect something was awry.

Nira took a cotton swab from a glass canister that sat on our bathroom counter. "If you choose the office over time at home, you have to accept the consequences," she said sarcastically, digging one end of the cotton swab into her right ear.

"You know I have deadlines. People expect things from me. I don't want to disappoint them."

She switched ears and subjects. "Did you eat the sandwich I packed?"

"Yes."

"You're lying."

"I'm not. I ate it. You can check my lunch box."

She tossed the swab into the garbage and squared her shoulders with mine. "I will do no such thing. I should be able to trust that my life partner is telling the truth. Don't you think?" Her gaze was fixed on me, this gaze that saw inside me, through me. It was the same gaze I fell in love with, years ago, the gaze that disarmed all the illusions I tried so hard to build around myself. Now, twenty years into marriage, the gaze detected my lies.

I couldn't hold my breath any longer, and when I released it, out came the truth. Well . . . half of the truth. "Okay. I ate a pork bun."

"Alma!"

"*Two* pork buns. That's all. Just two."

"Alma. How many times have I told you to park the car on the other side of the building, away from the Chinese bakery? That place is like your Achilles heel."

"It doesn't matter where I park. I can smell their buns baking through the walls of the editing suite."

Nira cupped her hands around my face. "I love you, Shortcake." Only Nira could come up with a nickname that was endearing and belittling at the same time. "And I want you to live a long time. Your son wants you to live a long time." I doubted that. Mateo rarely said a word to me these days unless he was asking for something. "Please think of your health. Please."

By the time I took a shower and washed three days' worth

of editor stink off me, Nira was asleep on our bed, softly snoring. We had recently bought one of those space-age beds that claimed to keep the peace between couples by adjusting its height to stop snoring. I used the phone app I had downloaded to adjust Nira's angle. Still dead to the world, she turned onto her back, transforming her throaty groan into an open-mouthed wheeze. So much for that.

I tiptoed down the hallway, hugging my pillow, to go sleep on the couch, as I had been doing for the last several months. Lightly sleeping on the lumpy couch with minor resentment was better than not sleeping on a three-thousand-dollar bed and fuming.

Passing Mateo's room, I could see his light was still on. I debated whether to knock and say hello. Maybe the light was on but he was asleep . . . only I could hear him talking to someone. Or was that his television? Why did we install a television in our teenager's room? To poison him with the kind of garbage I help edit every day? I stepped away from the door, too confused by all the bad parenting choices I had made.

I set myself up downstairs in the living room, making a mess of the sofa pillows and blankets until I felt comfortable. Somewhat comfortable. Not comfortable at all. The silence was unbearable. The smell of Nira's pork vindaloo was still thick in the air. How could she expect me to lose weight when she cooked so well? Several minutes passed as I watched the light from passing cars scan across the ceiling. Sort of like the suburban version of counting sheep, I guess. It only made me notice my bad paint job over the pantry doors. Nira had warned me to use paint tape and scoffed at me believing I had a steady hand, and now look. I have to redo it. Oh well. I added it to my never-ending to-do list and draped my forearm over my eyes, willing sleep to come. It didn't work.

Now . . . how would I edit what happens next if I were given the footage of my life? How would I best structure this sequence? I would start with an image of me sighing heavily, then reaching across the coffee table for the remote control, the plan being to turn the television on to something light-hearted, like HGTV. Nothing like a renovation show to let the mind go blank. But that's not what happens. Instead, the camera follows my hand about to touch the remote control before I lose my balance and fall headfirst into the table's sharp corner. Wide shot of me silent-screaming in pain, not wanting to wake my family.

Misleading the audience towards a comical moment, the camera follows me as I free myself from the tangle of bedding and make my way down the hallway, clutching my swelling face. Close-up of my free hand slapping the wall in the darkness, trying to find the light switch to the ground-floor powder room. I find it. I turn on the lights.

Over-the-shoulder shot of me looking in the mirror at my reflection. I gasp. Shot of my tongue as it touches the edge of my bloody lip. The taste of copper pennies. Extreme close-up of my iris as it dilates, followed by rapid flashbacks of the past.

Me. Sixteen-year-old me, in the back of that car, with a bloody lip. You. Twenty-year-old you, on Missing posters all over Scarborough.

If I were to edit this scene, the flashbacks would stop there. I would have me icing my face, going back to the couch and pretending all was well. But I have no control over this footage. What we lived . . . what you suffered . . . was no movie. I remember you, Victoria Ruiz. Last seen on your morning run in Colonel Danforth Park. And here you are, running back into my life.

Chapter 2

Our brown Mercury Cougar arrived at our Scarborough Orton Park home in the summer of 1987. From the back seat, crowded with houseplants and bags of clothes, my sister, Leah, and I peered at the bungalow sitting on a half-acre lot under the shade of an ancient oak tree. Although we were only a short drive away from our old apartment close to Toronto's crowded downtown core, it felt as though we had entered another world of wide-open spaces and strip malls.

"There they are!" Mom pointed at the movers filing out of the truck parked in our long driveway. She positioned the boat of a car far enough away from the truck to allow the workers to extend the ramp and begin transporting our furniture inside. It was a bit of a large truck, considering our meagre belongings, but Mom hadn't had a choice. She needed as much help as she could get. "Okay. Let's empty out the car and stay out of the movers' way, ha?"

Leah and I exited the car. I was happy to move my legs

from under the box I was forced to put on my lap. It was one of those last-minute boxes with things such as our umbrellas, jackets and yesterday's mail. I took a brief moment to assess my new neighbourhood, since I had not seen anything beyond the newspaper real estate listing Mom had shown me. It was like I had been transplanted into a living, breathing episode of *The Flintstones*. Mid-century house, tree, long driveway. Mid-century house, tree, long driveway. Mid-century house, tree, long driveway. Across the street, I saw an interruption in this pattern with a slight bend in the lace curtains (the same lace curtains everyone seemed to have), as though someone was looking at me from inside. I waved and the curtain slid closed.

"Is your father here?" I turned to find a lean man in coveralls standing by his parked cube van. I did as I always did when this question was asked and called out to my mom. She exited the house with a roll of packing tape around her wrist like a bracelet.

"What is it, Alma?"

I pointed to the technician, who lifted his toolbox and said, "I'm here to hook up the phone line. Is now a bad time?"

Mom looked at her watch with urgency. "No, no. Please come inside." I picked up the box and followed them both underneath the angled carport, through the side door, into the hive of activity, with movers coming in and out with lumpy mattresses and second-hand sofas. We walked along the narrow galley kitchen with avocado-coloured tile and appliances to match, through a dark hallway with sticky wood panelling, into the master bedroom. She pointed with the toe of her sneaker at the white junction box in the corner, buried deep in the mustard shag carpet as though the filthy fibres had grown around it. Mom would never let us walk into the house with shoes on, and seeing her wear her sneakers was a hopeful sign that she had intentions of replacing the carpet with something more hygienic. "I'd like to call my husband before he goes to sleep. So this is good timing."

"Sleep?" the technician asked, confused, as it was morning.

"Time zones. He's in the Philippines."

"Ah. Gotcha." The technician did a fake salute before getting to work with his tools.

"Okay," he said moments later. "All hooked up. Do you have your phone?"

Mom's eyes lit up. "Yes! We do." She turned to me. "Alma! Come." She dug her hand deep into the box I had carried in, tossing items she didn't want onto the floor. She retrieved our maroon rotary dial phone and handed it to the technician, who clicked the jack into place.

He picked up the receiver and listened. "Yup. All done." The technician had not even left the room before Mom was dialling my father.

"I need you to sign, please," the technician whispered while my mother held the receiver to her ear. Mom signed and waved the technician away. As she always did whenever she called Daddy, she fixed her feathered hair, as if he could see her. From where I was standing, I could hear the rhythmic beep of an overseas call, and I watched the slow deflating of my mother's face as the beeping persisted with no answer.

When she caught me looking at her, hoping alongside her, she placed the receiver back into its cradle. "We'll try again later."

Once the movers were done and gone, Mom made a second attempt to call, this time summoning me and Leah when he answered. "Carlos? Hello? Hello?" There was always the awkward first two minutes when the connection was bad and our ears had to get accustomed to the faraway sound of Daddy's voice. Sweetly, in that singsong way she always spoke to Daddy, she said, "Yes. I wanted to call you with our new number. That way, you can call us. Any time." She recited the number, even urging my father to write it down while Leah and I looked at each other. It felt uncomfortable to witness these calls unfold in disappointment each time. "I know it's late. I guess I can call you tomorrow when you do have a paper and pen." I bit my lip and looked down. Leah crossed her arms and shifted her weight from one foot to the other. "One sec. Here are the girls."

Mom waved her hands at us to come forward. We approached and she knelt at our feet before making us share the receiver between our two ears the way we always did. Even though Leah bent down slightly, she held the phone in a way that made me struggle to match her taller, spindlier frame even if I was standing on the toes of my wide feet.

"Hi, Daddy."

"Hello."

We both waited that long pause as the magic of telecommunication sent our words across the ocean to my father's house somewhere in Manila, somewhere I had never been.

We heard him clear his throat then greet us with his gruff voice. "Hello, Alma. Hello, Leah. Are you being good girls?" It had been a while since I had seen him. Years, in fact, and I had a difficult time recalling his face each time we were subjected to this ceremony. I started imagining him as Ricardo Montalbán from *Fantasy Island*, only darker brown, holding the phone while surveying his tropical surroundings through smoked glasses.

"Yes, Daddy," we said in unison. I looped my fingers into the coils of the phone cord, playing with it like I usually did, and my mother flicked my wrist.

"Stop doing that," Mom whisper-shouted. "You're going to ruin it." I obeyed and folded my hand into my armpit. It was as painful as a dentist appointment trying to figure out what to say to him, anything to keep him on the phone for our mother's sake. What had changed since we spoke last week? Mom rose a bit from her knees in excitement. "Tell him about your room. Tell him!" she urged Leah, sweat gathering in her neck folds.

Leah's jaw shifted to the side. She took a deep breath and said, "The house is . . ." Leah looked at the dusty stalactites of the popcorn ceilings. "It's really great. I have my own room now, so Alma and I don't have to share, and um . . . I start grade nine this fall . . . so . . . yeah."

"Fantastic!" exclaimed the Ricardo version of my father. Before I could tell him that I was generous enough to give away most of my toys to charity because I was a big girl now, he said, "Well . . ." I could already hear the departure in his voice. He was always creative with how he got out of conversations with us so quickly. "Daddy is tired because your mommy called me very late. So . . . take care and listen to her, okay?"

"Yes, Daddy," Leah and I said in unison.

Leah added, "Here's Mom," before handing the phone back to Mom, who eagerly put it to her ear.

"Hello? Carlos? Hello?" I could already hear the dial tone, and judging by Leah's widening eyes, she could too. Daddy had hung up on her. My mother's face reddened as she pretended to continue the conversation. "Oh. I . . . I love you too, Carlos," she stuttered over the high-pitched hum. Mom turned around, thinking we could not see her wipe tears from her eyes, then turned back to us, continuing this ruse with a smile. "Yes. The girls are so happy with the house. We can't wait for you to come here and join us finally." Her voice cracked on the last word. "Good night, handsome. Love you." She hung up and looked at us. "What? Why are you looking at me like that?" Leah and I carefully retreated from the room as Mom shamefully closed the door behind us.

The muffled sound of Mom weeping dog-whistled something deep inside me. I remembered another time when Mom and Dad were fighting. She had changed jobs from being a low-stress, low-pay bookkeeper for a family-owned construction company to a high-stress, higher-paid accountant at a law firm. On our kitchen corkboard, positioned on the wall underneath a velvet painting of Jesus's last supper, Mom pinned her hard-earned pay stubs and deposit slips into their savings account. I had been eating my morning cereal, reading our strictly observed monthly budget, which Mom had printed on dot-matrix paper from the office, when I overheard Mom on the phone speaking to Daddy. Same singsong voice, only pleading, "Darling, I'm not accusing you. I'm just—" Mom paused while my father shouted at her on the other end. "Yes, but . . . darling . . . I'm already saving for the down payment. And we're counting on you for the— Hello? Hello? Carlos?" She slammed the phone several times into the cradle on the wall, then there was silence. While twirling the cereal around in my bowl, I made the mistake of asking, "Mom? What's a down payment?" and she turned to me, screaming, "It's what I have to pay to make sure you have a home to live in!" I scrambled, thinking she would be buoyed by a token of appreciation. Using yellow construction paper, I made her a coupon with her crayon portrait on the front, and on the back I scribbled, *GOOD FOR ONE HUG.* She never cashed it in. Instead, Mom sat at the end of her bed and held the coupon to her face as she cried. I tried to rub her shoulder, but she recoiled at my touch. I left her alone, thankful she didn't throw it at me.

This time I was even more nervous, since the house was empty and I couldn't remember where I'd packed that yellow construction paper. Before I could knock on Mom's bedroom door and ask, Leah tugged at my shirt.

"Don't bother her. Come on. Let's check out downstairs!"

I reluctantly followed my sister, who was already mischievously running down the hallway, through the kitchen and down the stairs into the darkness of the basement, leaving me alone on the landing.

"We should help Mom unpack," I said, bending down and peering into the pitch black below. No response. "Where did you go, Ate Leah?"

"Ooooooooh! Ooooooooh!" Leah sang back like a ghost.

"Stop iiiiit! Turn on the lights. I can't see you," I whined.

"You do it. Come down and turn them on yourself." Leah's new, curt teenage voice felt sharp in the air.

Not wanting to be called a baby, I slowly made my way down to the basement. The air became several degrees colder. I sucked the drawstring of my hooded sweatshirt, as I always did when fear overwhelmed me. My eyes adjusted and I could see a laundry room to the left of the steps and a small storage room to the right. In front of me was a larger space that I could not make out. I stepped forward. The sound of breathing.

I removed the drawstring from my mouth and held the wet fibres tightly in my fist, trying my very best to appear confident. "Ate Leah? I can't find the light," I said, even though I wasn't looking. "This isn't funny. Come on. I can't see you." I was frozen, facing this big black void. Something clutched my shoulder. "AHHHHH!"

Leah switched on the light and rolled her eyes. "You're such a baby."

To deflect from my lack of bravery, I said, "We're supposed to be unpacking. Mom's gonna get really angry."

Leah tightened the elastic on her side ponytail and slotted her hands into the pockets of her pink windjammer. Dismissively, she replied, "Fine. Let her get angry. I don't care," as though Mom's past episodes didn't leave Leah in tears or hiding. Leah walked the perimeter of the basement's icy parquet flooring. "This place is buck."

I had to agree. The previous owners had tried to give the place Tudor-like character by installing brown framing and wainscotting. But with the faux candelabras and low ceilings, it resembled a creepy dungeon instead.

The main floor was no better. It was obvious that chain-smokers had lived here before us, as there was a yellow tint on all the surfaces. There was even this jaundiced circle on the ceiling in the living room. Judging by the chair mark in the carpet, this was where the man of the house sat and smoked his pipe.

By the time midday rolled around, Mom had gone back to unpacking boxes, albeit with swollen eyes and a red nose. She even called for pizza delivery, which I took as a sign that she was feeling better . . . at least for now.

"I'll start with the garage. Make that into our living room. That way, we won't have to be so cramped in here. We can spread out a bit," Mom explained over lunch in the kitchen, her arms sweeping over her grand vision. Leah and I sat around the pizza box and munched away silently, not wanting to interrupt her usual pipe dreams. She wiped her greasy mouth with a napkin and continued, sparkles in her eyes. "We'll remove the carpet and put in hardwood. Add a second bathroom. Then we'll redo the basement. That way Leah can have her own special space downstairs."

Leah's face lit up. "Really?"

"Really," Mom replied, rubbing her thumb over Leah's cheek with a wistful smile. "Of course . . . we'll have to wait until your daddy gets here. He's the handy one. He'll build you a beautiful room and—"

"But . . . he's not—" I made the mistake of interjecting. Once I realized what I had done, I tried to stop myself before I provoked the volatile storm that was our mother. It was too late.

Mom's face shifted yet again. Her nostrils flared. Her lips twisted. She threw her half-eaten slice back into the pizza box hard enough that a crumb ricocheted into my eye. "What are you talking about? You know your daddy is coming back. He's just away for his contract. You know this," my mother exclaimed, lying to herself and us, like she had for years.

As I covered my watering eye with one hand, I couldn't help my curiosity and stammered, "But . . . wha . . . what's Daddy's job? Why does he have to—"

"Alma! Don't!" Leah whined with a raspy voice, like she was stopping me from kicking a wasps' nest.

Mom stood up, seething at me. "What's wrong with you, Alma?!" Before I could duck, she grabbed me by the hair at the back of my head and slammed my face into my plate with every word. "YOU! AND! YOUR! STUPID! QUESTIONS!" Horrified by her own actions, she stepped back and looked at me, cheese and sauce all over my face, before storming out to her bedroom. The sound of Mom crying again. I started crying too.

As Leah left the kitchen, she said over her shoulder, "Shut up and eat your pizza, Alma. You always have to ruin shit."

My face throbbing, I obeyed. I took a bite of pizza and looked down at my feet. She was right. It *was* my fault. How? It was never made clear. But things were always my fault—from Dad's absence to heavy traffic to bad weather. I was reminded of this every single day. The pizza in my mouth was mushy and flavourless. I did what I always did back then when things went bad. When I was told I was bad. When I was a bad, bad girl. My vision went foggy, until everything was a blur, until my body was numb. Until my sister poked the pizza I had squirrelled into my cheek.

"Wake up, weirdo!" Leah screamed at me. I startled. Shame burned from where Leah had prodded me in the face. The pizza was nothing but a ball of paste in my mouth. "You're supposed to be setting up your room! Go!"

I looked around and outside the mildew-covered windows. The afternoon sun hung low in the oak tree and the sound of Mom's crying had stopped. How long had I been sitting there?

I shook my head out of my fog and went to the washroom to rinse the sauce off my face and out of my hair. I had to get started with my room. After my big mistake—whatever that mistake was—I was going to make it up to Mom. I was going to set up my bedroom lickety-split. Put everything in its place. Wipe all surfaces. Mom was going to come into my new bedroom and be amazed at the progress I'd made, all at lightning speed.

One by one, I took each of my outfits from the garbage bag they were stuffed into, draped them over hangers and arranged them neatly in my narrow closet. It was tight, but I managed to cram in all my second-hand, outdated ensembles by pushing the wooden slotted bifold doors as wide as possible. In my dresser drawers, my panties and undershirts sat in perfect rows. My socks in orderly bunches. On top of the dresser, I displayed all my special things. My Barbie container (the doll's legs were removed so that its torso sat on a margarine tub, hidden by a large crocheted dress). My coin towers (three locked burgundy cylinders measured how much loose change I had collected). And my lockbox. (A blue plastic box. With a lock.) I fussed with the placement of these objects so that it looked intentional. Maybe if Mom saw how established my room was, she would forgive me.

I kept waiting for Mom to look in on me. I kept waiting to show her so she could see all the hard work I had put into this task. I listened through the wall that I shared with her room and heard nothing. No banging of drawers or doors. Banging was my mother's unspoken language. And if I couldn't hear banging, how would I know if she was still angry with me?

I decided to keep on working, keep moving, to appear productive so that I was good enough to keep and not bad enough to hit. In this theatre of industriousness, I felt my body temperature rise. I tried to open the boxes of my books, but my hands were too sweaty to break through the tape that sealed them shut. I wiped my palms on my shorts.

"Nice to meet you. I'm Russ Stolks," I heard a voice say. I peeked through the silky beige curtain of my bedroom window and looked outside. My mother was shaking hands with a stout man in his sixties. His hair was styled with coils at the front like Ronald Reagan, but it was bright white like Donahue. Behind him, I could see his mower standing in the middle of his perfectly manicured lawn, halfway through making checkerboard patterns in the grass.

"Hello, neighbour. I'm Luz." Mom spoke to him in the same singsong voice she used with Dad, as if all was normal despite our quarrels behind closed doors. Nothing to see here. She even managed to say something under her breath to make Russ chuckle before he spotted me at the window and waved with his gardening gloves pinched between his thumb and forefinger. I hid behind the curtain, but it was made of translucent polyester. Through the fabric I saw Mom signal for me to come outside, Filipino-style, with her hand pointing down.

I was confused, considering our last hysterical exchange, but I did as I was told and exited the patio doors and stood a distance away. I could feel our lawn's long blades of grass scratching at my ankles. Mom and Russ were still engaged in conversation.

"Really? You wouldn't mind?"

"Absolutely not. I'm glad to mow the lawn until your husband returns." Russ paused and turned my way with a warm smile. "Well, hello, young lady."

Mom looked at me. "Go on. Introduce yourself to Mr. Stolks."

"Hello, Mr. Stolks," I mumbled, mostly to his shoes.

"And what's your name?"

"Alma."

"Well, isn't that pretty?" Russ turned to Mom with a false grin. "Just as pretty as she is." That was a lie. I knew Russ didn't think I was pretty. I knew my mom didn't think I was pretty either. I get it. I wasn't.

A meaty, hairy hand was extended in my direction, and I knew I was supposed to shake it, like I'd seen in episodes of *L.A. Law*. I knew it had to be firm. I did my best and squeezed his hand as much as I could, even giving it a good yank downwards as if we had made a deal. Just as our hands parted, Russ ran his finger along my palm. Lightly. Slowly. I cringed. The sensation tickled. Tickled? No, it made the hairs on my arm stand on end. I clutched my fist to my chest as if I had caught an insect that I needed to examine. Make sense of.

"Go help your sister" is what my mother said in response to my strange reaction to Russ's handshake. I went inside to continue unpacking.

Later, when Mom headed out to pick up more takeout for dinner, I went to my sister.

"Ate Leah?" I asked her while she was looping drapes over a curtain rod in her room.

"What is it now, Alma?"

Her exasperated tone made me worried I would make her angry again, but I had to ask. "I met our new neighbour. He's an old guy named Mr. Stolks."

"So?" Leah said, ascending a stepping stool towards the window with the curtain rod.

"He did this thing to my hand." I demonstrated, pretending to shake my own hand, then showing Leah the lingering caress that followed.

I searched Leah's face for answers, a reaction, anything to confirm that the muddy feeling in my belly was justified. There was a brief, ever so brief scowl, and a twitch between her brows. A fleeting moment of disgust, like the face she made when she had opened a forgotten container of leftovers and braced against the smell of rot. It was quick enough that had I blinked, I would have missed it. It was there, that look. Then it was gone.

With a sigh, she said, "Alma. He didn't mean anything by it. That didn't happen." I wanted to refute what she was saying, but inside I was already questioning if it had happened at all. Leah clicked the rod into the brackets.

Victoria, where were you at this time, when I was trying my best to sidestep the land mines of my family? Were you setting up your room as I was, but in your student residence just east of us? Were you excited about your first year at university? What posters and photos did you put up on your walls? Did you have to share a room? Wait. Yes. Yes, you did share a room. I remember now. Your roommate was the last person to see you alive. No. The last person to see you alive was your killer.

Chapter 3

The squeak of metal hinges pulls me out of my sleep. I sit up fast enough to catch a glimpse of the mailman stepping off our stoop and heading to our next-door neighbour's house. What time is it? If the mailman just visited, then it should be . . . mid-morning? Maybe? I slide my hands between the sofa cushions in search of my phone. I keep telling myself to put it on the coffee table before falling asleep. Where the hell did it go? I begin folding my blanket, hoping it will magically appear. Instead of my phone, a bag of frozen peas, now thawed and wet with condensation, falls to the carpet from the blanket's layers and I suddenly remember putting it on my face after last night's mishap. When I touch my lip, I'm relieved to feel the swelling has subsided. Like many things, only I know the pain that dwells there beneath the surface.

Another vague memory comes to mind of Nira kissing me goodbye before she headed off to the school. She gave me instructions about something, which I don't recall. I'm pretty sure whatever it was was important and I'll pay the price for not following the instructions. I'll text her today and ask. Hopefully, she'll get the text during her lunch hour and all will be sorted.

Shit. Still no phone. My stomach grumbles. I bet if I have a full stomach I'll be better equipped to find it. Inside the refrigerator, I see another lunch bag. A yellow sticky note adheres to it that reads, *Enjoy! Don't forget what I told you.* Holy hell. What did she say? Could she not have used the space on the chit of paper to reiterate her instructions, which she issued to me while I was still sleeping? Frustrated, I put the lunch bag into my backpack by the door. I'm so annoyed, I decide that this is my licence to search the kitchen for some fun food. As in, not the kind of breakfast we have with friends on the weekend with cute fruit cups and homemade granola, but the kind of breakfast I used to eat after pub nights in university. Yeah. That's the ticket. I deserve it. Late nights. Cryptic, snoring wife. I deserve at least one sugary treat. Maybe two.

Just as I am about to reach for the stepladder filed between the counter and the fridge, the stepladder that allows my short body to reach for all the fatty, artificially flavoured, chemical-ridden food on the top shelf, I hear keys turning the front door's lock.

"Oh. Uh . . . hi, Mama. You're still home?" Mateo stands on the stoop, his hand grasping the doorknob. I swear to god he's grown a couple of inches since yesterday. Or is it just the height of his curls? When he was a baby, he would go through these cycles of fat and wide, then a growth spurt would make him long and lean. Now that he's a teenager, he seems to be growing exponentially taller and skinnier. Perhaps one day his arms and legs will be the right size for his massive hands and feet.

I stop myself from observing my child with loving wonder and try my hand at a more assertive facial expression. "Um, yes. I'm still home because I have a late start. I set my own hours. Hello, Hong." I give a disapproving wave to my son's girlfriend, Hong, who shyly threads her long black hair behind her ears and hides behind Mateo. The two have been together for a couple of years and they've become pretty serious. Serious enough to skip school and have sex, I guess.

They both cautiously enter the foyer and remove their shoes. Hong places her flip-flops neatly with heels against the wall while my son uses his toes to remove his Vans from his giant feet and leaves them in a messy pile right in front of the door.

I put my hands on my hips. Since when do I put my hands on my hips? "You, however, *don't* set your own hours. Aren't you supposed to be in school, young man?" I wince at the sound of my own voice. *Young man?* Who am I? I realize I am still up on the stool, one arm's length away from the Bad Food Shelf, so I step down as gracefully as I can, without losing eye contact. I got this. I'm cool.

"Today was credit recovery day."

Instead of saying "Huh?" which is the first, clueless thing that comes to mind, I say, with the same tone as one of those investigators in *Law & Order*, "And what does *that* mean?" Yes! Excellent delivery. I'm staying firm. Sticking to my guns. Not looking foolish.

Mateo's eyeballs roll to the side the same way they did when I asked him how to post an Instagram story. Part confusion that someone wouldn't know something so basic. Part withholding a laugh. "It means, since I'm a straight-A student, I don't need to attend." We both slowly nod at each other as if doing so will make this conversation less painful.

"Hmmm," I say, pretending to still be suspicious. "And you, Hong? You didn't need to attend classes today?"

"No, ma'am." I hate it when she calls me that. "I took extra courses during the summer so that this year I'd have spares to wo—"

"—spend together," Mateo says, finishing her sentence. Hong looks down at her feet then at me, flashing a momentary smile. Has Hong gotten shorter since last I saw her? That's impossible. Teens don't shrink, do they?

After what seems like an eternity of awkward silence, me with my pyjamas and bed-head, them with their flushed faces, Mateo says, "So . . . can Hong and I study upstairs in my room?"

"What do you need to study if you're getting straight As?"

"We just need—"

"No, you may not." My lips tighten, trying my best to be authoritative.

Mateo steps forward while Hong remains by the front door. "What's the problem? It's not like we're gonna head up there and surf porn . . . smoke crack and . . . I dunno . . . have an orgy or something."

"I just . . . I don't feel comfortable with you both . . ." I try to find the words, and while I stammer, Mateo crosses his arms and shakes his head in disgust. I finally spit out, "I don't like you sneaking around, not asking for permission to—"

"I *did* ask for permission! I texted you and Mom that we were coming to the house."

Shit. I don't have my phone to prove he never texted me. He probably did text me. I sidestep this damning fact by saying, "Why are you shouting at me?" even though I too am shouting. Mateo lets out this heavy sigh and I'm tempted to change my mind. "If you texted me asking for permission and you never heard from me, is it asking for permission or are you telling me what you were going to do anyway?"

"Never mind," Mateo grumbles as he signals a departure to Hong. Hong quietly puts her flip-flops on again. "We'll head to the library. Unless . . . we need your permission to do that too?"

"What the hell are you talking ab—?"

Mateo and Hong head out and Mateo slams the door behind them before I can finish my sentence.

Well, that went splendidly. Raiding the Bad Food Shelf doesn't seem like fun now, not that that stops me. After filling my plate with butter tarts, I turn on the television to something mindless. Some talk show with five women sitting around a big table shouting at each other about a celebrity's love life. I hunker down on the couch, and while stuffing my face, I replay the sound of Mateo's heavy sigh over and over again in my head.

What is it that I can't stand about our conversations? What makes my spine stand up straight and brace against the crash of our conflict? Even before it happens, I'm already imagining the worst. For heaven's sake, my own mother didn't give a shit about my feelings when she'd punish me over the most random things, and here I am, completely inept in establishing basic-ass rules around the house.

As much as I understand that it's my job as a parent to lay down the law, the truth is, I hate disappointing him with rules. I hate upsetting him with boundaries. You don't even have to put a gun to my head to make me give you a list of each and every time I have done so. I can remember the circumstances. All the reasons why I screwed up while trying my best to be firm. All the wrong things I said, trying to be lax, then doubling down on those rules. The weather that day. The angle of the sun. What I was wearing. What he was wearing. I'm not kidding. I can describe every moment on this list, and the list goes all the way back to when he was born, seventeen years ago.

Nira went into labour two months early. The little guy's lungs were a mess with respiratory distress syndrome. The nurses encouraged Nira to bide her time pumping breast milk, saying it would give him a fighting chance. The pressure got to her and affected milk supply. It was heartbreaking to watch her plug her boobs into that godawful pumping machine. She would scream to the ceiling, "I need to do this one thing right! Please let me do this one thing right!" I'm not a religious person, but I prayed every day. I prayed to take away the baby's pain. Nira's pain. I had a secret thought that maybe, if I had been the one to get pregnant, he wouldn't be premature. I am three years younger than Nira. She even mentioned this when we began discussing having a family. Eventually, after opening up about all the reasons why I could not bear to be impregnated, the reasons why I knew pregnancy was not an option for my body and the memories that occupied it, she relented.

What did it matter, anyway? We were stuck in this terrifying hospital, wondering every day if that day would be his last, too uncertain about the future to name him. Not until we were discharged three months later and buckled him into his car seat did Nira look at him and say, "Hello, Mateo. Ready to go home?" My heart leapt out of my chest hearing Nira name our child after her grandfather back in Goa.

Naming him did not give me the confidence I needed to forget the precariousness of those first three months of his life, though. As he grew older, I handled him with kid gloves, believing he would break at the slightest touch, the slightest disagreement. Instead of making me a loving parent, this amoeba-like sense of structure made me an ineffectual one. Nira became the mother with the upper hand. I became the parent Mateo rolled his eyes at and dismissed. That's why I am here, stuffing my face with this dessert for breakfast, wondering where I went wrong.

Should I have let him and Hong upstairs? It's only sex, after all. He's seventeen. She's seventeen. It seemed consensual. I should have been cool. Asked him if he had protection. Yes. I should have focused on condoms. And the pill. The morning-after pill and the everyday don't-get-pregnant pill. That would have been the best thing to chat about. Because it's not just about avoiding pregnancy, right? Those damn STDs. Fuck. What a missed opportunity. There was even a bunch of bananas in our fruit basket. I could have done that thing that sex educators do when they show teens how to "wrap it up." I could even have used that term and sounded hip. Informed. Great. Now he will be scarred forever. He'll have a litter of illegitimate children, all of them from different mothers, all of them living hand to mouth because of Mateo's irresponsibility, and it will all be my fault.

I hear my phone ring. The sound of Britney Spears's first number one hit and a rhythmic vibration is coming from underneath my bum. Ha! I found it. "Hello?" I answer, all flustered.

"You didn't do it, did you?" Wow. Nira has such confidence in me.

"Look, I was half-asleep. I don't even remember what you said."

I can tell from the echo in Nira's voice that she has snuck out of her classroom and is talking to me while peeing in the staff washroom. "I told you to please make reservations at Aida's for six tonight."

"I can do that."

"I hope you still can. It's already eleven. Please call before the lunch hour rush. Try to work your magic with Ife and get the window seat."

I don't understand what Nira is talking about. There is

no magic between me and Ife. Nira teases me each time we have dinner at Aida's, which is our fave place to get injera. She believes that one day Ife will be inspired enough by my good looks to finally come out of the closet. She believes the repressed tension Ife has each time I'm present motivates Ife to dole out larger portions. This is completely absurd. I've compared the size of the dishes and Ife's temperament around other customers and there are no discrepancies. She's just a nice person. Besides, no one has ever had a crush on me. Ever. Not even Nira. I still don't know how she ended up marrying me. I had zero game.

"Okay. I have to go. My students are probably dancing around dismembered pig heads on stakes." I shudder at Nira's imagery, remembering yesterday's crime photo footage. "And Alma?"

"Yes, babes."

"Happy anniversary." Click. She already knew I had forgotten.

Shit on a stick. I rush to work, determined to get out of the office no later than five in order to pick up some flowers. Flowers are a good present for year twenty-two, right? Yeah. I'm an asshole.

I park the car crookedly in the lot, trying my best to ignore the smell of pork buns. I smile at my colleagues and rush towards the editing suite.

"Hey. Please check your email. Your tax form needs to be filled out no later than tomorrow," Lois says to me from behind the reception desk.

"Sure thing!" It's been weeks since I've dealt with any email messages outside this show.

The noise of the office all abuzz with creative meetings and administrative tasks annoys me, so I close the soundproof door. Nice and quiet. Just the way I like it. I begin downloading the footage of the newsreels the archivist sent me while I get on the phone with Ife to make a reservation. Well . . . anyone working at Aida's. Not just Ife. It would be nice to hear her voice, but . . . no. She's just a waitress. That's all.

"Hello, Alma."

My cheeks get warm hearing Ife say my name. God. Why does Nira do this? Draw attention to things that don't exist? Now I'm all self-conscious. "Hey, Ife! How did you know it's me?" I croak.

"I recognize your number on my call display."

"Really?" My voice cracks and I cough. "Anyway . . . can I make a reservation for tonight at six?"

"Hmm. Let me see. It might be too busy tonight."

"It's for my wedding anniversary. Nira and me. I really hope you have space."

"Ooooh." Was that disappointment I heard in her voice? "In that case, I can find you a spot. I can get you your favourite table by the window for 7:00 p.m. How about that?"

I'm suddenly ashamed by her generosity. "It's just our twenty-second anniversary. That's all." Why did I say that?

"Wow! Really? That's amazing. Well . . . you're all booked. I will see you tonight."

Did she say "see you" or "see you both"? I'm too embarrassed to ask. Why would I ask? Ife hangs up and I am relieved. Sweaty but relieved. The reservation is booked. I'll get flowers. Nira will forgive my forgetfulness. Or is it carelessness? Or both? Yeah. I'm an asshole.

I take a breath and begin cutting clips as per the director's paper edit. Footage of a reporter standing in front of an alleyway, a bright light shining in his eyes. I chuckle at his 1980s mullet and trench coat. His Walter Cronkite–like voice booms over my speakers, describing how a child found the body of one of the Scarborough Stalker's victims.

Chapter 4

The first time I saw reports of the Scarborough Stalker was when Mom was trying to set up our television in the living room. This was back when our television wasn't so much a device as it was a piece of furniture. Its wee screen was framed by a block of solid wood with intricately turned poles at the edges and carved leaves on its face. If the manufacturers had put as much effort into the technology as they did into the wooden box, the television would have been fabulous. Instead, it broadcast in squiggly lines whatever we could find on the airwaves. Mom didn't mind it because it was free. Free as in someone left it in a dumpster outside our old apartment building. As the saying goes, one man's trash is another man's trash that will do for now.

"A bit higher. No. Too high."

"Mom! I can't. You try." Leah switched places with Mom and let her adjust the antennas. If we tweaked it just right, we could get the signal from a television station in upstate New York. I was instructed to move all metal tchotchkes in the living room close to the screen to help amplify the image. Leah's track and field medals. Decorative serving spoons. An ashtray.

"Hurry! *Little House on the Prairie* is about to start."

Mom did her best but managed to capture the local news station instead.

"Do the police see a connection between the two incidents, Don?" said the anchor, who sat in front of a backdrop of an artist's illustration of the Toronto skyline, done in neon shades of pink and purple.

The reporter on site held an umbrella while the rain gently poured from overhead. "Carol, at this time they are not making any statements about these assaults being connected to one another. During today's press briefing, Police Chief Garrison clearly stated that there is no evidence at this time that the two incidents were committed by the same person."

Back then, I didn't know what an assault was, so what was being said mattered little to me.

"Sit down here, Alma," Leah instructed. She placed the large channel changer on the newly installed carpet (an updated low-pile dusty rose) and pulled its cord to give it more slack. "Play around with the channels to see what we can get."

By pressing firmly on the remote's buttons, I switched the channel just as the reporter began their walk and talk of the crime scene.

"Yes! We did it!" Leah cheered as soon as Michael Landon's mug appeared on the screen. Leah and I danced to the show's intro music, linking arms in a faux pioneer dance.

When did you first hear of the Scarborough Stalker, Victoria? Was it on the news, like us? Or was it your parents who called you, warned you, like so many parents at the time, hoping their daughters would be spared if only they took the necessary precautions?

My mother was too caught up in the act of setting up our new lives to pay attention.

First, we established St. Bernardine as the Catholic church we would attend. While Immaculate Conception was a more remarkable Gothic monument and its choir angelic, it took too long to drive there. The timing of their eleven o'clock Mass had Mom rushing through our cherished silog breakfasts. It simply wasn't enough time to air out the stink of pork and garlic fried rice from our clothes and arrive for the opening procession.

So we settled on St. Bernardine, which was a convenient five-minute drive from our new home. On our first visit to St. Bernardine, I noticed that the sad brick building had a confused architectural identity. Like it wasn't sure if it was a church or a discount outlet. Inside was even worse, with gaudy red carpet that was buckled and stained in high-traffic areas. I did not want to dip my fingers into the holy water at the entrance to the nave. By the looks of the calcium crust around the bowl's edge, it had been a while since someone had cleaned it. Instead, I mimed the action just over the bowl and a young woman did the same right after me, before we both touched our foreheads, hearts and shoulders in a cross. It was you, Victoria. We did that thing Filipinos do when we see each other in the wild and raised our eyebrows in recognition.

The exchange was quick. I'm pretty sure you wouldn't even remember me, an unremarkable and plain kid wearing a hand-me-down floral dress two sizes too large. But I most certainly remember you and your nicely feathered hair. Your hairline in the front, under your teased side bangs, met in a pointed widow's peak. I could never figure out how to make my hair feather like that, no matter how many times I brushed my tresses back from my ears to the nape of my neck. You managed fine, though, wearing what looked to be your Sunday best, with a padded shoulder blazer and pleated skirt. I watched you shuffle with your mother, father and brother into a pew. Your mother handed you a songbook and you began turning the pages with your manicured hands while singing along with the entrance hymn. The church's lone singer looked like Anita Baker but sounded like a heavy smoker.

I picked at an itchy scab on my elbow, wondering when that magic moment would happen that would transform me from an awkward kid to a pretty girl like you and Leah.

I'd had my first Communion in our old neighbourhood, where I was taught to ceremoniously cup my hands and receive the Eucharist. But in this parish, things were different. I lined up with my family to join the rest of the congregation in Communion. We filed out of our pews and into orderly lines to approach the priest, who fed us all the thin wafers of bread, symbolizing the body of Christ. When it was my turn, I cupped both my hands and extended them towards the priest, expecting him to place the wafer in my palms. He did not. Instead, he held the wafer up high as if I were a dog that he was training to do tricks.

"Not in your hands, young lady," Father Michael said, his spectacles sitting at the end of his gin-blossomed nose. "Open your mouth." My skin crawled listening to him say this at the top of his voice, loud enough that everyone could hear him, loud enough to make me an example. I quickly turned to my mother behind me, confused.

Was she embarrassed? Enraged? Resigned? I'm not sure. Maybe she didn't want to draw any more attention to us, one of the few brown families in the congregation. She looked at me and nodded.

Now with my mother's approval, now confused by my mother's approval, I turned back to Father Michael and opened my mouth slightly. Was he going to throw the Eucharist in like a Frisbee? I was nervous. I wasn't very good at sports. My aim was definitely subpar.

"Wider," he said.

The volume of his voice made my mouth clamp shut. From behind me, my mom squeezed my shoulders. *Do it*. I opened my mouth a little more.

"Come on. Open wide."

I did, and he reached in to place the wafer on my tongue, his fingers brushing my lips.

"Good job!" he said in a tone that made my arms hot with shame. "Thatta girl."

After Mass, we piled into our car and Mom announced

that we would drive to McDonald's to get ice cream sundaes. She said it while looking at me from the driver's seat and gently patting my knee, like the sundaes were some kind of apology to make up for something bad that had happened. It was weird, because I had never seen my mother apologize and I didn't know what she was apologizing about. I happily accepted this treat since I would eat anything to get the sour taste of that wafer out of my mouth.

At McDonald's, we put in our orders at the counter. As usual, Mom got a strawberry milkshake. Leah wanted an apple pie.

"And what about you?" said the cashier to me with a smile. Her lips were that dark-brown shade all the girls were wearing in those days, defined with an even darker lipliner. My heart fluttered. This would be one of thousands of times I was smitten over feminine women.

"Hot fudge sundae, please. Double fudge. Double peanuts."

"Someone knows what she wants," the cashier giggled.

Completely overriding my order, my mother stepped forward and said firmly, "Just the hot fudge sundae for her. No extra fudge. No peanuts." She tapped me on the head, making me feel a foot shorter.

We ate our desserts around a plastic table with built-in chairs. Even though I didn't ask, Mom told me I was too old to go into the playroom. That was fine by me. It smelled like feet in there anyway. Looking down at the space between the table and chairs, which were bolted to the floor, I could see my belly. Round and soft. The delight of eating this sweet treat quickly turned sour in my mouth because, in my mother's opinion, my body was much too fat for me to have something in its entirety. I said nothing. I did not complain. I did not mention what had happened with Father Michael during Communion. Just like that handshake with Mr. Stolks, none of it ever happened.

• • •

My mother established which schools we were to attend. The closest Catholic elementary school was St. Xavier. I really wanted to go to Bishop Stevens because it had an indoor pool and art studios, but it was far outside our catchment area.

St. Xavier was nearby but always on the verge of being torn down due to low student numbers. It was badly placed in a neighbourhood that was made up predominantly of Protestants, who would rather shuffle their children to public schools. I wished I could have joined them and jumped from what felt like a sinking ship.

I'm sure my teacher, Mr. Fletcher, felt the same way. His sad eyes and droopy posture told me he had given up on life. Rather than teach us, he would point to a shelf full of *National Geographic* magazines dating back to the 1960s and say, "Find an article. Tell me what you learned." I spent my first month at school clipping pictures about the life cycle of pearl oysters while Mr. Fletcher sang country songs about life's losses. His favourite position was with his right bum cheek on his desk and his left foot on a chair to prop up his acoustic guitar. One day, I asked him if I could try playing it and he refused. "You can play music during band class."

Band class was held in a converted storage room. It used to be where the sports supplies were kept, back when the school had enough students for sports teams.

"Choose whichever instrument you want!" Mrs. Jenkins said to all eleven of us. We looked around the cramped room. Mrs. Jenkins's lone enthusiasm didn't make up for the obvious lack of resources. Could we call ourselves a band when the only options for instruments were flutes and clarinets, some of them broken? I doubted that. But with some digging through the detritus of dusty sports pennants and deflated soccer balls, I was able to find one snare drum, two mismatched sticks and a cymbal. Yes, I had to set the drum on top of a desk. Yes, I had to steady the cymbal stand with my foot to keep it upright. But the drum "set" made our rendition of "Three Blind Mice" rather lively.

Leah chose Our Lady of Perpetual Help high school. Although this meant a whopping two-hour commute one-way on Scarborough's subpar transit, my mother was delighted because it was an all-girls Catholic school, and she assumed this would keep Leah away from hormonal boys. Her plan didn't work. Within a few weeks, Leah was regularly accompanied home by some guy named Len.

Len was unlike any Filipino boy I had met before. I was accustomed to the well-mannered sort who were eager to please their elders. Smart haircuts. Even smarter grades. This dude Len smelled like CK One. He smelled like CK One from a mile away. A city away. The cologne did a poor job of hiding his body odour. The peach fuzz on his top lip was sparse and uneven. His eyes were always half-closed as if in a dreamy state around my sister. With these dreamy eyes he would sniff my sister's fourteen-year-old neck, whisper things into her ear. He and my sister would sit on our couch in the living room for what felt like an eternity, giggling with each other until it was close to the time our mother was due back.

During these make-out sessions, I would hide in my room and fume, wishing I could watch television. Their incessant giggling infuriated me. What could they possibly be talking about that was this funny?

At the end of their first rendezvous, Leah lovingly waved goodbye to him from our foyer, shut the front door, then turned to me with a snarl. "Don't you dare tell Mom."

I replied, "Or what?" because it was something cool that somebody had said in the latest episode of *Magnum, P.I.*

My sister's face shifted, the same way our mother's did just before she was about to unleash her animosity towards us. Leah jabbed the middle of my forehead with her pointer finger. My face flushed. "If you breathe a word of this . . ."

She continued to jab me until my back was against the wall of the entrance hall. I tripped on our neat line of shoes near the front door, and still she jabbed me smack dab between my eyebrows. Bull's eye. Bull's eye. Bull's eye. ". . . I will fucking kill you."

She only stopped once I closed my eyes and just endured the jabs instead of fighting. I could hear her breathing hard, her face just inches away from mine. When I dared to open my eyes, she casually dismissed me with "Who told you to stay?" I wilted and scurried into my room.

I had already set up a safe place, although I would never have called it that back then. I don't think I even knew what I was doing, creating a spot in my room where my family could not hear me cry. It certainly wasn't a conscious choice. It existed in the dark corner between my dresser drawers and my closet. There, I could sit on the carpet with my knees close to my chest, the fibres of my hung clothes and the surface of the wooden bureau absorbing the sound of my misery. I could remove the mask of the dutiful child and sob until the collar of my shirt was damp, until the cuffs of my sweaters were smeared with the snot I had wiped from my nose. My safe place was far enough from everyone that they could be spared my drama while being close enough that I could listen in on the conflict and assess risk. At that very moment, the risk was high; high enough that I would rather get in trouble for not doing my chores than suffer any further interactions with Leah. So I stayed there until I heard my mother come home that evening.

Later that week, I walked home from school, banging my drumsticks on any surface I could find. If I was going to be as good as Sheila E., I would have to practise. I passed the oak tree on our lot, now painted with white insecticide to keep the tent caterpillars under control. I walked up the stoop and used my keys to open the door. The door did not swing open easily, so I pushed harder. Two sets of shoes sat on the welcome mat. My sister's and Len's.

"Hello?" I said into the silence of the house. I went into the living room. The afternoon sunshine bathed over Mom's houseplants. Her floral sofa. The glass coffee table. Mom's porcelain potpourri bowls. "Ate Leah?" If the two were here, why couldn't I hear them?

Down the hallway, I could see movement in the slit underneath Leah's bedroom door. The silence made me uneasy. They were obviously doing more than kissing.

Outside, I heard our car pull into the driveway, two hours earlier than usual. My heart pounded in my chest. I ran in a circle, wondering if I should alert Leah. I managed to grab Len's shoes and throw them into the closet. I slid the closet's mirrored doors closed as a key turned in the lock.

"Hi, Mom," I said nice and loud, like an announcement.

Her face was weird. She didn't even greet me back. Did she already know? There was a sound of something banging in Leah's room, which I covered up with a cough. Not that Mom noticed. She draped her trench coat over a kitchen chair, dropped her car keys on the table and made a beeline to the kitchen. Huh? No complaining that our chores weren't done to her standard? No traffic horror stories? She just started heating leftovers, staring at the Corelle serving dish through the greasy window of our oven.

I tiptoed to my bedroom and shut the door. Outside my bedroom window I could see Len running down the street with his clothes still undone. His shoeless feet curled with every step over the rough asphalt. *That was close,* I thought.

Dinner was unusually quiet that night. I was accustomed

to my mom griping about work over spoonfuls of rice and oxtail. Part of decompressing from the day was grumbling to us about the clowns who brown-nosed their manager, or about her colleagues who belittled her despite having only half her qualifications. This would be followed by us showing her our completed homework. But this night was different. Even when Leah chimed in with the good news that she had been made captain of the volleyball team, our mother barely nodded. The silence was finally broken when the phone rang.

We jumped at the sound and expected Mom to eagerly snatch it up, as she usually did, hoping it was Dad. This time, Mom continued to play with her half-eaten meal. By the third ring, Leah got up. I saw Mom's hand touch Leah's wrist. "Don't answer i—"

"Hello? Oh. Hi, Tita Lorna. Mom? Yeah. She's okay. Why? Um . . ." Still holding the receiver to her ear, Leah tried to make eye contact with Mom. I could hear our aunt on the other end speaking a mile a minute.

Despondent, Mom said, "Hang up the phone."

"One second, Tita. What did you say, Mom?"

Mom got up, took the phone from Leah and placed it back in the cradle. "Sit down, please. I need to talk to both of you."

Leah looked at me. The muscles in my shoulders started to kink at the thought of Mom confronting us about Len's stealthy exit. Should we run? Hide?

"I don't want to speak to your Tita Lorna right now. I don't want to hear all her *I told you so*'s." She took a deep breath and added, "Your daddy . . . he's no longer with us."

"He's dead?!" I exclaimed.

"No, Alma." Mom stared into space. "He's gone."

A long moment of silence.

Carefully, Leah asked, "Where did he go?"

"I don't know. But wherever he went, he went with some-one else."

"Does that mean he won't—" I stopped when Leah pinched me under the table.

We all sat in silence for a long while, looking down at our food and considering the ramifications of our dad's departure. Leah was the first to rise, signalling me with her eyes to help her clean up. Again with the dog whistle. The larger our mother's despair, the cleaner that kitchen had to be. We did the dishes, put away the leftovers and wiped all surfaces as if our lives depended on it. As I was drying cut-lery, I watched Mom make her way to the living room and turn on the television. Her face practically catatonic, barely listening to the news.

"According to eyewitnesses, he is approximately six feet tall, with brown hair, blue eyes and . . ."

I was too distracted by my worry to notice my dishtowel was damp enough that the serving dish was still wet. I looked out the kitchen window at the cotton candy pink of an early autumn sunset. *What are we going to do?* I thought. *What's going to happen if Mom is the only breadwinner? Will we lose our house? The car?* Biting my lip, I ran through the possibilities in my head. I thought of getting a job. One that would pay cash under the table, because I was just ten. Eleven in October. I would be a hard worker. But it's not just about earning money, it's about saving money, I'd heard a financial expert say on the radio once. Maybe I could eat less. Much less. Then it would be killing two birds with one stone: I would be skinnier and the family budget would be spared my enormous appetite. And Mom would be so proud of me. I pictured her face, relieved to have such a thin and devoted child.

Click. Click. Click. Mom pressed the buttons on the converter to another station. The sound of *Dynasty*'s intro music. I wanted to join her on the couch to watch the latest episode, but knew better than to share her company. There would be too many opportunities to disappoint her. I tiptoed to my room and cracked open one of my Nancy Drew mysteries instead. Lying on my bed, I fell asleep fantasizing about Nancy and George kissing, the hardcover book tented over my face.

• • •

The next day unfolded calmer than I had expected. Leah and I quietly had breakfast. Mom handed us our lunches and told us she was taking the day off work. She never took time off work and she certainly never left her room without wearing a full face of makeup. I wondered at the shape of her eyes without the contour of eyeshadow and the thinness of her lips without gloss. I dared to feel hope as she lovingly hugged us goodbye before school. Maybe Dad was the source of all

Mom's problems. Maybe things would be better now that he was gone. Not dead. Gone with someone else.

Things got even better at school when the librarian, Mrs. Bartkiewicz, served as substitute teacher. Mr. Fletcher had the flu. I was delighted to see her at Mr. Fletcher's desk, gingerly clearing the mess of documents and half-eaten granola bars to one side. The corner where Mr. Fletcher stored his guitar sat empty. He must have really needed his guitar to battle the flu.

"Impending. Im. Pend. Ing," Mrs. Bartkiewicz said as she paced the aisles between our desks. She looked over our shoulders with her owl-like face and oversized glasses. I tried not to look around the room, but the faces my classmates were making while struggling with the surprise spelling test were too amusing to miss. "Come on. Break down the word and try your best. Thirty more seconds then I'm moving to the next word." Some sighs from the back of the class. "Okay. Moving on. Admonish. Ad. Mon. Ish." I quickly wrote down the word and saw Mrs. Bartkiewicz's shoes stand by my desk. "Alma, right?" Her eyes scanned my test.

"Yes, ma'am."

"Come see me during recess." A few giggles. "Quiet! Okay. Put your name on your test and hand it to the person on your right and we'll mark them together. On your right. On your right. Your other right, Jennifer. Good."

Before the bell, Jason, the only boy with a cool earring, shoved me into the wall of coats by the classroom door. "Have fun with Bartkiewicz." This did not warrant my standard comeback, "I know you are, but what am I?" so I scowled silently instead. As our fellow classmates emptied the room, he added, "You know what they say about her, right?"

"No. What?"

"She's a big ole lesbo. That's why she has short hair and no husband."

"That's not true," I scoffed, even though I had no idea what he was talking about.

"Why don't you ask her yourself? Ask her if she's a dyke." Another word I didn't understand. He laughed and ran outside, a snack bag of ketchup chips tucked under his arm.

I approached Mrs. Bartkiewicz.

"You did well on the spelling test, Alma. You were the only one who got twenty out of twenty. I was especially pleased with you spelling the word *ineffable*."

I was unaccustomed to someone complimenting me, so I just nodded. I was lucky, I guess. I had seen the word in one of the nature magazines at the doctor's office the other week. My mom and I were in the waiting room trying to get a new prescription for my asthma medication. I was leafing through an issue of *Birder's Digest* and I saw an article where the writer described a hummingbird's feather colouring as "ineffable magic."

"Would you like to be my assistant in the library? This would mean you coming in during morning recess and lunch. Does that sound interesting to you?" she asked.

I looked outside the window at my classmates playing a game of tag. I didn't understand the point of it. I didn't understand the point of throwing balls. I didn't understand the point of hanging out with anybody when all I wanted to do was be alone with my thoughts. I accepted.

At lunch hour, I entered the library. Mrs. Bartkiewicz sat at one of the empty tables, eating sushi from a plastic container. I had never seen a white person eating Asian food before. Her chopstick use was clumsy. "Hi, Alma," she said, the wasabi making her eyes water.

"What do you need me to do?" I put my jacket and backpack on one of the chairs.

"Have you had your lunch yet?"

"Not yet."

"Then why don't you join me?" I thought about what Jason had said. I didn't know what a lesbo was, but it didn't sound good. Maybe this was a trap. "You can't do this kind of work on an empty stomach."

I cautiously took out my lunch bag and opened up the container full of adobo and rice, still lukewarm from when my mother heated it up this morning. The smell that made me embarrassed around my classmates filled the air.

"That smells lovely!" Mrs. Bartkiewicz said while opening another package of soy sauce. "You know, some people think it's sad to be indoors in a library all by yourself. But I kind of like being in here, especially when there is a winter storm outside."

When we were done our meals, she took two Wet-Naps from her purse and handed me one so that we could both clean our hands. It was time to get to work.

She showed me how to shelve returned books using the Dewey decimal system. I thought the system was bullshit, but I did it anyway. I thought it would be better to categor-ize everything under genres, then alphabetize under author's name, like at the bookstore at the mall. But I didn't want to be insubordinate on my first day on the job.

Mrs. Bartkiewicz was right. The quiet of the library was a nice place to be while my classmates played pointless games outside. I especially enjoyed making all the book spines line up at the edge of every shelf.

"Great job!" she said. I flinched. The volume of her praise was similar to the volume of my mother shouting at me, and I knew that sound well. "Sorry, did I scare you?" I shook my head and she continued. "I'm not accustomed to students tak-ing a job this seriously."

Mrs. Bartkiewicz showed me a special place in the library, behind her desk, underneath the shelf where she kept the bor-rowing cards. "This is a printer. If you keep on doing a good job, you can have access to this printer any time you wish. That might come in handy when Mr. Fletcher gives you one of his assignments. And here's another thing." She walked me back around to the main part of the library, into a darker corner that I had never seen before. "This is our film section. Usually, I only allow people to view the videos in the library, but for you I will make a special exception. As long as I can trust that you'll return them in one week's time, then I will let you bor-row as many of the movies as you wish."

My heart soared. I had never received preferential treat-ment before. If this was what it meant to be a lesbo, then I was all for it. I immediately signed out two Russian animated films. They weren't blockbusters, but I was happy to watch anything other than our bootlegged copies of *Big* and *Three Men and a Baby*. I skipped home that day, eager to tell my mother what had happened, eager to see the look on her face when I told her I was given special treatment.

When I arrived at the house, however, I sensed that something was wrong. I heard my mom downstairs in the basement.

"Alma!" she screamed. "Come down here now."

My chest suddenly felt like concrete as I tiptoed down to the basement. I found her sorting clothes in the laundry room, the bug-stained fluorescent light above her head. She stopped what she was doing and looked at me with a strange expression on her face, as if to appear neutral, but anger filled the air around her. I knew from the look in her eyes that she was scanning me. I ran through the events of the last twenty-four hours, trying to remember something that I might have done wrong, in the laundry room specifically. Did I accidentally put a coloured T-shirt into a white load? Did I not use the right water level? Or use the wrong detergent?

Mom stepped over her pile of whites to stand closer to me, her face towering above mine. "Alma. Did someone come to the house yesterday?"

I manufactured the best smile I could, pretending I knew nothing. I opened my mouth and let the word spill out as naturally as I could. "No."

And that's when she slapped me. Or rather, that's when she backfisted me. I know she backfisted me because I still remember the sensation of her knuckles hitting my cheekbone.

I stood there like a soldier with my arms tight against my body. My head had turned to the left because my mother used her right hand to discipline me. My eyes were shut tight, bracing against the sharp pain.

"Liar!" From underneath the sink, Mom presented Len's shoes like a smoking gun, evidence of Leah's wrongdoing. She dropped them on the ground, where they landed on the pinky toe on my right foot. I didn't feel that, though. My body was too numb to feel anything else. Even as my mother walked up the stairs, my body went into its foggy place again. How long I stood there, I do not know. But the next sound I heard was Leah entering the house and having a screaming match with Mom.

"You slut! How long have you been bringing him home?"

"I'm not a slut! Len is my boyfriend!"

I found myself at the top of the basement stairs and watched as Mom punched my sister's face hard enough that it chipped her tooth. I knew she chipped her tooth because Leah reached into her mouth, her bloody mouth, and produced a tiny piece of what looked like white porcelain.

Chapter 5

"Where are you right now?" Nira says to me.

That's a good question. I look around, unsure of the answer. Oh yes. We are in our favourite gelato joint, the same gelato joint we went to on our first date. I realize that the tips of my fingers are touching my right cheek, no longer swollen and tender from my mother's aggressions. Suddenly, I am an adult, now facing a display of endless flavour options, the hipster behind the counter waiting for me to make my choice.

I scramble to make it seem as though I was paying attention and autopilot my selection. "Sorry. Peanut butter and dark chocolate."

"That's not what he was asking you, babes." Nira smiles sheepishly at the hipster. "He was asking you if you wanted a waffle cone or plain."

"Waffle, of course!" I say, feeling like my shoes are two sizes larger than my feet, and my shirt a foreign fabric. I can't wait to get out of here. This place is not what I remember it to be. It used to be simpler back then, back when we were in school. Back then, there was just a small counter with flavours such as chocolate and vanilla and mint. Now the hipsters have moved into this neighbourhood, and with them they brought their ridiculous gastronomic tastes. I don't need black bean. I don't need activated charcoal. I just want things to be simple. Why can't things be simple? I can see from Nira's nostalgic expression that she is trying to relive our romantic moments from long ago, so I try too, and I hold her hand as we stroll down the street. But I'm not really holding her hand. It's more like I'm hoping she can pull me out of this water I am drowning in. I just want to surface.

"Oh look! Our favourite bench is up for grabs." Nira leads me to our bench, located under an oak tree in the Toronto Metropolitan University quad. I don't remember what made this bench so special. It doesn't have much of a view of the commons. But the seats are within arm's reach of the emergency phone, which is meant to give students a sense of safety if they are walking through here late at night. I wonder if it works.

Nira helps to jog my memory. "Remember this bench?"

"I do. It took a lot of convincing on my part to get you to go on a date with me."

"Well. I didn't like you at first." She continues to tell the story. I watch her mouth as she recalls the mythology around our courtship, all smiles. It was pub night. I was a bit tipsy and playing darts for the first time. I was never good at sports or drinking and I narrowly missed her arm. I begged her forgiveness and claimed that all would be well if she went on a date with me. She refused. I asked around about her so that I could wait for her outside her classes and beg again for a date. Finally, on attempt number five . . .

"Lucky five," says Nira, ending the story we have told a million times at barbecues, cocktail parties. "That's when I finally looked at you and said, 'Okay, Shortcake. Let's do this.'"

When she finally gave me a chance, we talked for hours at that Thai restaurant that's now gone because of the condo developments. The owners had to tell us to order more food or please leave, so we left. I had hardly any money, but I had enough to buy Nira an ice cream.

Nira points and says, "There used to be a bush right here, just across from us, and no one could see all the nasty things we did to each other." She leans into me and takes another suggestive lick of her pistachio ice cream. Given my state of mind, I'm not sure if I can make love tonight. I hope she cools down. I finish my ice cream in several efficient bites. No drips. I wipe my hands. I barely remember the taste of the ice cream. What flavour did I get?

Nira uses one of the thin napkins that the parlour gave us to wipe a spot of green from her fancy dress. Fuck. I forgot she wore that dress to impress the school board and I didn't even ask about it. I scramble. "How did your interview go?"

"Well. Thanks for asking. But . . . to be honest . . . I don't want to discuss it because I don't want to jinx it. Janet says I'm a shoo-in, but I don't know, so . . . anyway. Let's talk about something else, okay?" Nira closes her eyes and shakes her head as if to temper her expectations, pushing the dream away to avoid disappointment. "Let's list all of our accomplishments over the last twenty-two years."

"You achieved your master's in education *and* you completed the Principal's Qualifications program," I offer immediately. I'm surprised by myself. I think I'm feeling more normal now. Maybe I can still save this evening. "I can't tell you how proud I am of you for doing that while raising a kid."

Nira pinches my cheek and says, "Why, thank you. And you managed to save enough money for our down payment. And that was nothing short of a miracle. Damn banks!" She's right. Between Nira's modest teacher's income and my freelancer status, mortgage lenders were reticent to deal with us. I was thankful for a feature film gig, which granted us enough money to put a whopping 30 percent down. It was a miracle, indeed.

The warmth is returning to my hands. I can hear the birds chirping in the trees even though the traffic is busy on the street outside the quad. I rub Nira's back and say, "And we raised a teenager."

"We're still raising a teenager, Alma. He is far from being done cooking yet. I know we agreed on being progressive parents, being all sex positive and shit, but do you find yourself acting like . . . you know . . . a puritan? Like . . . remember when we sat down and told ourselves that our child wasn't going to have sex in some alleyway? Or that we were going to celebrate his changing body? Remember how self-righteous we were? But there's something about his burgeoning sexuality that makes me want to lock. Him. Up!"

I laugh, grateful that she's experiencing the same challenges. I tell her about my exchange with Mateo and Hong that morning, but leave out the part where Mateo corrected Hong about how she would spend her extra time and how badly I failed at controlling the situation. I just tell her the basics: Mateo thought he could bring his girlfriend home, but I happened to be there. I keep it simple, hoping Nira won't reprimand me for being soft. If our family were a corporation, she would be the CEO and I would be that dude in the mailroom.

She rolls her eyes. "See, that's what I'm talking about. I used to wipe his bum. Do you remember when he had pinworms? Do you remember me spreading his ass cheeks apart while you rubbed coconut oil on his anus? Do you remember teaching him how to retract the foreskin on his teeny tiny penis before urinating? Now he's putting his teenage penis into the vagina of a teenage girl. Wrap your head around that, Alma." I do as she tells me and instantly regret it. "Anyway . . . this isn't a conversation for our anniversary, but when we have the calories for it, we need to discuss boundaries with him. I don't want to clean up his room and find . . . you know . . . things."

"What things?" I don't know why I asked.

"You know what things. The condoms. Like . . . I can't, Alma. I don't know if I have it in me to see a condom in his garbage can. A used condom." She does this to herself. She grosses herself out. I have to stop her before it goes too far.

I cradle her sweet brown face, trying to be as present as I can be, despite the knot behind my belly button and the phantom sting on my cheek. "Okay, okay, now. I will take over garbage collection until he moves out."

She laughs and puts her head on my shoulder. Nira's curly hair gets in my mouth and I pat it down to tame it. I fail. I always fail. Nira's curls are untameable.

"We did okay, right?" Nira asks.

I kiss her forehead. Replaying Mateo's behaviour today, I am not so sure, but I rarely get to be the one to reassure her. It feels good to be in this role for once, so I say, "We did. I'm proud of us."

"Me too." Her hand wanders to the inside of my thigh, and I stand up suddenly.

"We should get back. There's a Jays game today and the traffic is gonna be shitty." I don't know if there is a game today. I don't even know if it's baseball season.

On the ride home, I think of ways to manage Nira's expectations, the way I always do on "Cactus Days." I call them Cactus Days because my painful memories leave me feeling prickly, untouchable. Not that I can even explain those feelings to her without Nira feeling unwanted. She's desirable. Of course she's desirable! Unbelievably so. But on Cactus Days, my body memory fogs over my sensations, and that includes sensations *down there*. Do I pretend to be sick? Do I just make love and get it over with? Make all the sounds, all the movements as believable as possible until she is satisfied? One of our friends told me once that marriage is made up of compromises. Could I not, just this once, on the day of our anniversary, compromise for the sake of Nira's feelings?

In the car, my wife sits in the passenger seat and lovingly runs her fingers through my hair. Suddenly, she winces and burps. "Oh my god. Sorry. That's so gross." She doubles over and unbuckles her seat belt.

"What are you doing? Put your belt back on."

"I can't. I need you to stop."

"Stop now? Stop where?"

"Stop! You need to stop! Stop the car!"

Miraculously, there is a parking spot in front of a Tibetan dumpling restaurant. Nira runs in. I know better than to run in after her; she doesn't like me witnessing her weak moments. Twenty minutes later, when she comes back out, her mottled face is a distinct shade of green. Weary, she re-enters our car.

I touch the back of her clammy neck, her curls kinky from sweat. "How are you doing?"

"Babes. I think it was the gelato."

"Oh no!"

"Yeah. It tasted kind of funny. I should have known. I'm so sorry to ruin our evening."

"Don't say that. You didn't ruin anything." I drive home, avoiding the potholes. I am thankful we don't have to make love. I am ashamed that I don't want to.

Chapter 6

When was the first time you saw your killer's face? Or rather, when was the first time you saw the composite sketch of his face?

For me, it was one morning when I took out the garbage. That was one of my chores, along with raking leaves, ironing shirts, drying dishes and general sweeping. On a Tuesday morning, like all Tuesday mornings, I rushed through my breakfast to get outside and carry our garbage bags to the curb. Kids nowadays don't know how easy they have it with those wheeled garbage bins. Back then, you had to strong-arm each bag to the curb one at a time, hoping the flimsy plastic wouldn't burst. That one Tuesday, I stuffed my cake-hole full of Cheerios and an apple before I hightailed it to the carport and grabbed our trash bags. I managed to place them by the end of our long driveway just as the truck approached. I froze. Plastered on the side of the truck was a poster of the composite sketch of the Scarborough Stalker, but drawn as a puzzle with some of its pieces missing. The words above the image, in bold yellow lettering, read, *DO YOU KNOW WHO THIS IS?*

The garbage collector, who was hanging from his perch off the side of the truck, stepped down and collected our bags. As he threw in each bundle, he looked at me. "See that?" he said behind a lush moustache. His orange reflective uniform was stained with mud. He pointed to the poster with his thumb. "You gotta pay attention out there, little lady."

"Why?" I asked, pulling up my corduroy pants over my widening hips.

"See this guy right here? If you're not careful, he's gonna snatch you up and rape you like the others. Is that what you want?" I shook my head even though I didn't know what rape was. "Good. Always look behind you." And with that, he stepped back up onto his perch and the truck drove off to our neighbour's home.

Unease bloomed in my stomach for a moment. *What's rape?* I shrugged off the exchange, as I was ready for what was going to be the highlight of my day: riding my bicycle to school for the first time.

I didn't know it was unusual for no one to have taught me how to ride it. My mom was too busy. She didn't even give me the bike. Not officially, anyway. I had found it in a pile at the back of the garage, most likely hand-me-downs from Tita Lorna. I had put down my peppermint-striped hula hoop, which I had been spinning around my waist, and pulled it out from behind plastic bins full of our winter clothes.

It felt as if I had stumbled upon some ancient relic. The

bike had a banana seat and tires that were so soft they made a flip-flip sound when I wheeled it out of the garage. I figured out how to mount the seat and push off with my legs. I must have looked like Fred Flintstone, using my feet on the ground to run it forward the way he did with his stone car.

"That's not how you do it, stupid." Leah had emerged from the house, putting on her jean jacket. She went into the carport and produced an air pump. She pumped my tires until they were plump, then said, "Now use your feet on the pedals or you'll embarrass me."

I tried it her way, but it was harder. Of course it was harder, because it actually demanded balance and skill, but over the course of a week I figured it out, thanks to my sister's ridicule.

And today, I had promised myself, would be my first ride to school. On my short journey to St. Xavier, I imagined I was in the provincial countryside, like in that French film I saw on late night television. All I needed was a front basket loaded with baguettes purchased from the local boulangerie. Wind blew through my bowl cut. I waved at motorists who honked at me to get the hell out of their way. It was exhilarating.

"Look at Alma's shitty wheels!" Jason said as soon as I pulled into the schoolyard. I looked down at my bike and compared it with everyone else's, all of them nicely chained to the fence out front. Theirs were much more current in their design. While they had things like pink handlebar streamers and neon spoke beads, my ride had more subdued maroon colouring. The most obvious difference was their stamp-sized seats. Mine looked more like something the milkman would ride back in the 1940s. A milkman with hemorrhoids. "Alma's got a banana seat because she's got a banana-sized pussy!" Of course, this inspired my classmates to chant "Banana Pussy" over and over again as I made my way to class.

It wasn't one of my finest hours. Not that Mr. Fletcher noticed. He was already strumming on his guitar as my band of troubadours continued their jeering in a line behind me. They did not stop. No—it was Jason who did not stop. His desk was behind mine and from there he kept on whispering, "Hey. Banana Pussy. Why are you so ugly, Banana Pussy?" This continued through our morning pop quiz, where Mr. Fletcher tested our knowledge of the solar system.

"Psst. Alma. Do you know which planet is after Jupiter? I can't see it because your banana pussy is in the way."

"Watch out, you don't want to slip and fall on Alma's banana pussy."

After recess, we moved on to math. I was relieved that Jason had cooled it with his taunting.

"Let's get out our geometry sets, everyone." Mr. Fletcher wanted us to experiment with making circles using our compasses. Or rather, he wanted us to keep busy using our compasses to make circles while he strummed on his guitar. I opened the Oxford set Mom had bought me at Grand & Toy. I removed the plastic film that attached the protractor, set squares and compass together in the packaging. The smell of something new excited me and I got to work, pinning the needle of the compass to the page of my notebook and twirling it around to make a perfect circle.

"Alma. Why are you so ugly?"

You'd think that Jason's omission of the term *Banana Pussy* would make his mockery less painful, but it had the opposite effect. It felt crueller. Perhaps that was by design. I had not paid attention before; I was definitely paying attention now.

He continued whispering. "Everyone thinks you're so ugly. You ruined our class picture. Go back home and fix your face. You're so fucking ugly!"

I stopped making circles. In one graceful movement, I stood up and turned around. I plunged the needle of the compass into Jason's palm. I meant to stab his face, but he shielded it with his hand. At first, the entire class laughed. They quit laughing when I dug it in deeper. I pushed and pushed until I felt bone. Until I heard Jason screaming. Or . . . was it when I heard Mr. Fletcher say my name? I can't remember which came first.

"Alma! We do not stab our friends." Mr. Fletcher put his guitar down, which meant this was serious. "Apologize to Jason right now."

I refused.

The principal called my mother at her office. It took her two hours to commute from downtown to the suburbs to witness Principal Jenner scold me.

"What you did was unconscionable. However, with your formidable grades, we will spare you a suspension," he said. Mom sat in the chair beside me with a tight jaw, as if she too was being punished by this uptight man with his uptight comb-over and uptight bow tie.

"But . . . he's been bothering me for forever!" I looked at Mom, whose eyes darted back and forth between the deadpan Principal Jenner and me, her pleading daughter. I could see words forming right behind her lips, but she didn't say a word.

Principal Jenner rearranged the pens and highlighters on his desk into a straight line. "You can't let silly boys bother you, Alma. I bet this young man has a crush on you. That's what they all do. Boys can't help themselves. Sometimes they have these . . . these new feelings, especially around your age, and they don't know what to do about it. So they hit and curse and tease, but they don't mean anything by it. You understand?"

I looked down and nodded, even though it made no sense to me.

I paid the price when Mom and I returned home. What I had done wrong, according to her, was to shame her. She cared very little that I had stabbed someone. She cared very much that she was called out of work, that she had to explain things to her executive officer, who then berated her for not being a reliable worker.

Funnily enough, after she disciplined me, I did not cry. Even as I sat in my safe place, it didn't matter that a bruise was swelling on my arm, where my mother had hit me while calling me an idiot. I just sat there, scared and delighted at how much I'd enjoyed stabbing that fucker in the hand. Replaying the sensation of needle against bone fuelled my rage until I fell asleep on the carpet.

• • •

In the library, Mrs. Bartkiewicz sat across from me during lunch hour the next day. She ate a chickpea curry. I ate a corned beef and pandesal sandwich. She broke the silence between us by saying, "I heard what happened between you and that boy Jason." The congealed fat in the corned beef smelled off to me, but I continued to chew, slumped in my chair. "I want you to know that if you're being bullied, you can talk to me, okay? I've handled some mean people in my day and I am happy to—"

"Is it true?" I interrupted sharply.

"Is what true?" Mrs. Bartkiewicz snapped her pea-green Tupperware shut and wiped her utensils with a napkin.

"Is it true you're a lesbo?" I said as curtly as I could, trying on the role of bully myself. I still didn't know what it was, but I knew the question would hurt her.

"Do you think that's an appropriate question?"

"Everybody says you are."

"Interesting." Mrs. Bartkiewicz shifted in her seat and crossed her legs, her chin proud. "Well, according to the Catholic school board, no, I am not. But according to me, I am. I have a partner, she and I have been together for fifteen years, we are happy and in love. Does that satisfy your curiosity?"

Her consonants were clipped and her face was red. I thought I had hit the mark, but she smiled. I hated her for being the only person who cared for me. I hated her for being kind. Why couldn't she be like everyone else? Why couldn't she do what was most familiar and belittle me? Couldn't she see what everyone else saw in me? That I was a horrible person. I was a mistake. A burden. I deserved an uninterrupted stream of hate towards me. Wait. What did Mrs. Bartkiewicz say about "she" when referring to her partner? Did she mean she had a wife? A *wife*? Women can have wives?

"If you don't close your mouth, a bug might fly in," Mrs. Bartkiewicz said with a chuckle.

I spent the rest of the period reorganizing the card catalogue, looking at Mrs. Bartkiewicz out of the side of my eye. Lesbo. That's what a lesbo was.

• • •

I was looking forward to trick-or-treating with Leah, but when Halloween finally arrived, she told me she had other plans. Now that she was no longer grounded, she was eager to join her friends in her first-ever teenage party.

I stood by the door frame of Leah's room, watching her apply black lipstick. My sulky whimpers of disappointment went unnoticed, so I sullenly said, "How is this a Halloween party? You're not even wearing a costume."

Leah rolled her eyes at me, looked in her vanity mirror and drew whiskers on her face with her eyeliner, and slid a headband with cat ears over her crimped hair. "There. Happy now?"

"Why are you a cat? You said you'd be a priest." I was about to lay on the guilt trip, jogging her memory about how I had worked so hard crafting her white collar, but she cut me off.

"Alma. Only kids dress up like that. When you get older, you just want to do things like . . . you know . . . dance to music and stuff."

My stomach turned, wondering if Len would be at the party too. Surely she wouldn't risk seeing him again, would she? Not after having to get her tooth filled, and lying to our dentist Dr. Hertz about chipping her tooth during volleyball practice.

"You'll get it once you're my age."

I doubted that. Being as cool as Leah one day seemed impossible. I didn't even have friends to trick-or-treat with. My only substitute for my sister was my own mother.

Mom suggested we start our trick-or-treating route at Mr. Stolks's home next door. I protested, saying there was a rumour the old lady in the opposite direction gave out tennis balls instead of candy. She reminded me that I did not play sports. Point taken.

In my nun's costume, I stood on Mr. Stolks's porch and pressed the doorbell. No one answered. His main door was open, but his thin screen door was shut. I looked through the window and could see only darkness.

"He's not there?" Mom asked from the curb.

"Let's go to the next house," I said, about to rush down the steps. Then I heard a sting of spooky music from inside the house. I turned around and saw a ghost-shaped flashlight twirling in a circle within Mr. Stolks's hallway. He switched on the hallway light and put his arms out like *tah-dah!* I crossed my arms, remembering the sensation of his finger along my palm.

Mr. Stolks slid the metal toggle on his screen door to prop it open. "Were you scared?" he asked, already pleased with himself.

Before I could answer, my mother had scaled the steps and was shaking his hand. "Hey, Russ! Thanks for your tip about the pancake social. We registered for next week."

"No problem at all. Hey, I've been meaning to ask if any of your little ladies would be available to babysit my grandson next weekend."

"Next weekend? Well, Leah has a volleyball tournament, but Alma is available."

"Oh yeah? That would be much appreciated. I would pay, of course."

"No, no. You don't need to pay."

"I insist. Does five dollars an hour sound good to you?"

"Uh . . . okay. If you insist. Sure."

"Excellent. He'll be arriving on Saturday. It'll be great if she can arrive before we have our brunch guests. I want to give my son and daughter-in-law a bit of a break from him while we eat. He can be quite the handful."

"How old?"

"He's two."

"She'll be there."

Neither of them looked at me as they negotiated over me. I just stood there, my eyes below their chest level, as they discussed my time and my labour.

•••

I arrived at Mr. Stolks's house at ten on Saturday morning. I had babysat cousins before, but this was my first time doing it outside my family and for pay. The excitement of having my own cash helped assuage my feelings of dread about sharing space with Mr. Stolks. Immediately after ringing his doorbell to be let inside, my hands were in fists, as though it would keep him from giving me the same creepy handshake again.

My working day began in the foyer, which was the centre of activity, with various relatives greeting each other with hugs and kisses. It was extraordinary how quickly I became invisible in that mass of people. I was handed this toddler and suddenly I disappeared from view, with none of them asking who I was, all carrying on their conversations as if I didn't exist. One woman even handed me her jacket as though I were the coat check. This was a relief. I didn't want Mr. Stolks or any of his guests to talk to me anyway.

I took little Carl downstairs to the basement to play. As in our home, the basement was several degrees cooler than upstairs, only Mr. Stolks's home was renovated to look like a stately lodge. The adults upstairs chatted among each other while I kept Carl occupied downstairs. We rolled a ball between us, steering clear of a bearskin rug that sat underneath a lead glass table. I wasn't sure if it was real, but if it was, I certainly didn't want to touch it.

"It's real, you know," Mr. Stolks said.

I startled. I hadn't heard him come down. His stairs weren't as squeaky as the ones to our basement.

He swirled his champagne flute, making the raspberries spin in the amber liquid. "That rug over there. It's a real bear."

"Cool." I didn't know what else to say. I just wanted him to go away.

"I shot it when I visited the Yukon. Square in the eyes. And see this?" He walked to the fireplace and leaned on the mantel, where a stainless steel jar stood. "These are my late wife's ashes."

Carl jumped at my feet, begging me to build train tracks with him. I let Carl lead me to his bin of toys, hoping this would cue Mr. Stolks to leave us alone. He kept talking.

"It's amazing how light our remains are after being burned. Here. Hold it." He outstretched his arms, trying to get me to hold the urn.

I shook my head.

"Come on. Hold it."

I took it, just to end the conversation. The urn was cold against my chest.

"See? That's all there is to us. Just a few pounds." When I handed it back, Mr. Stolks chuckled. "Looks like you may need a sweater." He grinned and pointed at my hard nipples, poking through my shirt. Taking a swig of his drink, he headed back upstairs.

Embarrassed and ashamed, I crossed my arms over my breasts, willing my nipples to go soft. But the chill of the basement made them stand at attention. I knew exactly what I was going to buy with the money I earned.

•••

"Mom. I need a bra." Or was it a burial site? I wanted to dig a deep, deep hole and place my boobs into it, with no marker so that no one would ever know about them ever again.

Mom was busy frying ground beef over the stove, pressing

her large spoon into the sizzling meat to make torta for Saturday breakfast.

"Why do you need a bra?"

"Because I'm growing. There. I'm growing *there*."

Without looking at me, she said, "You're not growing there."

"I am. People are noticing."

Mom put down her spoon and turned to me, alarmed. "Really? Who?"

"People. Everyone." I stopped short of telling her about Mr. Stolks's comment. Why even bother? I desperately changed tack. I was determined to hide my body as best I could. "And I have money. I'll buy it myself."

"Okay, fine." I knew me paying for it would change her mind. "We'll go to Zellers." She went back to cooking, pouring egg over the cooked meat to scramble.

I sighed. Where I truly wanted to go was one of those real lingerie places at Scarborough Town Centre mall. I liked looking at the headless mannequins wearing French front-clasp bras with demi-cups. It gave me pants feelings. Zellers was better than nothing, though. Anything to cover up my nipples and the growing hard mass behind them. The swollen gland was tender to my touch and the size of one of my shooter marbles. I experimented with various arm positions to conceal them, but the only thing I could do was hide behind my desk at school, or the kitchen table.

There was a knock on the door. Whoever was on our stoop tried to press the doorbell as well, but Mom didn't know how to repair it.

"Answer the door, Alma," Mom said, measuring a spoonful of *patis* to season the torta.

I did as I was told. It was the same white lady who had come to our home the month before, asking us to sign a petition against the development of affordable housing down the street. "We don't want *those* kinds of people in our neighbourhood," she had said to Mom, who threw the pamphlet into the garbage as soon as she left. With a shake of her head, she explained to me that "*those* kinds of people" were people like us. Not white.

Now the woman had returned, this time with information about an upcoming community event.

"Are your parents home, young lady?" The autumn wind blew through the trees, but her Flock of Seagulls hairdo was immovable.

Mom stepped into the foyer, wiping her hands on her apron. "Can I help you?"

The woman looked at the threshold of our house, hoping Mom would invite her in. She did not. Instead, Mom held the doorknob to make a boundary the lady could not cross. It was the thing she did when salesmen arrived. It made it easier to slam the door shut.

"Hello again. My name is Gladys. I live at 357. Just down this way." Gladys pointed in the direction of the cul-de-sac at one end of our street. "I'm taking the time today to inform everyone about the safety workshop happening Monday night."

"Safety for what?"

Gladys handed Mom a letter-sized poster. "Safety from the Scarborough Stalker. I'm not sure if you've been keeping up with the news, but there have been three women and one little girl who have been attacked."

"They were killed?"

Gladys looked at me out of the side of her eye, leaned in to Mom and whispered, "Raped. All of them barely got out alive. Whoever it is is some maniac right here in Scarborough wanting sex with women and girls!"

In my head, I pieced everything together. *Oh. That's what rape is. It's when a stranger forces you to have sex with him.*

"He's targeting people getting off buses late at night. Children left alone to play on the street. It's terrifying."

Mom glanced at the date and time on the poster. "I'm not sure I can make it."

"You should be there." Gladys pointed at me. "Is this your only daughter?"

"No. We have an older one."

"I have daughters too. Three of them. And one son. Thank god for him. Things are much easier raising a boy. You don't have to contend with this nonsense, worrying who's going to attack him. But for my three girls, they need to know how to defend themselves. They need to know how to fight back and escape. If only these last victims knew how to throw a punch, they would have gotten away."

As soon as the lady left, Mom did the same thing again and threw the poster in the garbage, convinced the timing of the workshop was too tight for her return home from work.

Zellers was crowded the next day. At the entrance, two store clerks handed children balloons and greeted customers, saying, "Happy Zuper Zunday!" Everything was 25 percent off. I was thrilled. It meant I could buy more bras with the twenty-five dollars I'd folded into my Velcro wallet. I declined a balloon because I was no longer a child. I was growing boobs, and therefore was much too sophisticated for balloons, thank you very much.

Mom pointed me in the direction of the bras. "Find what you need. I'll be here." She pointed with her mouth, Filipino-style, towards the toys. "I have to get a present for your cousin Belinda's birthday next week." This gave me relief. I didn't want my mother around to sully this important rite of passage with her usual cheapskate antics.

Disappointingly, the bra section was not as fancy as the storefronts at the mall. Half-open boxes stored misshapen cups in shades ranging from light beige to bright white. Nothing was brown like me. Unlike places such as Blossom & Pearle lingerie shop, there were no mannequins for me to gawk at, only cartons with images of middle-aged women smiling, as if satisfied that their breasts were simply contained and hidden. Although that was my agenda as well, I couldn't help but want cleavage. It looked pretty cool the way women in Mafia movies would put money down there. It was the only good thing about having boobs.

I finally found the shelf holding a selection of training bras. I opened one of the plastic cases and ran my finger along the thick fabric with daisy patterns. The packaging read *A32*. What the hell did that mean? I had to try it on. Only, when I arrived at the dressing room, there was a long lineup, with everyone wanting to take advantage of the zuper zavings.

A store clerk with crimped blond hair looked at me in the line and said, "Hey. I can get you into the dressing room in the men's formal wear department. It's on the other end of the store. No one goes in there." I shrugged my shoulders and followed her, relieved to not have to wait my turn. She sorted through her fob to find the key to open the dressing room door. It was weird being in this empty space with mannequins displaying the latest tuxedo trends.

She told me, "Whatever you don't like, just hang it on the door here." And then she left.

The store muzak played an instrumental version of a Madonna song while I stripped off my windbreaker, fanny pack and Mickey Mouse T. I accidentally hit my chest gland and held it for a moment until the pain subsided. Naked from the waist up, I took the bra out of the carton and tried to figure out which way was front and back. Recalling a scene from a made-for-television movie I'd seen about teen pregnancy, I remembered that the boy tried to unbuckle the girl's bra at her back but she slapped him on the arm before he could do so. Buckles in the back. Right. Okay. I looped my arms into the straps but couldn't figure out how to fasten the hooks from behind, so I turned the hooks to the front, fastened them and spun them behind me afterwards.

Looking in the mirror, I sucked my gut in and puffed my

ed me and put it into my non-existent cleavage. I took
it out again and imagined I was being bribed. Cocking my
shoulders seductively, I said to my reflection, "If that's what
you want me to do, it's gonna cost you." Then I took the bill
and placed it into my bra again. Yeah. This bra was perfect.

As I made my way back to the lingerie section to get a
few more of the exact same bra, I heard my mother screaming.

"Alma?! Where are you? Almaaaa!"

A circle of people had gathered around her.

"Where was the last place you saw her?" asked one man.

"Here! I left her here."

"You left her?" said another woman.

"She was supposed to—" Mom's eyes locked on me. I
thought of running away. Her face was a frightening combination of fear and fury. "Alma!" She grabbed me, and to my
surprise she did not hit me. She held me close to her chest.
My arms were at attention, stiff at my sides. "Where the heck
did you go?"

"The lady brought me to the other dressing room."

"What lady?"

"The lady . . . who works at the store."

While Mom hugged me again, a woman with her toddler sitting in their shopping cart chimed in. "You can't leave
her alone, you know. The Scarborough Stalker is around here,
stealing and molesting kids. You have to pay attention."

85

Mom let go of me long enough to flash the woman a look of animosity. The woman scowled and continued shopping. Mom held me by the shoulders and jostled me. "Don't do that ever again, okay?"

While we waited in line for me to purchase my bra, I saw Mom's head hanging low with shame and worried that I was definitely in trouble now. She didn't even peruse the trashy magazines on the shelf while we waited our turn. I must have really embarrassed her. But she did not hit me, even after we exited the store, even when we were out of sight of concerned onlookers. From the passenger seat, I watched her drive us back home visibly shaken, her eyes somewhere far away.

Later that night, Mom raced to the television to turn up the volume. "SHHH! Everyone. Listen!"

Leah and I were in the middle of a game of Operation and my tweezer touched the sensor. BEEP!

"Turn that off, Alma!"

I begrudgingly flicked the switch on the side of the fake operating table and we all positioned ourselves towards the screen. Usually the news was more of a background noise, a soundtrack to our dinners. What was so important?

"Breaking news. Yet another victim in the Scarborough area, this time a young woman aged . . ."

This was the first time we devoted our entire attention to the situation. A rapist was on the loose in our neighbourhood. Not somewhere far away. The attacks were happening within a five-kilometre radius of our house. It gave me the same creepy feeling I had when I first heard that other families believed in

Santa, this man in a white beard who came into your house to give you presents at Christmas. But with this man, you didn't know if or when he was coming for you. And it didn't matter if you were naughty or nice.

Mom watched on the couch, her legs crossed tightly and her fingers forming a cage over her mouth. When the segment was over, she suddenly stood up and went through the house to close each curtain and check the lock on each door. She began digging into the kitchen trash. Leah and I looked at each other, sensing the erratic nature of our mother's movements. "Yes! It's still here." Mom pulled out the flyer the lady had given us from underneath discarded eggshells. She wiped it clean with a paper towel and smoothed out its crinkled edges.

• • •

The self-defence workshop took place at Heron Park Community Centre that Monday. The gym was full to the brim with people, mostly families, claiming blue plastic chairs arranged in front of an overhead projector and screen. When we arrived, one police officer was splitting the room in two by pulling a divider attached to a ceiling track across the width of the gymnasium. In that other space, parents encouraged their sons to go and play with the riding toys and basketballs provided so that the women and girls could learn, uninterrupted. It was standing room only. Mom, Leah and I were lucky to find lone seats that were somewhat close to one another. Unfortunately, my chair sat behind a rather tall man who emphasized his stature with poufy red hair and a baseball cap. Even with my jacket rolled up under my bum, I had to move side to side to catch what was going on up front.

Another police officer walked to the microphone in front of the screen. His boots click-clicked across the wooden floor. "Good evening, folks—" Feedback. A parent volunteer fiddled with the placement of the speaker until the squeal stopped. We all uncovered our ears. "Let's try this again, shall we? Good evening, folks. My name is Constable Leary and—" The officer placed a transparent sheet on the overhead and that same composite sketch I'd seen on the garbage truck was projected onto the wall. The words *Scarborough Stalker* came out backwards. He tried to rectify this by turning the plastic film, but then it was upside down. He cursed to himself until it finally projected the right way around. His annoyed exhale distorted the microphone feed.

"Thank you for joining us tonight for this important self-defence workshop. I am aware that a lot of you are scared, knowing there is a predator in our community. It makes sense. Four victims have been attacked and I imagine many of you are worried about who is going to be next. Your daughter? Your wife? Your sister? Your mother? That's why we wanted to host this event, because if we empower women to learn the skills to fend off a perpetrator, we will never have another victim."

He paused and looked at the audience. The sound of little boys running around in the other half of the gym echoed into our space.

"Before we start with the physical part of the workshop, I wanted to tell you that no self-defence is better than prevention." Constable Leary looked directly into the eyes of the women and girls in the front row. "You have complete power to prevent these attacks by using common sense," he continued, lightly tapping his temple before putting another transparency on the overhead, this one with bullet points. The shadow of his finger pointed to the words on the screen. "Don't put yourself in a vulnerable position. Don't come home late at night. Travel in pairs. Let your loved ones know what your plans are. Check in with each other. And always look behind you. We know that whoever the Scarborough Stalker is, he preys on women and girls who are alone, who are careless about their plans and aren't aware of their surroundings. Tonight, that ends. While our task force works to find him and put him in jail, you all can work together as a community to keep each other safe."

I looked around me and saw the crowd nodding in agreement. One man looked at his teen daughter, who had his same ruddy cheeks, and whispered, "See what I told you? You've got to be careful." The daughter rolled her eyes and repositioned herself away from him.

"Now let's give a warm welcome to Morgan, who will show us a few moves."

I shifted back and forth behind the red bush of hair in front of me. Constable Leary led the applause and a beefy man in a tank top and cargo pants emerged from the crowd, waving and cheerful.

Morgan moved the microphone to the side of the gym and said at the top of his voice, "I'm a pretty loud guy, so I doubt I need this." Laughter. Two volunteers dragged a crash mat to the centre of the clearing. Another volunteer unplugged the projector and wheeled it away. "See, your voice is an important tool in protecting yourself. Hands up if you were taught to be quiet and nice." All of the women and girls raised their hands. "Exactly. That's what this guy is looking for. A quiet, nice person who will bow down and do what he wants. So the first thing I'm gonna ask you to do is get loud."

I looked back at my mother, sitting two rows behind me, hoping for her permission to do as the man said. She did not return my glance. She was too focused on the presentation, clutching her large purse on her lap.

"At the count of three, I want you all to shout, 'GET AWAY FROM ME!'" Scattered laughter. "Ready? One . . . two . . . three!" Everyone made a mild attempt. "You call that shouting? I know you can do better than that. Come on. One . . . two . . . three!"

"Get away from me!" everyone said in unison.

"Louder!"

"GET AWAY FROM ME!"

"I KNOW YOU'RE FOLLOWING ME!"

We repeated, "I KNOW YOU'RE FOLLOWING ME!"

"GET AWAY FROM ME OR I'M CALLING THE POLICE!"

"GET AWAY FROM ME OR I'M CALLING THE

POLICE!" we repeated, although some of us were off rhythm and laughed about it.

"Awesome! Doesn't that feel good? Doesn't it feel like you have power? That's what you have inside of you. With that power, we're gonna learn some moves. Can I get a volunteer, please?" A teenaged girl at the end of one of the middle aisles raised her hand and made her way to the clearing, tying up her waist-length brown hair with a scrunchie. "Hello, pretty young lady. What's your name?"

"Camille."

"Can you shout that nice and loud, though?"

"CAMILLE!" she screamed with her fists tight. Camille's smile was wide as she looked out at the audience.

"Awesome. Okay. Here's what we know about the Scarborough Stalker. He has subdued his victims in the past by putting them into a chokehold and threatening them with a knife. Let's start with the chokehold." Morgan put his hands on Camille's delicate neck. "What you need to understand is that you have six seconds before choking leads to unconsciousness. Six seconds. That's all. And when you're out, he can do whatever he wants to you. So you gotta act quick." He turned to Camille. "What would you do in this situation?"

Smiling, Camille feebly attempted to punch Morgan's face. Her arms did not reach.

"See? She can't even reach my face."

"Kick him in the crotch!" said someone in the crowd. Laughter.

"Yes, while that is an option, you might miss, which will get him angrier than before. Another thing to consider is the fact that attackers could be on drugs or sometimes it's just the adrenalin. They feel nothing. You don't want that. I always think that being smarter is better than being stronger. So in this situation, Camille, I want you to praise the Lord." Camille smiled, not sure what this meant. "Show me how you pray, Camille." Camille put her hands in prayer position. "Exactly. Now lift your hands up through my arms as I'm choking you." She did as Morgan said and it deflected his arms. "See how easy that was?"

Morgan surprised Camille by putting her in a chokehold from behind. Camille's face went red. "What we also know about the Scarborough Stalker is that he would come up from behind his victims, much like this." He lugged Camille from one end of the cleared floor to the other. Her feet kicked helplessly out in front of her. "This is how he dragged his victims to ravines and ditches." I clamped my hand over my mouth. It was as if I were witnessing the act itself, all the things we had heard on the news, live, right in front of us. "What would you do in this situation, Camille?"

Camille struggled and tried her best to elbow Morgan in the stomach. Morgan was unmoved. He finally let go. "Okay. Try it on me and let me show you."

Flustered, Camille switched places. Morgan demonstrated a sidestep pivot that weakened Camille's hold. Morgan turned Camille's arm until it was behind her, then tapped the back of her leg in a way that made her fall to her knees on the crash mat. "See? Smarter. Not stronger."

Applause.

Morgan showed two more manoeuvres using Camille's body for demonstration. One scenario had Morgan straddled on top of her. Another had him holding her from behind at the waist. By the time he was done, Camille's face was red and her hair was a mess. Her smile had long faded.

"Can we give a round of applause for Camille?" Everyone clapped. Camille waved weakly back at all of us, her arms still marked from where Morgan had demonstrated how to get out of someone grabbing you by the wrists.

As we left the gym that night, we were all gifted rape whistles. While other girls my age made a racket blowing them to try out the high-pitched trill, I examined mine closely. I tapped the elbow of the volunteer handing them out.

"Excuse me, ma'am?"

"Yes, young lady?"

"This is a whistle?"

"Yup."

"How does it work?"

"You blow into it."

"When?"

"If you're being attacked. That way, if people passing by hear it, they can come and rescue you."

"I'm supposed to blow it . . . while being attacked?"

The woman's smile got wider, as though she were having difficulty opening heavy drapes at either side of her cheeks. "Yes. Exactly."

"While being choked?"

The woman waved goodbye to someone she noticed, then returned her gaze to me, annoyed and confused as to why I wasn't pleased with her answer. Was she being mocked? "Yes. I suppose so."

"So . . . we have six seconds to get out of the chokehold *and* blow this whistle? Should I get out of the chokehold then blow the whistle? Or should I blow the whistle then get out of the chokehold? Wait. That doesn't make sense. If you're being choked . . . how can you blow on a whistle?"

Mom ushered me away from the woman before I could get a proper answer. I put the whistle's lanyard around my neck as my family piled into the car. We hadn't even left the parking lot when Mom turned in the driver's seat and glared at me and Leah. Her eyes were wide with determination.

"Those whistles won't do anything. When we get home, I'll make something you can carry with you in your purse at night." I didn't have a purse, nor did I travel at night. But whatever she was talking about sounded better than some silly whistle.

Mom took out three forks from our kitchen drawer and bent the forks using a set of pliers. The volume of her voice, the way she paced about the kitchen with sweat on her brow, made me nervous. This was a familiar pattern, a high-speed train I could not stop. Leah and I were passengers now and there was no way of getting off. Fearful of upsetting her, Leah and I kept quiet.

"Here." Mom showed us her handiwork. The metal handle curved around her fist while the two prongs of the fork stuck out menacingly from her knuckles. "See this?" Mom punched her fist forward at an imaginary opponent. "If the killer comes at you, you do this!" Mom moved her hands in various combinations from stabbing to slashing. I stepped back, worried she would aim at me. "Now you try, Alma."

I shyly took the handmade weapon.

"No. Like this." Mom showed me a tight fist. "Be strong."

I changed my stance. Leah stood beside me with the other fork gadget and tried it out herself.

"See your sister? Ate Leah knows what she's doing. See how strong she looks? Do that, Alma."

I tried again.

"Good. Better. Now lunge forward and stab him. Go. Pretend he's right here."

I sensed Mom was approaching the apex of her rage, so I kept trying.

"That won't hurt him. Again. Harder."

I did as I was told. At least, I thought I did. Finally, Mom took me by the shoulders. She shouted into my face, strong enough that her breath moved my eyelashes and her spit sprayed across my nose. "I SAID HARDER, ALMAAAAA!"

Silence. She pushed me away. I managed to remain standing, even though my eyes were downcast. I could feel myself slipping into my foggy place.

Mom was in tears. "I read the newspaper. Do you know what he did to one of his victims? He . . . whoever he is . . . he is a sick, sick man. Do you understand, Alma?" From my foggy place, I willed my head to nod. "I don't want that to happen to you . . . to either of you!"

Leah cautiously placed her hand on Mom's shoulder. As usual, Mom flicked it off. Leah sighed and looked at me. "Alma. Apologize to Mom."

I was still floating outside myself but felt Leah push me forward.

"Do it!"

I had no idea what I was apologizing for, but knew I had to obey.

In my foggy place, I pulled the strings of my puppet body to step forward and wrap my arms around my mother. She hugged me back and sobbed.

Chapter 7

In the middle of the night, a familiar warm trickle runs down the crease of my bum. Half-asleep, I stand up before my blood stains the couch. I clutch my crotch and run to the ground-floor powder room. Wait. No. There are no tampons in the powder room. I quietly jog to the second-floor washroom, hoping not to drip anything onto the stair runner. I had told Nira that a paisley-patterned carpet would hide stains and she scoffed at me, saying something along the lines of "Exactly. We need to see the stains so that we know it needs to be cleaned," which is why I have to spot-treat and shampoo the damn thing every month.

I narrowly make it to the toilet. My flow has been stronger and less predictable these days. Friends keep telling me it's a sign of perimenopause, but I dismiss them because . . . well . . . because having a uterus fucking sucks. Like . . . could we get a sweet spot in life where we don't have to worry about procreation and we don't have to worry about the "change"? Could I get a fucking break where I don't have my period *and* I'm pain free *and* my boobs look up at the horizon? Is that too much to ask? Perhaps if I ignore my friends and their well-meaning warnings, I can get that reprieve.

I reach my arm as far as I can into the cabinet underneath the vanity and search for a tampon. Ultra Super. If I keep this flow up, I will need Military-Grade Extreme Maximum absorption. I stick it in. Might as well be a king-sized mattress. Maybe this is why I'm so emotional lately. Maybe this is why I had such an extreme reaction to the footage the other day, and remembered you. Maybe. Yes. Hormones.

I tiptoe my way back downstairs to my couch/bed, and as I pass Mateo's room I hear him on the phone. Is he crying?

"I don't understand."

Silence.

"You can't send a gift back. No one does that."

Silence.

"It was supposed to be a surprise! That's all. That's why I went into your locker."

Silence.

"You don't mean it. Don't say that." His voice is pleading.

Silence.

"But you said you loved me!"

Should I knock? Check in on him? No. I can't help but listen. I lean forward, and just as I am about to put my ear to the door, I hear Mateo throw his phone across the room. He opens the door and sees me standing there, his face blotchy and red.

I scramble. "Hi. I was using the washroom . . . and—"

"What is it?" he says to me sharply.

"Nothing. I just . . . Are you okay? You sounded upset. I was worried."

"I'm fine." He removes his glasses and wipes his face with his sleeve. When was the last time he brushed his hair?

"Do you need to talk?"

"I said I'm fine!" Mateo pushes past me to the washroom and slams the door.

I sleep poorly and the drive to work the next morning is difficult. Thoughts keep swirling in my brain. He went into Hong's locker? How did he do that? More importantly, why the hell did he do that? I'm distracted enough that I run through a stop sign. A sharp horn blares and I come to.

"What the fuck are you doing?!" says a woman in an SUV, her baby crying in the back seat.

I hold up my hand and say, "Sorry," but then realize I have the window rolled up. I really am sorry. I should have been paying attention. It's odd. I was prepared for Mateo's first sexual experiences. Well . . . I was as prepared as I could be, imagining that moment as soon as he was born into this world and I changed his preemie diapers. There's something about seeing your child's innocent body that makes you want to protect it at all costs. I have rehearsed the tough conversations around safe sex over and over again in my head, imagining how well I was going to keep my cool, how healthy I was going to be around the subject matter. That said, I never practised conversations around his first heartbreak. As I've said before, I hate disappointing him. But what if disappointing him is beyond my control? I guess that's exactly what's happening here. It's beyond my control. If someone in his life, someone he loves, breaks up with him, I can't solve it.

Another sharp sound. A cyclist bangs on the passenger window. I don't know why I do, but I roll it down so that I can hear him curse at me at full volume. He spits out the whistle between his lips and cranes his sunburned neck enough that the visor of his helmet protrudes into my car.

"This is a bike lane, motherfucker."

"I'm so sorry. I didn't see—"

"You'd see if you were paying attention."

"You're right, I—"

He pushes off the car and cycles away. I realize that I am supposed to turn right on this next street to get to the office. The vehicles behind me honk their horns in frustration because I am now too cautious in my speed. Another cyclist pulling two children in a cart waves her arm, urging me to hurry up and turn right already. Today is not my day.

Things get worse when I have to edit footage of interviews with victims' family members. It's proof positive that "time heals all wounds" is a bullshit sentiment. These people are far from healed. Sure, some of them make it through the interview without crying, but their eyes. Their eyes. Jesus Christ. I can't get over their eyes. Most of the time, their eyes are weary and full of anguish. Yet when they recount horrifying moments, such as that first phone call when they learned their loved one was missing or when they identified the body, their eyes become fixed and wide. Comparing interviews immediately after the murders to them now, after rampant substance use, dissolved families, unemployment, mental illness, is even more heartbreaking. There are lines on their faces, between the brows, around their lips. It's not age. It's agony. They must have been asked these same questions for decades. And what is it all for? For our entertainment? Because it's like a murder mystery but real? That's what the True Crime genre is, isn't it?

"I'm not sure what was more painful," says one brother of a victim. "Waiting and hoping Gwen would show up at our doorstep or accepting that she was never coming back." He coughs to stop himself from crying. The cough occurs extremely close to the word "back," making it difficult for me to cut where the story editor has told me to cut. It takes me several attempts, but I manage to trim the sound out. What I truly want to do is push back and tell the story editor to include the brother's emotion. Best not to rock the boat, though. I just want this project to be over and done with.

●●●

I remember watching your parents on television.

It was a Wednesday night and my family sat around the coffee table in the living room to eat dinner. It had been months since we ate at the kitchen table with chairs under our bums. It was located too far from the television. Our mother's single-mom schedule now included filing people's taxes on evenings and weekends in addition to her day job at the law firm, so we had to combine eating with viewing to catch the best shows when they aired. *Designing Women. Golden Girls.*

Growing Pains. The Waltons. Leah wanted to watch *Married...
with Children*, but Mom thought it was too obscene.

Leah filled everyone's glasses with cola. Mom shovelled
rice and Filipino beefsteak onto everyone's plates. "Alma, turn
the TV on," she said to me, the human remote control. The
real remote wasn't as remote as we had wanted, given its short
cord. So I was in charge of pressing the buttons and adjusting
the antennas.

When I flicked the switch, the nightly news appeared. I
turned the knob to change the channel. "Go back!" my mother
shouted. "What was that?"

I went back to the news. Your photo filled the screen. A
soft smile and feathered hair with a widow's peak. Lip gloss
and heavy mascara. In the photo you were sitting on a picnic
table, smiling at the camera.

Leah pointed. "Don't we know her?!"

That pretty girl from church.

"Victoria Ruiz, a student at Centennial College, has been
reported missing since Tuesday. Her classmates have joined
the search party to scour Colonel Danforth Park for any sign
of her whereabouts," said the reporter's voice over a shot of
the search party in reflective vests, walking in a line through a
forested area. Cut to a map graphic showing where you were
last seen on a morning jog. Cut to footage of your parents at
a press conference.

"To the person who took our daughter, please. Please.
Please. Bring her home to us. She is my joy. She is a bright
light. Please do not harm her," your mother begged. She held

a piece of paper but did not read from it. Instead, she looked directly at the cameras, pleading. "And to you, sweet Victoria. We are searching for you. We will not stop. We will not give up. We love you, wherever you are."

The anchor asked the reporter, "Doug, is there any suspicion from the police as to whether or not this disappearance is connected to the Scarborough Stalker?"

"At today's press conference, Police Chief Garrison said they do not believe there is a connection to . . ."

I looked back at my family. Mom clasped her mouth. Leah had taken a spoonful of steak and rice but had yet to eat it.

I barely slept that night, pondering your disappearance. The police said there was no connection, so . . . did that mean there was more than one person out there attacking people? If that was true, we only had a police sketch of one of them, but what did the other one look like? He could be anyone. He could be anywhere.

The dark around me suddenly felt menacing. Even with the night light on, it cast shadows that transformed my dresser into a caped villain and my closet into a dungeon entrance. I curled up tightly, worried that if the attacker was under my bed, he would snatch my feet first. I felt under my pillow for the homemade weapon Mom had made me, remembering what she said about striking hard.

My eyes grew heavy, but I couldn't help imagining you trapped somewhere, cleverly freeing your hands from ropes and sneaking away while your perpetrator wasn't looking. Maybe I would hear a tapping on my window.

"Psst. It's me! Victoria," you would whisper. "Please! He's right behind me!" And I would break through the screen of my window, grab your arm and pull you with all my might into the safety of my room. I kept imagining the various possible scenarios until the elements of the story were made absurd and nonsensical by my dreams.

I woke up the next morning to an unfamiliar sensation. I scratched at an itch in my crotch so acute that I thought a bug was crawling on me. I stretched the elastic of my pyjamas and underwear and saw hair. Hair?! Down *there*?! I quickly snapped the elastic back into place and stared at the ceiling with eyes wide. This growing-up business was pure and utter bullshit.

I decided to take control of the situation. I snuck into the washroom before Mom and Leah woke up. I had witnessed Leah shave her legs a couple of times while I brushed my teeth, so I assumed it wasn't going to be too complicated. After shaking the can of shaving cream, I pressed the nozzle and sprayed the foam onto my crotch just like I had seen in commercials with people putting Cool Whip onto their Jell-O. One big swirl. Then I ran Leah's razor over my mound, and rinsed the blades clean of any evidence. I breathed a sigh of relief. That should do it. No hair down there for the rest of my life.

Over breakfast the following day, Mom announced to me and Leah that we were installing a security system in our home. She had sourced an affordable one from a family friend. Some guy named Tito Ned whom our dad went to college with back in Manila happened to live just half an hour away with his wife and son.

I was busy stirring boiled water into my porridge and reading the sage advice on the side of the Quaker oatmeal packet when Mom said, "Tito Ned's son, Gary, is coming this afternoon. When he comes to the door, please let him in, okay?"

I absent-mindedly nodded and crossed my legs tightly.

"What's wrong with you? Do you need to go pee?"

I shook my head, not wanting to tell her the horrific fact that hair down there has the audacity to grow back immediately after, and when it does, it can be even more itchy and inflamed. Now I tried my best to be as convincing as possible and pretend nothing was going on.

On my slush-filled walk to school, I dug my hands into the pockets of my sweatpants to pinch at my irritated skin and alleviate the pain. During class, I pretended to need things from my bag in the back of the room so that I could furiously scratch my crotch in privacy. Each time I did so, my eyes rolled to the back of my head with relief. At lunch, I walked down the hall to the library with my legs entwined in agony.

"Are you all right? Do you need to use the restroom?" Mrs. Bartkiewicz said, crunching on a carrot. She wiped her hands on her skirt and walked over to me, concerned. I didn't want to go pee. The last time I went, I saw welts on my pubic bone. It hurt so much and peeing made it sting even worse.

In my desperation, I had no choice but to tell her what had happened. There was no time for shame. I needed a solution, and I needed it quick. If it meant my school librarian was to drive me to the hospital to operate on my wounded front bum, then so be it. Quickly and furiously, as if I were on a 911 call, I explained what I had done.

"Oh dear. That must be unpleasant," Mrs. Bartkiewicz said, looking around the empty library for a answer. Was she trying not to laugh? I wasn't sure. "Okay . . . so . . . listen. I am not supposed to give you any medication." She walked to her desk, opened a drawer and pulled out a tired old grey leather purse that sagged at the edges when she rifled through it. Mrs. Bartkiewicz placed a tube of cream beside her reading lamp and said in a contrived voice to no one in particular, "I'll just put my cream here on my desk. If anyone takes it, it is beyond my control and I have nothing to do with it." She exited the library.

At first I didn't understand, but when I looked at the tube, I figured it out. *Anti-itch cream specially designed for intimate areas*, it read on the label. I ran to the girls' washroom and slathered it on. Relief at last. When I returned to the library with a look of satisfaction, Mrs. Bartkiewicz sat down beside me. "I know that this is a bit late to hear, but you can't just shave your vulva. The stubble will hurt when it grows back in."

"What am I supposed to do with it?"

She looked around the empty library. "It's your choice, really. Some women use chemical creams that dissolve the hair, but that can hurt too. Some women let it grow out naturally. It's your hair. You can decide what you want to do with it."

"Really?"

"Really."

She had thought I meant "Really?" as in "Really? You can grow or get rid of your hair?" when what I really meant was "Really? I can decide what to do with my body?" I wanted to ask her what her choice was, but we had to get to work, sorting through late notices.

Before the period was over, Mrs. Bartkiewicz was already putting on her coat and changing out of her ugly teacher shoes to get into her ugly winter boots.

"You're leaving?"

"Yup. I'll close up now. My daughter has a ballet recital downtown today." Whoa. Lesbos could have kids? She held the keys in her hands and added, "Shoot. I forgot to give you something." Mrs. Bartkiewicz searched her fob for another key. She made me follow her to a backroom of the library, where all the AV equipment was stored. Her arms were full of her lunch box, purse and backpack, so she pointed with her foot at a case sitting at the base of the VHS trolley.

"What's that?"

"It's a video camera. I found it the other day. The battery has to be charged, but there's a tape inside that has footage of an old lacrosse tournament. Go ahead and tape over it."

"What do you mean, tape over it?"

She shuffled me out of the library and locked the door. Walking away from me down the hallway, she explained over her shoulder, "Shoot anything you want. Make a movie. Interview people. Whatever you want to do." And that was that. I became a filmmaker.

But first, I had to figure out how to operate the damn

thing. I rushed home that afternoon with the heavy nylon bag slumped over my shoulder. The padding on the strap had been worn down and it cut into my bra strap. The lampposts I passed were plastered with posters of your face, with big block letters reading *MISSING*. Once I got home, I immediately plugged the camera battery into the charger and sat by the outlet on the new linoleum kitchen floor, waiting impatiently for all five indicator bars to become a hopeful shade of green.

There was a knock on the door. I opened it to find a handsome young man on the other side. "Hi. I'm Gary. Ned's son?" He was taller than most Filipino guys. He removed his Blue Jays baseball cap when he came inside, and I saw that his hair was tidy and smelled like Leah's Dippity-do gel. "And what's your name?" He extended his hand.

"Alma," I said as I shook it.

"What a pretty name." He smiled a genuine smile as he removed his shoes at the door. "Do you have an idea of where your mom wants the alarm sensors?" I shrugged. "Hmm . . . Well . . . let me take a look here. Are there any other doors?"

"There's a side door too. Oh, and a patio door."

"Okay then. Three door sensors. I'll count the windows too." He stood by the frame of the open front door and ran his thumb along the wood. Something caught his eye and he waved. "Hi. I'm Gary. Ned's son."

I could hear my sister approaching. "Hi. I'm Leah."

"Nice to meet you, Leah."

Leah shyly pushed past Gary in her school uniform. She had yet to unroll her blue-and-white kilt back down where it was supposed to be. It was school policy that kilts were down to the knee, so as not to attract unwanted attention. But only losers kept their kilts long, Leah once explained to me.

Gary's eyes travelled from her shoes to her smile. "Have we met before? At Lora-Lee's wedding?"

"Oh my god, yes. I remember you now."

"I didn't recognize you. You're a lady now."

"Hardly."

Even after Gary had installed the alarm system, he lingered, sitting on the couch in front of the TV. Relaxed and casual, he sprawled out with his hands interlaced behind his head. Leah sat with her legs folded under her bum and a pillow on her lap, which she giggled into any time he said anything.

The battery had finally recharged. I locked it into place on the side of the camera and played around with the knobs and buttons to get a sense of what they did. Zoom in. Zoom out. Zoom in. Out. Cool. I took the VHS tape and placed Scotch tape over the tabs so that I could record over it. Shouldering the camera, I walked as steadily as I could towards the laughter in the living room and pressed Record.

"What do we have here?" Gary said, looking squarely at the lens.

"Fuck off, Alma. Leave us alone."

"Hey. She's cool." My face heated. Gary thought I was cool. I thought he was cool too. "Are you recording?"

"Yup."

"What for?"

I didn't know. What was this for? I thought of *60 Minutes* and how journalists engaged their subjects in tough conversations. "Mind if I ask you a few questions?"

"Shoot."

"Okay. Um . . ." I zoomed in, then out, trying to figure out the best frame. "Please state your name and where you live."

"My name is Gary Suarez. I'm from Mississauga, but I live in Toronto right now because I'm going to U of T."

"University!"

"Yup. University. I'm in engineering."

"That means you're old."

"Alma!"

Gary put his hand on Leah's arm and rubbed it affectionately. She looked at his hand there and smiled. "No, no. It's all right. I'm twenty-three. Twenty-four next August." He returned his gaze to Leah, grinning. "And how old are you?"

"Um . . ." She sunk her face into her pillow.

Before she could answer, I shouted behind the camera, "I'm eleven!"

"Awesome. Eleven is a great age."

Leah mumbled through a closed fist, "I'm fourteen. Fifteen in June."

Mom's keys opened the door and she slammed it open with her foot because her arms were full of groceries. "Alma? Leah? Help me with these, please."

Gary walked with all of us to the entrance and began taking bags from Mom's arms. "Hi, Tita Luz."

"Hoy! Hi, Gary. How is school?"

"Good, good," Gary said as he helped us all put away the groceries.

"Will you stay for dinner? We're having pork asado."

"No, that's okay. I should get back."

"Really? It was already cooked last night. I just have to heat it up."

"That's all right, Tita. I have to study for my mid-terms."

Mom playfully hit his arm. "Always working so hard. Okay. Well, we will see you soon. Maybe when we visit."

Gary snapped his fingers. "Oh! I forgot, I have to show you how the alarm system works."

With all of us looking over his shoulder, Gary went through the steps for arming and disarming the system. "Let's say someone tries to break in." Gary opened the kitchen window over the sink and a loud siren went off. He pressed a series of buttons and silence. "See?"

"Wow. It really works."

"Of course it works! The system is foolproof. No one can get in without you and all of your neighbours knowing."

"Good. We need protection here in Scarborough." Mom wagged a finger between me and Leah and Gary. "Did you listen to all the steps your kuya Gary told you? We have to remember to lock all the doors now, ha? Otherwise . . . hala, that stalker guy will come in here looking for you girls." Leah and I nodded dutifully.

If I hadn't needed to leave and slather on more of the anti-itch cream Mrs. Bartkiewicz gave me, I would have been able to say goodbye to Gary. By the time I re-emerged from the washroom, he was gone. Maybe I would see him again and I could continue the video interview.

The following week, I got my first period.

The signs of its impending arrival were all there. Tying my shoelaces that morning seemed too difficult a task to complete. I wanted to scream. I got teary-eyed walking through the snow that morning, worried spring would never come. In the afternoon, I had to do my presentation on Christmas Island's annual red crab migration (yet another chapter in Mr. Fletcher's lazy *National Geographic*–based curriculum). The question-and-answer portion of my presentation represented a quarter of my final mark. I did not do well. It wasn't that I didn't have the answers, it was more like my classmates' questions were plain ignorant. That is . . . if they even were questions.

Fucking Linda Lowry, the pretty girl in class, whom everyone adored and pitied because she was the first and only person whose parents were divorced, raised her dainty little hand and said, "Look! They're gonna make babies in the water!" to which I snapped, "Is that a question, Linda?"

Linda stammered, "Uh . . . they're making babies and—"

I karate-chopped the air to emphasize each word. "Linda. Do. You. Have a question. About. The. Red. Crabs?!" My tone was sharp enough that the classroom was suddenly silent and everyone's eyes were wide and cautious, especially Jason, who knew from past experience not to cross me.

A heat had spread across my face and I couldn't help but scowl. Scowling felt good. Anger felt good. A stab of pain rocked me from behind my belly button. What the hell was going on?

After my presentation, I rushed out at the end of class, went into the girls' washroom and pulled down my pants. I saw a brown stain across my panties. Did I poo my pants? No. It was blood. Oh, great. I had officially become a woman. First boobs and hair, now my period. What was next? Growing a third eyeball? I looked closer and was mortified to see that the stain had spread to my pants. What if someone saw?!

I rushed to the main office and shyly tried to tell the school secretary what was happening.

"Mrs. Grimaldi. Psst. Mrs. Grimaldi," I whispered on the other side of the reception desk.

She did not take her eyes off her typewriter. "Hello, dear. How can I help you?"

"I need help. I . . . I think I just became a woman."

"That's wonderful to hear." Mrs. Grimaldi's cluelessness made me want to rip her head off.

"I said, I think I just became a woman. You know. Down there."

Mrs. Grimaldi pulled the carriage return lever on her typewriter. "Wonderful. Wonderful."

"MRS. GRIMALDI!"

She came to and looked at me over her reading glasses. "Young lady, do not raise your voice at me."

"I'm bleeding. Down there. Please help me!"

"Oh goodness me!" Mrs. Grimaldi exclaimed before walking me to the nurse's office (there never was a nurse around) and unlocking a cabinet where a half-empty box of ancient maxi-pads was stored. She handed me one of them. It felt as thick as the sleeping bags Mom bought for the camping trips we never went on. We then perused the lost-and-found section of the office for a pair of pants for me to wear. She held up each item for me to consider. A pair of toddler leggings with frills on the bum? No. Snow pants with the Teenage Mutant Ninja Turtles logo on them? No. Finally, a large pair of overalls was found in the pile.

"There you go. Take everything and change in the girls' washroom."

"Perfect, thank you!" I said, about to rush out the door.

Mrs. Grimaldi stopped me. "You have to hide the pad, though."

"Why?" I asked, holding my legs together.

"Well . . . you don't want people to know you're . . . you know."

"Bleeding?"

"Exactly. So you have to do this. Watch." Mrs. Grimaldi demonstrated the secretive way to hide one's maxi-pad. "Then you say something like this." She paused and pretended to wave at an imaginary group of people. *"I just need to use the ladies' room. Be right back!"* She looked back at me. "Now you try."

"But I—" A warmth between my legs.

Mrs. Grimaldi gestured for me to do as I was told. I took a deep breath and waved at the imaginary group of people, these people who must not, under any circumstances, know

I had a body that had bodily functions. *"I just need to use the ladies' room. Be right back!"*

"Exactly." Mrs. Grimaldi gave me an enthusiastic thumbs-up as I ran out of the office. "Let me know if you need any help in there," she sang quietly down the hallway.

In the washroom, I crammed that duvet of a maxi-pad into my crotch and then I was sent home early. I walked all the way home with my legs spread wide. The loaner overalls were much too small for me and the cuffs were halfway up my calves, but I barely noticed with the gnawing pain at my pelvis.

I came home relieved to be in an empty house. This meant I could raid the snack cupboard where Mom hid all our left-over Halloween candy. I wasn't sure what was happening to me, but I needed all the snacks. Salty, sweet, crunchy, soft. I needed it all. Just as I removed my winter coat and boots, I heard a noise. It was coming from Leah's room.

"Ate Leah? Are you home?" Why was she here? She usually came home after me because of her commute. "Ate Leah?"

Gary opened the door. I screamed.

"Whoa! Sorry, kiddo." His coat was draped over his arm. Behind him, Leah was putting on her school cardigan.

"Kuya Gary? What are you doing here?"

"I forgot to put a sensor on Leah's window. Her window faces the street, so it's super important to keep her safe."

"Hi, Alma!" Leah smiled and waved at me, which wasn't like her. She rarely was nice to me.

"But we live on a corner. All of our bedrooms face a street."

Gary looked back at Leah. He shrugged his shoulders. She shrugged her shoulders. "You are so smart, Alma. Wow. Well ... it's done now, so ... I'll be heading out. See you, Leah. See you, Alma." And then he left.

Before I could ask any questions, Leah smiled and asked, "Wanna get some Fudgee-Os from the corner store?"

"Really?"

"Really." Leah smiled wider at me. "Oh. And don't tell Mom he was here, okay? He doesn't want her to get angry about him forgetting the sensor thing." I nodded, even though the only thing that made sense to me was avoiding Mom's anger.

Later that afternoon, I watched any show I wanted. Leah let me. I got to watch any show while dunking my cookies into a tall glass of milk. I split each cookie in half, ate both chocolate wafers, then relished the creamy centre, slowly forgetting what I had seen, one bite at a time.

•••

That winter was pretty calm. As calm as things could get in my household. The unusual lull in family drama was attributable to the fact that Mom got a promotion at work, now managing the finance department. Her previous manager was caught having an affair with one of the secretaries, and the staff shuffle finally gave my mother the step up she deserved. Her pay increase meant she could happily part with filing taxes in the evenings and on weekends. In one fell swoop, our dated Immigrant Special electronics were replaced by a high-tech stereo system, a less bulky television with a wireless remote control and, most importantly, a microwave.

"Don't stand beside it or your head will explode," Mom said as I cheered on the microwave's timer by dancing and singing the countdown numbers on the display. "Go and set the table for dinner."

I got to work putting the placemats on the coffee table as a news segment played on the television behind me. "We are strongly considering establishing a curfew for women and children," said Constable Leary to a reporter. "The Scarborough Stalker has, in all cases, attacked at night and ..." I put the cutlery in place, Filipino-style. Spoons and forks only. I heard the microwave beep and knew hot rice was on its way, so I put down a trivet in the middle of the table. "The police's call for curfew comes after the sudden disappearance of Victoria Ruiz two months ago. There are still few to no clues as to her whereabouts. Police say ..."

I stopped what I was doing to look at the television screen. *Where were you?* I wondered. Surely, if you had been murdered, there would have been evidence. Maybe you just ran away. Maybe you didn't want to be found. One day, maybe I would see you again at church and you would tell me it was all a mis-understanding. You'd tell me how foolish you felt for scaring everyone. We would laugh about it, then you'd head to the pew with your parents to join in singing the entrance hymn.

"Alma?" My mom's voice snapped me out of my fantasy. "Can you please empty this out? It's starting to stink." I walked to the kitchen and saw Mom pointing with her mouth at the garbage can beside the fridge. "Then wash your hands, because dinner is almost done."

Thank god. I was as hungry as a horse. I was hungry all the time and my new hips showed it.

I tied the ends of the bag into two neat knots before pulling it out of the plastic bin. Mom was right, it did stink. And it was heavy. I walked the bag to the carport, slid the door open and was about to place it into our metal trash can when I noticed a smaller yellow grocery bag underneath. To make it fit better, I wanted to combine the smaller bag into the larger one. The ends of the grocery bag loosened when I pulled at its handles. I saw a large cardboard box inside that read, *First Detection Pregnancy Test. Results in 20–30 minutes!*

My pulse quickened. With the innocence of a kid with zero sex education, my first thought was, *Mom is pregnant? Which means . . . I'm going to be a big sister?* I reached for the box and looked inside. Nothing. I rolled the bag back and forth to see if there was any other evidence without having to touch the soiled tissue and crumpled paper. Just some empty plastic containers.

I returned to the house with a big smile on my face. I washed my hands as I'd been told to, fantasizing about the little brother I was going to have. I would dress him up like my Cabbage Patch doll, but he'd be real. In fact, I could use the same clothes my doll had. Surely they'd be the right size. Mom would be so happy. She'd be so proud of me reading him bedtime stories. Teaching him how to read and write. I'd call my family to the living room just in time to watch him take his first steps. What would his name be? Maybe my mom would let me choose.

"Alma! Leah! Dinner is ready."

Leah joined us at the table, her eyes weary and red.

• • •

I waited and waited for my mom to tell me the good news. Days passed and she never did. One Sunday afternoon, I was sketching out a blueprint of where the crib would be placed in our shared bedroom when I heard a commotion.

I raced down the hall to Leah's room to see her curled up in a ball on her bed, her knees tight to her face. She braced against the force of my mother's punches, which rained down, swing after swing.

"YOU HAVE NO SHAME! YOU SLUT!"

It was a miracle I did not retreat to my foggy place in that moment. Instead, I felt my legs run towards my sister. I felt my body drape over Leah to intercept Mom's punches. Mom stopped once she realized she was now hitting my back instead of Leah's head.

"I trusted you! What are people going to say, ha? What am I going to tell everyone?!"

No one ever mentioned anything about Gary being nine years older than Leah. No one mentioned anything about Leah being underage. No one mentioned anything about Gary's choice to have sex with a minor. Instead, there was much discussion around Leah making her bed and lying in it.

Chapter 8

My phone rings at work. I pause the video playing on my monitor and put my phone to my ear without checking who's calling.

"Tita Alma. It's Jess."

I squeeze my eyes shut. I should have looked at my call display. It's not that I don't want to talk to my niece. It's because I know why she's calling.

"Mom's been trying to get a hold of you. We're all wondering if you can make it to Lola Luz's birthday next weekend."

"Oh . . . is it coming up already?"

"You know it's coming up."

I love my niece, but I find her curt honesty off-putting. Only eleven years younger than me, she acts like I'm her sibling more than her elder, and it's annoying. Did I not help toilet-train Jess? Teach her how to zip up her jacket? And yet she speaks to me the same way everyone else in my family speaks to me: as if I were garbage.

"Lola would love to see you." She sounds as if she's outside somewhere, like a park. I look around the dark editing suite and make a mental note to go outside and get some vitamin D.

What I want to say back, in a sarcastic tone, is "Really? Does she want to see my wife as well?" with a special emphasis on the word *wife* to allude to my mother's homophobia. I know it's not worth it, though. Instead, I say, "That's nice. Will it be at the home?"

"Yup. Mom is making the usual spread. I'm making the cake. Can you bring . . . I dunno . . . drinks or something?"

I sigh. I am a fabulous cook when I put my mind to it, and my family has never, in the history of family get-togethers, invited me to cook something. "Sure."

"Just . . . no pop. Maybe flavoured fizzy water or something. The nurses told us she's off sugars for the time being."

"Suuuure she is."

"I know. I know."

• • •

The following weekend, I find myself mentally preparing for my mother's birthday. My wife knows the drill. Nira understands that it's probably best she and Mateo do not attend. The last two decades have taught us that the best way to deal with conflict on my side of the family is to avoid it altogether. I kiss my wife goodbye while she finishes her bagel, and we share a knowing look, a look that says *Good luck with all that*, before I leave through the door. She knows I won't be gone long. I'll just show my face and come right back. The faster the better.

It's sad, really. Nira's family have always been so welcoming to me, even though I'm horrible at eating spicy food, even though I don't speak their language. Every occasion I have attended they have included me in conversations, asked me how I am and congratulated me each time I got a new contract. I wonder sometimes if Nira feels shortchanged for not having the same experience.

The old folks' home is emptier than usual. I imagine it's because the weather is glorious outside, and everyone's relatives want to take advantage of the tranquil walkways around the property. I consider suggesting that we move our party outside. Not that it's much of a party. I think better of it because most likely I'll be labelled as difficult yet again, coming up with some idea that will inconvenience everyone. Instead, we remain inside the home's main hall. The walls have been treated in that 1990s style of peach-coloured smooshing paint that looks like old grease stains. I'm not sure what we were thinking back then to believe that it made the walls look like marble. It doesn't look like marble; it looks like there was a shortage of paint. The ceiling fan spins above us, its blades covered in a thick layer of grey dust. It's much too high in the rafters of the room and I can barely feel the air move. Is the air conditioning even on?

"Wow. You're sweating a lot." Leah points to the sweat stains on my button-up shirt. I want to reply and tell her, *No shit, Sherlock*, but she gets pure joy from pushing my buttons, so I try my best not to react and continue arranging the pop cans I brought into a neat line on the table.

She and Jess walk back and forth from the communal kitchen. Both of them have chosen the tallest heels to wear for this occasion, which make an obnoxious clickety-clack sound with every step. It helps them make a big show of all the food they made for the party. I could have made something. I could have lessened their load. But the two of them really love to make my gestures seem small in comparison. While others may believe it's the thought that counts, for Leah and Jess, it's size and scale.

"Tita Alma, did you want to sign the birthday card we got for Lola?" Jess asks while placing serving spoons in all the dishes. For a brief moment I am astounded at how much she looks like my sister. The same straight-ironed hair. The same over-contouring of their cheekbones. It looks like they even chose the same shade of foundation. The only difference is that Jess's face has this dour expression, as though she smells something foul but doesn't want to let on.

I try not to roll my eyes. "No, thank you. I got her a gift myself."

Jess nods silently, as if it's a surprise that I thought to get a gift at all. I know I sound as though I'm making mountains out of molehills when it comes to my blood family's every move, but they are truly, truly toxic people, and there is biting intention behind everything they do.

"How is Nira?"

I want to slam the table. It irks me that Jess never calls her Tita. It irks me that she's only asking out of obligation and not out of genuine curiosity.

"She's fine."

Jess lets out an obligatory "Cool" and nods as if to congratulate me.

The general lack of interest in my life makes me want to scream. None of Nira's accomplishments, of Mateo's accomplishments, are acknowledged as much as those of members of our family who are straight. Hell, Jess could remove a splinter from her thumb and get more praise than Mateo being an astronaut and going to the moon. I remember when Mateo did his first piano concert, when he was six years old. Back then, I was still under the impression that somehow a grandchild would soften my family towards my queerness. I invited them to shell out the whopping five bucks a ticket to watch him. Even that early on, Mateo's teacher could see the promise in him. His musicality. His ability to read sheet music. Even the graceful length of his fingers convinced the teacher he was the kind of student worth investing in. Even after I explained this to my mother and sister, they still dragged their feet. "Will you stop worrying? We'll buy our tickets soon. It's not like it's a real concert at the Carnegie Hall or something," Leah said while she and Mom painted each other's nails. Of course, just before the show, there were only four tickets left. If I wanted my family to see my child, see him shine, see that the life I had made for myself was a good one, I had to buy three tickets myself. One ticket for each of my thankless blood family members. I shouldn't have, but when I saw that it was general seating, I thought the impact of Mateo's cuteness would best be felt if everyone was closer to the stage. So I nabbed a bunch of seats in the front row. Beside me, Nira and my in-laws, I placed my jacket, scarf and hat on the three remaining seats and waited. And waited. Even when the kids all came out for a bow, I kept looking at those empty seats, vowing never again to believe they would ever change. I should never have used him as bait to lure the love of my family, which will never come. I just pulled my focus to my little guy onstage, bowing in his wee tuxedo. I stood up and applauded him. I gave him four people's worth of applause.

Now, I find my hands in fists and loosen them. The past is the past. At least, that's what I tell myself.

"Jess, can you put the birthday cake into the fridge? I'm worried the icing might melt in the heat." Leah wipes her forehead with the bottom edge of her apron.

"Sure, Mom!"

While my sister and my niece go about their usual business of making martyrs of themselves, Mom comes into the hall with the aid of her nurse. This nurse is a new one, with deep-red hair pinned in a neat chignon. I stand up, wipe my sweaty hand on my shorts and reach out to shake the nurse's hand.

"Hi. My name is Alma."

She shakes my hand weakly. Just the tips of her fingers with no grasp. "Oh yes. I heard about you. You're the other one."

What the hell does that mean? Of course, I know what that means. I don't know why I'm asking. The nurse does not make eye contact as she settles Mom into her chair at the head of the table. She does not offer me her name in return.

"And . . . what's your name?"

"Beth." I am about to say that it's nice to meet her, but she's too busy lifting the lids off the dishes that Leah and Jess have made and inspecting the contents. "Did you receive my list regarding your mother's nutritional needs?"

"No, I haven't. Maybe—"

From across the room, Leah rushes to the table holding another Dutch oven full of something hot and heavy. "Hi, Beth! I did get your email and you can rest assured that we followed your nutritional advice." Jess places a trivet on the table in time for Leah to place the pot down, and she removes her oven mitts. They are so in sync with one another, it's scary.

"Even this one?" Beth pokes at a tray of lumpia. "These are deep-fried, aren't they?"

"Oh no, not that dish. Those are off limits for Mom. I made those for the young people in the room."

Beth smiles a tight smile that warps the freckles on her cheeks into blurred lines. "I appreciate it. Your mom's blood pressure has been alarming these days. And her diet has a lot to do with it." She bends at the knees so she's just above my mother's eye level and speaks at the top of her voice. "Okay, Luz. I'll leave you to it. Have fun with your family!"

"Happy birthday, Mom," I say as I reach in and kiss her liver-spotted forehead. The one thing I appreciate about her dementia is that she doesn't wince when I try to be affectionate with her. She hasn't been very affectionate since I came out of the closet. No. Who am I kidding? She has never been affectionate with me. Closet or no closet. Perhaps it was my fear of her that helped me stand back at a distance while still observing her closely. After all, I was the one who started noticing the signs of her dementia in the first place. Not that Leah would admit it. She likes to tell people she was the first to get Mom to go to the doctor, where she was later diagnosed with early-onset Alzheimer's disease. But deep down I know she knows I was the one who spotted it first. Mom started putting these random objects into the fridge. Things that had no place in the fridge, like her car keys, her toothbrush or her Oil of Olay lotion. I smell that lotion on her forehead as I kiss its crepe texture. The scent is familiar; the feel of her skin touching mine in a loving gesture is not.

Mom quietly surveys the spread. You can tell by the way her eyes light up that she is happy to finally eat real food.

Leah looks over her shoulder to make sure Beth is no longer in the room and slides over a plate full of spring rolls, adobo, and spaghetti with hot dogs.

"Alma. Did you get the ice?"

"No. Jess only mentioned drinks."

"Yes. However, if you're going to get the drinks, don't you think you'd get ice too?"

I sigh and pat Mom on the back. "I'll be right back."

Sure, I'm frustrated that Leah and Jess managed to leave a detail out, setting me up for failure yet again, but I'm glad to drive off and go to the grocery store. I would rather share space with the dude who is stacking apples in the fruit and vegetable aisle than spend time with my own blood family.

While I'm in line at the store, with my forearms freezing

from the bags of ice, I see your mother pass me with her shopping cart.

"Are you in line?" says the man behind me. I realize that I am next and the cashier is patiently waiting for me to step forward. I shake my head and find myself following your mother down the spice aisle, trying to keep my distance. I pretend to peruse the baking supplies while she considers the wide selection of spices.

Her face looks different now, different from all those times she had to speak to the press. However, I recognize your mother's widow's peak, the same widow's peak you had. Those first few months of anguish, waiting for you, wondering if you were still alive, dug deep lines between her brows. Her eyes were always this shade of purply red and her hair grew grey over the short time that they shifted from hoping to rescue you to searching for your remains.

Here, right now, right in front of me, your mother is faced with a very simple task. She is trying to choose a steak spice. Such a simple problem. Not a dilemma at all. I can see from my vantage point that she is considering whether to get the bulk bag or the tiny shaker.

I want to introduce myself to her, to tell her how much I worried about her well-being, how much I prayed that her daughter would return. Before I can, she is already pushing her cart down the aisle to the left.

Even though I am carrying bags of ice, I am covered in sweat. I secretively switch the melted bags for new ones at the store's freezer and stand in line yet again. While waiting my turn, I contemplate how strange it is that when memories of you popped back into my mind, I happened to cross paths with your mother.

Before I can make any sense of it, the cashier tells me to step forward.

•••

"You would not believe who I saw at the grocery store," I say, and no one acknowledges my return. The main hall of the nursing home is now raucous and loud with the sound of Tita Lorna and Tito Benny. Tita Lorna must have swallowed a microphone at birth. Her volume usually hovers between rowdy and ear-piercing. As usual, twenty minutes after their arrival, Tito Benny is asleep in an armchair in the corner while his wife tells her latest story about discount clothing shopping adventures in Buffalo.

My arms are full of ice bags and everyone is happily drinking sodas—without ice. Great. I guess I'll just put these away. I pass through the swinging door of the main hall's kitchen and try to jam the bags into the freezer. Someone from a past party has left a box of Fudgsicles. You know what? If things go downhill at this shindig, I'm gonna pocket those. I may eat the entire box in my hot car later.

I can hear Tita Lorna's high-pitched voice echoing through the wall.

"And then I told the border guy, 'I'm only here for the day! Chicken wings. You know . . . a little tour here and there, then home. No shopping.' And he was like, 'Ma'am. I can see the clothes you're wearing are brand spanking new!' And I said, 'No, sir. That's because I take care of my clothes! Maybe *you* don't know how to do laundry!'" Ear-piercing cackle. "Of course, he had to let us go. No tariff paid. See? This cardigan I got, only $19.99."

Leah swings the door open, still looking behind her. "Wow, Tita Lorna. What a deal!" As soon as the door closes, she turns to me and whispers. "Okay. Don't make it obvious. But when you go back in there, look at Tita Lorna's face."

"Why?"

"I swear to god, she got work done."

"Okaaaay."

"Like . . . surgery or something."

"Botox?"

"More than that. It's like she tidied up her bed and tucked all the sheets into the right places . . . well . . . sorta all the right places."

I see her body language change, as though we are in cahoots with one another. Like we're two girlfriends whispering to one another at a slumber party. She always does this. Treats me like crap when I'm useless to her but then gives the impression we are the best of friends if she wants something from me. It's taken years of building awareness and I catch myself delighting in this gossip. I decide to not engage in this triangulation. I'm better than this.

"What do you mean?" I know what she means, but I enjoy making her squirm. Something about watching her struggle to express herself gives me minor satisfaction.

Leah reaches below me for the container of ginataan for dessert. "It's sorta uneven or something. And it's hella obvious."

"What's wrong with it being obvious?" I finally get the last goddamn bag to fit. I close the freezer door and step back. "Isn't the point of a facelift to create a noticeable change? To look youthful?"

"Sure. But not that obvious. Who is Tita Lorna kidding? We're all from the same family and have the same nose. It's not like she can fool us into thinking she's in her twenties again."

"Well . . . good thing it's not for us."

Leah mixes the ginataan with a serving spoon and gives it a taste. "What do you mean?"

"If she got surgery done, she didn't do it for *your* approval. Or mine."

She shifts again. Best Friend Leah fades away and she resumes her Asshole Leah tone with me. "Shit. This needs more sugar." Sure enough, as soon as I say something that rubs Leah the wrong way, she's ignoring me. She pretends to rifle through the cupboards for sugar.

Leaning on the counter, I push harder, just to see if I can get a reaction out of her. "You remember what happened way back in the day between her and Tito Benny, right?"

"Yeah. So?"

"If my husband was not only a gambler but a cheater, I'd want to have some fun with my life too."

Leah grabs some sugar packets from the coffee cupboard and rips them open. "What are you talking about?"

"It's Tita Lorna's turn to have some fun in her life. And if that means looking the way she wants to look, then I'm all for it. And to be honest, I wish Mom had had a little fun after what happened between her and Dad. It would have been better for all of us."

Leah stirs the mixture one last time before picking it up in her arms, and looks at me with contempt. "Oh my god, Alma. When did this become a philosophical debate? You always act so high and mighty because you went to university. Just look at her face and tell me if you think she got her nose and chin done. Jeez."

We both head back into the main hall, me trailing behind. Leah puts the ginataan on the table and begins spooning out bowls for everyone. Everyone except for me. I sit down and do not ask to be served. I want to pretend that her intentional error doesn't affect me by casually sitting among them at the table with my arms crossed.

"Tastes good," says Jess to Leah.

Mom quietly chases a sliver of jackfruit around the Styrofoam bowl with her spoon. Tita Lorna swallows her mouthful then says, "Hoy. Alma. Are you still making movies?"

"Yes, Tita. I'm actually an edi—"

"You know, I keep telling my branch manager, Gordon, 'Gordon! Did you know my niece edited that commercial for Canuck Coffee?' and he's always like, 'Wow! Amazing. You have a niece in Hollywood.'"

I edited that commercial fifteen years ago. This woman and her memory.

"I don't work in Hollywood, I work in—"

"When is your next movie coming out?"

"Well . . . it's not *my* movie, but I edit for—"

"Which movie stars have you met? Have you met Brad Pitt?"

I shake my head and lean back in my chair, hoping for the conversation to end. It's hardly a conversation anyway. As usual, there are no questions about my Indian wife or our mixed-race child. Looking at the clock, I see I have only burned an hour with these people. That's all. I decide to bide my time by doing what Leah told me to do and examine Lorna's face. While she tells us all how well her daughter, Belinda, is doing at the University of Guelph, I confirm in my mind that yes, her nose has been done. And yes, her chin has been given one of those clefts.

"Um . . . Tita Lorna. Sorry. I have to interrupt you. Have you . . . ?" I let the question stand at the edge of a cliff for a couple of breaths. Long enough to make Leah's eyes widen. Long enough to make Tita Lorna smile.

"Have I what?" Tita Lorna looks around the room uncomfortably. Tito Benny rouses out of his sleep to witness this awkward moment I am orchestrating.

"Have you been doing something with your skin? Because you look . . ." Again with the long pause. "You look . . . amazing."

Leah sighs in relief.

Tita Lorna gently smacks my hand. Not too long of a touch. She hasn't hugged me since I came out of the closet. "No! Really?"

"Really. Even Leah was saying . . ." Another long pause. Leah's mouth is full of ginataan and she's chewing the fruit like her life depends on it. "Leah was saying that you looked ten years younger. Maybe twenty."

Tita Lorna clutches the beads of her costume jewellery necklace and cocks her head to one side coyly. "I'm so glad you noticed, Alma."

"It wasn't me initially. It was all Leah. She told me, 'When you go out there, look at Tita Lorna's face. Tell me she doesn't look younger.'"

Leah's face is beet red, exactly the colour I like it to be.

"What's your secret?" I say, leaning my elbows on the table, my chin on my fist.

"Oh, you know . . ." Tita Lorna says with a scattered chuckle. "Fruit and vegetables. Lots of water. Things like that."

"Well, it's working. It. Is. Working."

Leah glares at me from across the table.

A little while later, when Leah and Jess leave the table to get the cake, I put a birthday hat on Mom's head. I have a tough time getting the thin white string to tuck under her chin.

"There. Does that feel okay?"

She doesn't answer me. I don't think she recognizes me anymore. Or she's stopped pretending she likes my company. Either way, it hurts a little.

I turn to Tita Lorna, who is reapplying her lipstick. She knows there will be a group family photo. "Hey, Tita. You won't believe who I saw at the grocery store."

Tita Lorna closes her mirrored lipstick case and smacks her lips together. "Who?"

"Mrs. Ruiz. Remember her? The mother of that girl, Victoria?"

Tita Lorna looks up at the ceiling, where all her memories live. "The mother of . . . Oh yes. Victoria Ruiz. How did you see her?"

"No. I didn't see Victoria. I saw her mother."

"Oooooh. Paula Ruiz. I know her."

"You do?"

"I did. Before. They used to do missions with me and your Titi Benny. We went to the Dominican Republic together. El Salvador. Places like that. When Victoria was killed, she stopped coming along. But see . . . that's when you're supposed to do mission work. When you're in pain." I resist the urge to roll my eyes. "You don't turn your back on Jesus when he is trying to help you find your way."

I shift the conversation slightly. I don't want to listen to my aunt proselytizing the way she did in all those countries she just mentioned. "Are you still in touch?"

"No. No. I have not seen her around. What a tragedy. Did you know that Victoria jogged every morning?"

"Okay." At first, I'm not sure what she's getting at.

"Every morning. Even on weekends. She would wear these short shorts and even makeup and she'd run through Colonel Danforth Park."

"Lots of people jog through that park, Tita."

"Not looking like *that*. Of course, the killer was watching her. He must have been waiting for her. What a tragedy. She was still a student. And so pretty."

Jess and Leah emerge from the kitchen holding a sheet cake topped with lit candles.

"Happy birthday to you . . . happy birthday to yooooooou!"

Mom gently claps her hands. Everyone else sings. I do not join in. I'm too enraged by Tita Lorna's comment. If only you weren't wearing short shorts. If only you weren't wearing makeup. If only.

Chapter 9

It's your turn," Linda Lowry said to me at her thirteenth birthday party.

I could tell by the silence in the room that the boys were scared I'd spin the bottle and it would point at them. Nobody wanted to be kissed by me. I didn't want to be kissed by them either. I just wanted to be included. And the way my mother dressed me, in a frilly pink dress and matching barrettes in my hair, didn't help. I looked like the doll my mother had purchased in Chinatown back when I was a child, the one that closed its eyes when you laid her back and creepily opened them again when you stood her upright. The other girls at the party wore jewel-toned denim and pigtails like Punky Brewster, topped with Blossom-like bucket hats. I regarded their synchronicity with the same awe that I regarded the mystery of how ancient Egyptians built pyramids. How did they know to all dress the same? Did they all call each other to coordinate their outfits? That's why I looked different. No one had my phone number. No one ever asked for it. Not that I

137

would want them to call my house. The thought of my mother picking up the phone and my classmates hearing her Filipino accent made my hairs stand on end.

The Molson's beer bottle that Linda had picked out of the trash spun in a circle and landed on Randy. Randy, like the other boys, had yet to shoot up in height, standing at a modest four and a half feet. But his face already displayed adult acne. It made him a confusing combination of unattractive for having blemishes and super cool for being a glimpse into the future and a promise of puberty. The entire room exploded in a moan sung in unison, pitying Randy for having to kiss me. I was grateful that Randy gestured with his hands for everyone to quiet down before he bent over and met me halfway in the centre of our circle.

I had seen many kisses in films before, pretending to turn away and cover my eyes with my hands when I was really peeking through my fingers to see how it was done in case the opportunity ever arose. I watched with wonder as characters violently smashed their faces against one another and ripped each other's clothes off, twirling about the room until their rocking bodies descended from the frame. I had imagined my first kiss would be as well choreographed, and just as graceful. But here I was, on all fours, reaching my face towards Randy, wondering if I should close my eyes or not. Perhaps closing your eyes made the kiss real. Our lips had barely touched before Randy was already seated with his buddies, who were high-fiving him for being such a stud. I sat back down on my heels, glad the ordeal was over and done with.

"Okay, it's time for movies!" Linda exclaimed, ending the game. She led us all down the hallway towards her living room. As we walked through her expansive home, I looked out the windows and saw the Scarborough Bluffs at the edge of her backyard, and the lake beyond, the white waves crashing against the base of the cliff. I had never seen a house this large and I wished I could snoop in all its many corners rather then watch a slasher film. Everyone crowded into the room as Linda inserted the rented VHS tape into the machine. "Alma, can you hit the lights?" I did as she asked, preferring to stay near the door, not that anyone would have wanted to sit next to me.

Where were Linda's parents? I was amazed at how much freedom she had for this party. All my birthday parties were spent in the presence of my family and the ladies who pushed the carts around the dim sum restaurant. I had yet to see a single adult in this home.

The slasher film began with a bunch of teenaged girls gathering for a slumber party.

"Look at their stupid hair," said Linda, pointing at their outdated fashion choices. Everyone giggled. It was true. This movie looked like it was made ten years ago.

In the movie, there was lots of gossiping over boys and talking about drama among their sorority sisters, drinking alcohol and doing each other's makeup. Then the main character, the one with the Farrah Fawcett hair and heavy eyeshadow, got up, exclaimed, "Pillow fight!" and began hitting all her friends playfully with a pillow. I'm not sure about my classmates, but I was kind of confused about what this pillow fight had to do with the genre. I thought this was a horror movie. I became even more confused when the main character started to remove her pyjama top and bottoms, and her friends followed suit. I didn't know what to do with my body. If I looked away, my classmates would call me a baby. If I looked too hard, all my classmates would call me a pervert. I could feel saliva gathering at the sides of my mouth. I willed myself not to swallow, otherwise everyone would know I was getting aroused by what I was watching. Everyone would know I was getting turned on by the bounce of their breasts and the jovial way the actresses slapped each other's bums. I wanted to look around the room to see everyone else's reactions, but I knew from the stone cold silence that everyone else felt just as conflicted.

Then a murderer busted through the front door of the house and there was a close-up of Farrah Fawcett Hair screaming at the top of her lungs. Several shots of a machete slashing throats were seen, and all of us jolted back. In the film, the one survivor escaped the blood-drenched house and ran, barefoot and buck naked, to the nearest pay phone. "Please! Somebody help me!" she pleaded to the 911 dispatch. "My friends and I . . . we were doing things we weren't supposed to be doing . . . and now . . . now they're all gone!" Before she could complete her phone call, the killer wielded his machete, slashing her neck. Blood spilled all over the phone booth.

The relentless gore got boring pretty quickly and my classmates raided bowls of junk food in the kitchen instead.

That's when Linda proposed we play a game of hide-and-seek. To make it more creepy and fun, she thought we should do it outside. She was right. It was super creepy around her house now that the sun was quickly setting. The fog coming in from the lake added to the ambience. We donned our jackets over our party outfits and took to the lawn outside. Just ahead of me, I saw Jason walking alongside Ruth, Linda's best friend. As Ruth looked over the Bluffs, Jason grabbed her at the shoulders, pretending to throw her over the edge. Ruth laughed and playfully hit his shoulder. He plucked at her bra strap then ran away.

We kept walking until we reached a patch of woods beside her house. "Everyone run and hide!" squealed Linda. We did as she told us, finding places of refuge in the various bushes and trees. I sat cross-legged under the droopy arms of an old pine and realized, without the distraction of my immature classmates, that Linda's home was pretty spectacular. In fact, it would have made the perfect location for a film set in the 1800s. A romantic film with the ingenue standing at the edge of the cliff, longing for her lost love. I imagined the shot as it would look through my video camera. I heard Linda pass by with Ruth, arm in arm. I could tell I had chosen a good spot from the way they walked right past me, whispering to each other, not knowing I was there.

"So why is *she* here?" Ruth asked.

"I don't know. My mom told me I had to invite everyone."

"She smells like bacon."

"Totally. Well . . . she looks like a pig, so . . ."

The two snickered then ran off. I knew they were talking about me, and my face burned with anger. No wonder Linda handed me her birthday invite without looking me in the eyes. Maybe if I snuck into the house, I could take back the gift we got her. She didn't deserve a set of flavoured lip gloss.

I'm not sure how long I sat there under the boughs of the tree, but it was long enough to notice that the forest had gone quiet. I looked through the branches and saw Linda's house in the distance, the white clapboard now darkened by night, the lights shining through the thick of the fog. The cold evening air gave me goosebumps. Everyone must have gone inside, I thought. I carefully emerged from under the pine tree and brushed the needles off my bum.

Behind me, I heard leaves rustling in the wind, and I felt I was being watched. "Hello?" My heart pounded in my chest. Is this what happened to you? Did you call out into the forest? Did you sense something was wrong and turn back on that trail? When was it too late?

I didn't care about the game anymore. Hide-and-seek is a stupid game anyway. I heard a branch break somewhere in the distance and I began speed-walking through the woods towards the house. I walked as fast as I could, looking over my shoulder again and again, certain there was something behind me.

Suddenly, a tree limb clotheslined me and I fell flat on my back. Laughter erupted in the forest and my classmates emerged from their hiding places. All of them, Jason, Linda, Ruth, Randy, all my classmates, stood over me in a circle, pointing and laughing at me.

"Look at her. She's scared!" said Ruth.

"Did you think it was the Scarborough Stalker?" Randy said with a cruel laugh. As if answering his own question, he added, "She thinks it was the Scarborough Stalker! As if he'd ever want to rape *you*." He kicked cold, muddy leaves onto my face.

They left me there on the ground. They walked as a group back to the house, with their same hair, same clothes, all of them laughing at the same inside jokes. None of them looked back.

Did I know that your killer lived a stone's throw from Linda's house? No, I did not. I had not thought about you for a couple of years because I was too busy adjusting first to Leah's pregnancy and then to the addition of Jess into our lives. A crib was built, a baby was born, there were diapers to change, and lots of damage control in the Filipino community.

Trying to save face after Leah brought shame to us all was an arduous journey. For a long while, people at church refused to make eye contact with us. Mom was smart enough to not demand that Gary or his family pay any support. It made us appear self-sufficient. It made the pregnancy look more like an accident than a manipulative gold-digging move. As long as Leah and the baby stayed out of the way of Gary's future career as an engineer, we were good. Good enough. Acceptable.

Many nights I listened to Leah walking the hallways trying to rock Jess to sleep. Since Leah had a baby, there had been four more attacks. Two teenaged girls. One child. One elderly woman. On these occasions, there were no survivors. While I was busy learning how to properly burp a baby, the victims' photos circulated on the news. Smiling faces. Bright eyes.

I had very little room in my brain to commit to fear. That is, until that very moment. As I brushed myself off, wet with mud along the back of my frilly dress, something shifted in me, although I could barely discern what exactly was happening. Sure, I was familiar with being the loser at school. And yet something about this moment pushed me from being an outsider to considering that I was in fact a target for harm. A *target*. That word. Like I had a bull's eye on my forehead, around the area where Leah jabbed me. Target. This word was used to describe your killer, that he targeted young women and girls. His targets were often unaware of his presence until it was too late. And what made me any different from those victims? I had to know. If I could make myself as different as possible from them, I would not be attacked. Not by the Scarborough Stalker. Not by my family. Not by my classmates. I would stop being a target.

I thought about what Randy had said. That I didn't need to worry about the Scarborough Stalker raping me. Was that true? Was being ugly enough to keep him away from me?

"Did you have a good time?" Mom asked me on the drive back home from the party. I positioned myself so that she could not see the stain on my dress, this dress I did not choose to wear.

As soon as we were home, I went straight into my bedroom, to my safe place, where I undressed and cried in my underwear. It felt good to allow myself to surrender to the sorrow I was truly feeling, to be nothing but a messy puddle on the carpet of my room. Not until my stomach grumbled did I realize I had not eaten much, except for the few handfuls of corn chips at the party. The acidic sensation of my hunger felt like the right punishment for not being good enough. Mom wasn't punishing me at the moment, and I had to do what I found most familiar and punish myself. For a finishing touch, I slapped my own face while mumbling something to myself about being a stupid bitch. The sting on my cheekbone made my eyes water and my hands buzz. My tears flowed freely until I was sobbing in hacks and hiccups that no one ever heard. My safe spot was the perfect place to hide.

That night, I dreamed that the summer evening wind was blowing through the curtains of my bedroom window. Crickets and grasshoppers were singing their song when a doglike figure appeared just outside the screen and peered in at me. It was the shape of a Doberman pinscher, but its silhouette was pure darkness, except for the twinkle of its spiked collar and its menacingly glowing red eyes. In a voice I will never forget—demonic and robotic—it said to me, "You think you can hide from what's out here. But they're in there with you." Was it smiling at me? I woke up with my muddy dress under my head as a makeshift pillow.

From that night onwards, I wondered who among us was the Scarborough Stalker. Was it my dentist, Dr. Hertz, who always had his gloveless finger in my mouth, even when his receptionist interrupted the appointment? He would turn away from me and chat casually about something funny that had happened over the weekend while I reclined on his chair, mouth wide, his finger hooked into my cheek like I was a caught fish.

Was it that guy who stocked shelves at the grocery store? The one with the sandy-blond hair who eyed me up and down when I reached up for a bag of pasta on the top shelf? He was tall enough to retrieve it for me, but he chose to stand back and watch me, his eyes lingering on my bum.

Was it that white guy whom my Tita Ida married? The one at their engagement party whom I caught whispering to Leah? While leaning in to my sister, he said, "Why are you so sexy in that skirt? What's the reason? You have to tell me!" before Leah walked away.

Or was it my neighbour, Mr. Stolks, whose house I could see through my bedroom window? While he didn't fit the physical description, his creepiness fit the bill.

They were everywhere. All of them. These men lurking and leering. Touching and rubbing. All of them. But supposedly, there was just this one guy.

Chapter 10

I come home from a long day at work to find Nira digging trenches in our front garden. Why does she always tend to the beds in the middle of the summer instead of the spring?

"I know what you're going to say." She stands up and brushes off her knees, making old-people noises with each movement. Those groans have gotten louder over the last year. So have mine.

"I'm not going to say anything, because what's the point? You never listen." I shut the car door, activate the alarm and walk towards her with my hands on my hips. I rarely am the one in the right, so I need to milk it for all I've got.

Nira removes her gloves and points at the lavender seedlings. "I know we only have another month to enjoy these, but lavender is a perennial not an annual, so I didn't waste money like last year." I throw her a look. "Okay, and the year before that. They'll be in bloom come spring and you'll thank me then."

Hoisting my backpack higher on my shoulder, I give her a kiss on the cheek. I get it. Nira is a teacher. The last thing she's thinking about in the spring is readying her garden bed. Come March, she's already counting down the days until her shithead students can get out of her hair. It's tiring for her, to say the least.

"How was work?" she asks while stabbing a spade into the soil.

I give her a noncommittal shrug and a meh sound. I don't want to go into too many details about spending my day blurring out the faces of the Scarborough Stalker's surviving victims and altering their voices. Their testimony echoes through my skull and there's a dull pain at the base of my neck. I'm just glad this series is short. Ten episodes in total. When it's over, I will happily return to editing commercials, even cooking competitions.

As I'm stepping onto our stoop, she says, "Can you do me a favour, Shortcake?" Nira wipes one of her curls from her face, leaving a streak of mud on her jawline. Do I tell her? Nah. "Can you please use last night's chicken to make a pot pie? I'm having a fierce hankering for one of your pies."

I change my mind. I step back down and wipe the mud off her chin before I kiss her again. I love that Nira knows I am a good cook. I love feeding her. It's the one thing I do right by her, every time. No fail.

"Hey. Don't start something you can't finish," she says with a laugh, before slapping my bum. Then she sees something behind me and pulls away. "Hi, Mateo. Hi, Hong."

I look behind me and there they are. My stomach knots a bit, remembering that troubling phone call the other night.

From the sound of it, I thought they had broken up. It looks as though I was mistaken. I am ashamed by the relief I feel that I need not have a conversation with Mateo about it all, especially about him invading Hong's privacy. Or should I anyway? If I do, it will betray the fact that I overheard their argument.

Maybe not. He looks to be in better spirits. Mateo's hair is back to its normal shiny curls. He looks like he's wearing clean clothes. He waves (with a smile!) and says (clearly, not mumbling!), "Hey, Mom. Hey, Mama."

While I am relieved by his cheerful demeanour, there's something about the image of him and his girlfriend that I do not like. He has his arm around Hong's waist, but her body language is all wrong. She is leaning away from Mateo and looking down at her feet. What has happened since that phone call?

"Did you guys want to join us for dinner? I'm making chicken pot pie," I offer, trying to make eye contact with Hong.

Mateo speaks for both of them. "That's okay. I'm treating Hong to a movie tonight. I'm just changing my shirt upstairs." Mateo points towards the house and I notice a large bandage on his hand.

"What happened to your hand?" I ask him. Part of the bandage has a spot of blood.

"Oh, this?" Mateo laughs. Hong does not. "Chemistry class. It was a stupid mistake." He rolls his eyes.

149

Nira and I watch the two of them ascend the stoop and enter the house together. Arm around waist. A three-legged race.

I whisper to Nira, "Do you think Hong is okay?"

"She's always been shy, that girl. Don't read into things. She's fine."

"But . . . I dunno. I get the sense that she's not into Mateo as much as Mateo is into her."

"Alma, you can't speak for Hong. If she doesn't want to be in a relationship with him, she has the ability to tell him, and vice versa. They're their own people. We have to let them figure things out on their own."

"I just . . ." I try to edit the phrase in my head so as not to give away that I was eavesdropping. "Do you think we've taught Mateo how to be in a relationship? You know . . . how to treat people right?"

"What are you, Dr. Phil?" Nira puts her hand on my shoulder and laughs, slapping her garden gloves on her thigh. I should have left the streak of mud on her face. "My love, we taught him the basics. Sharing is caring. Say please. Say thank you. Say sorry. We gave him sex education and—"

"The *basics* of sex education. There wasn't a whole lot of detail."

Nira rolls her eyes at me because she knows her abridged birds-and-bees talk was rushed through and badly executed. It was the most nervous I had ever seen her. I admit it was funny to watch her crash and burn.

She continues. "My point is, we can't coddle him anymore, Alma. If he needs to talk, he'll reach out to us."

I keep this in mind as I head inside to get dinner started. Sort of. For a while I stand in the kitchen, all alone, training my ears to the sounds upstairs. Maybe the call wasn't as bad as I had originally thought. And maybe I'm mistaking Hong's shyness for agitation. But going into someone's locker without their permission? I will have to talk to him about that. Someday. I will broach the subject in a way that won't seem too pointed and obvious. Or maybe not. If I say something, he won't listen anyway. I might make things worse, I think while kneading the cold butter into the flour to make the pastry dough.

By the time I get the pie in the oven, Mateo and Hong are heading out the door, Mateo tightly grasping Hong's hand. He waves goodbye to me over his shoulder.

Chapter 11

We were the picture of Catholic family dysfunction as we descended the escalator at the Eaton Centre mall. To assist my sister, a teenaged mother, I was in the front, holding Jess's stroller up from the bottom wheels. Leah was above me, holding the handles, urging Jess to "be nice to Mommy and stop spitting out your soother!" Our single mom was behind her, holding a garment bag full of my clothes.

"Alma. The escalator is ending."

"Yes, Mom."

"It's coming. Look behind you."

"I can see that."

"Step down. Don't fall, ha?"

"Yes. I heard you."

At the base of the escalator was our destination: Glamourpuss Portraits. I had envied all the cool girls who got their photos done there before. Portraits weren't something on my mom's radar, especially since my family often joked about how I ruined family photos. Even though I experimented with different poses, different smiles, they would inevitably point and chuckle at how ugly I was. So as not to be labelled ugly *and* difficult, I would laugh along, even though I thought it was far from funny. Eventually, I stopped posing in group photos altogether and offered to be the one taking them instead. They never argued with me.

Now things were different. Somewhat. I was auditioning for a new Catholic arts high school, which was being built twenty-five kilometres away, in North York. There were four majors to choose from: music, dance, visual arts and drama. I chose drama just so I could access the school's state-of-the-art film lab. The promo booklet that had been mailed to us featured glossy artist renderings of several editing suites and shiny new VHS cameras. For this audition, I needed to memorize a monologue and issue a headshot to the jury.

Tita Lorna suggested we go to Glamourpuss Portraits. It was a new craze that disrupted the cheesy mall portrait business by being an even cheesier mall portrait business. Parents could send their young daughters to this chain of storefronts and have them photographed professionally, with real studio lighting, a makeup artist, a new hairdo and wardrobe.

"See this?" Tita Lorna had reached her hand into the thin plastic wrap and pulled out a pile of photos.

"Wooooow! Belinda is so photogenic."

Peering over my mother's shoulder, I watched her leaf through the images. Belinda in front of a backdrop of roses, leaning on her forearms covered in purple-bow evening gloves. Belinda pretending to spray her towering bird's nest hair while winking coyly at the camera. Belinda doing jazz hands in front of a paint-splattered backdrop. All with a soft-focus filter. Mom was right: she looked incredible. To look that good, to have hair that high, seemed much too lofty a dream for me. Mom had booked an appointment anyway.

So there we were, at the entrance of Glamourpuss Portraits, the sound of C+C Music Factory blaring over the speakers.

"Okay, I'm gonna look for some new shoes for the baby," said Leah as she wheeled the stroller away. What a relief. There was only so much I could take of them embarrassing me. Mom remained, though, and I prepared myself for all the ways she would make my skin crawl in a public setting.

She handed me the garment bag and put her giant purse on the front counter. "Hello. We booked an appointment for Alma Alvarez."

"Welcome, welcome." The receptionist bopped her head to the repetitive music. "Package A, right?"

"Yes." I knew what was coming. Mom made a big show of taking out her massive wallet and positioned herself so that I had a clear view of the transaction. "How much will it cost?"

"Depends. How many poses?"

"Two, please."

"It'll be fifty-five per pose."

Mom did not make eye contact with me but raised her eyebrows and pursed her lips to perform hardship in front of me.

"Cash or credit?"

"Cash."

Mom counted the bills out slowly, right in front of my face, stage-whispering her sums, until she handed over the money with a look of suffering.

I sighed. "Thanks, Mom."

"Anything for my children," Mom said with piety.

The receptionist came out from behind the desk. "I can bring her back to get her hair and makeup done. Will you be staying?" she said to my mother.

"Oh. I can leave?"

"Yeah. No problem. It's kinda crowded in the studio anyway."

"Oh. Okay. Alma, I'll wait for you outside, all right?"

I waved. Once Mom was gone, the receptionist looked at me and said with a sly grin, "It's not crowded. We just want you to have a fun time without your mom around."

I blushed. Her lips were painted a deep purple on the outside and a soft taupe in the middle. Surprisingly, once we were in the "studio" portion of the place (i.e., an empty backroom), the receptionist took an apron off the back of a director's chair and looped the strap over her shoulders. While tying it around her waist, she said, "Have a seat. I'll get your hair started."

Sitting down on the chair's canvas fabric, I felt my body buzz with excitement. I couldn't wait to sit down in a chair like this one day and be a real director.

"My name is Jillian, by the way. And you're Alma?"

My mouth was suddenly dry. Why was it dry? "Yes," I croaked.

Jillian got straight to work by setting my mushroom cut into Velcro rollers. While she teased my hair into a remarkable sculpture, some tattooed guy walked in, carrying a Styrofoam container. "You're late, Izzy."

Izzy rolled his eyes. "Let me finish my lunch and I'll be right there." He disappeared somewhere and the smell of sweet-and-sour chicken balls filled the air.

Now that my hair was rock solid, Jillian began working on my makeup. She squeezed a dot of moisturizer on her palm and rubbed her hands together before massaging it into my face. "You have nice skin." I felt dizzy at her touch, especially when she applied salve onto my lips with her ring finger. "What are we doing today?"

I didn't know what she meant. "Taking photos?"

"Yeah, but what look are we going for?" She faced her makeup table and considered her variety of palettes. "Like . . . are we going for the no-makeup look or are we going All. The. Way?"

"What do you mean by no-makeup look?"

She looked at me through our reflections in the mirror framed by bare bulbs. "You know that bullshit around makeup that looks like you're not wearing any? Soft pinks, blushes, a little mascara? It's supposed to look like you're not trying."

"Trying for what?"

"Trying to look pretty. For boys, mostly."

"Oh." I didn't know how to answer this.

"Well . . . how about this—what are these photos for?"

"An audition."

"So . . . not for your family's mantel or something?"

"No."

"Okay then." That same sly grin played on Jillian's face again. "Shall we go All. The. Way?"

I crossed my legs, overwhelmed by the waves of desire washing over me. "Yes. Let's do it!"

With an air punch, Jillian began to spackle on foundation that was two shades too light and one tone too pink. That was the closest we could get back then for brown people. "Look up," she said while poking liner into my bottom lid. "Look down," she said while brushing mascara onto my lashes.

My favourite part of the process was her applying gloss. While her eyes were focused on my lips, my eyes were fixed on her magnificent cleavage. Two brown mounds swelled into mountains behind her low-cut shirt and met in the middle in this mysterious crevasse. I wanted to dive head-first down into the depths of her. From my vantage point, I could see something lodged in its fold. A chit of paper with something scribbled on it. Was it someone's phone number? Her grocery list?

She smiled. "All right, Alma. Are you ready to see yourself?"

She stepped aside and I looked in the mirror. Holy shit. I looked like a woman. How Jillian managed to transform my mushroom cut into a towering architectural masterpiece is still a mystery to me. Her contouring skills brought out my cheekbones. The eyeshadow made me look alluring. Pretty, even.

Jillian tossed my mother's garment bag full of subdued pantsuits aside and put me in a white jean jacket and acid-washed pants.

"IZZY! She's ready."

Izzy magically appeared, tossed his empty Styrofoam container into the garbage and grabbed his SLR camera. "Stand here," he said unceremoniously while positioning the studio lights. "Turn your collar up. Yeah. Hold your collar. Yeah. Like you're cool. Yeah. Head to the side. The other side. Yup. But look at me. Perfect."

The process happened all over again in a fuchsia dress with a cluster of frills on one shoulder. "Hands on your waist. Yeah. Like . . . don't mess with me. Exactly. A bit more attitude in the face. Yeah."

The photos arrived a week later. Thanks to the soft-focus filter, my headshots were good enough to grace the pages of a magazine. Or rather a catalogue.

So you can imagine the faces of the jury when I entered the audition room a month later, looking like my normal self, wearing a plain face with my signature mushroom cut.

"What do you have prepared for us today?" one of the jury members asked. He was an older man wearing that typical wool sports coat that all drama teachers seem to buy from the Drama Teacher's Store.

I stood in the centre of the room and performed a scene from my favourite Fred Astaire and Ginger Rogers film. It was no regular ho-hum monologue. No sir. I wanted to give the jury an unforgettable experience, performing both as Fred (with top hat on) *and* as Ginger (with silky boudoir gown). It took a while to set up my various props and costume pieces, long enough that I heard one of the jury members, a woman with a chunky knit sweater and neck scarf, also acquired from the Drama Teacher's Store, sigh before taking a sip of her coffee.

When I finally got started, I pretended to be Ginger, struggling to sleep in the apartment below Fred, who is carelessly tap dancing on the floor directly above Ginger's bed. "Hello?" I said into my toy phone with a weird mid-Atlantic dialect. "Is this the building manager? There is a ruckus upstairs and it needs to stop immediately!"

Then I switched to being Fred, putting my costume felt hat on and tap dancing to my heart's content. I answered the toy phone that, in my imaginary world, was ringing. "Good evening. Yes. This is he," again with that mid-Atlantic dialect, only this time with the earnest cadence reserved for leading men of the period. "A ruckus, you say? Well, tell that young lady not to worry. She'll be asleep in no time." I pulled on my prop paper cigarette, blew out imaginary smoke and put it out into a vase I pretended was one of those lavish ashtrays of that time. I mimed taking sand from the ashtray and spreading it along the floor. Using *ch-ch-ch, ch-ch-ch, ch-ch-ch* sounds with my mouth, I mocked soft-shoe dancing.

When I switched back to Ginger, I was lulled back to sleep by the comforting rhythms of Fred upstairs. It was quite the feat. There were multiple voices, costume changes, a musical soundtrack, which I hummed all by myself. But I wanted to capture what fascinated me about films: the convergence of many disciplines to tell a story. This was a scene I had acted out many times in the solitude of my bedroom, where my imagination could run wild. It wasn't enough to just borrow those VHS tapes from the library and watch them. I had to live them. Make-believe was the safest place to be.

I brought my acceptance letter to Mrs. Bartkiewicz, who was in the middle of eating lunch in the library. My backpack was still on as I sat opposite her and watched her pull out the paper from the frayed envelope. She swallowed the food in her mouth as she read the first paragraph.

"My goodness! Alma. Congratulations." Mrs. Bartkiewicz's arms opened towards me. "May I give you a hug?" No one had asked me before. I nodded yes. We embraced hard enough that her clip-on earrings pressed into the pillow of my cheek. "Oh my goodness. This is great news. But . . ." She scanned the letter again. "Oh. It starts from grade seven? How unusual."

"Yeah. Because it's a new school, they are starting with three grades leading into high school. There'll be students in grade seven, I'll be in grade eight, and there will be one class of grade nine students."

"Oh. This is for this next school year. Oh." I watched Mrs. Bartkiewicz's smile wane a bit. "Does this mean you're not graduating from St. Xavier?"

"I'm starting this September!" I said excitedly.

She knew how little I was getting out of St. Xavier. By that time, the school's funding was so low we were sharing textbooks, three to one. My beloved drum "set" was now just a cymbal because the snare drum's springs had snapped. The gym was closed for mould remediation that was never going to happen. And while I was relieved not to have Mr. Fletcher anymore, my new teacher, Mrs. Casings, loved to belittle me when I didn't understand arithmetic.

I thought Mrs. Bartkiewicz would be just as excited. Instead, she refolded the letter and looked at me solemnly. "Well. Teachers always want their students to go on to do great things. I will miss you, Alma Alvarez." Tears began pooling in her eyes. I thought I had done something wrong. "The library will probably fall into quite the state without you." She took out one of her Wet-Naps from her lunch box and wiped her hands clean. The smell of rubbing alcohol filled the air. "I hope you will visit when you can. And I hope you know you can come to me any time . . . to tell me anything. Do you understand?" I nodded. "Maybe you don't. Let me be clear. Alma. If there is anything going on . . . if ever you want to chat and need a safe place to express yourself . . . about anything happening in your life . . . at home . . . whatever. I'm here. Please promise me you'll remember that."

This was the first time a teacher acknowledged their suspicion about the abuse I was enduring at home. When I think back, I suspect a few must have wondered why I was painfully quiet and horribly awkward. Even my first-grade teacher at my school downtown went so far as to ask why there were bluish contusions all over my legs. I never answered, and that teacher never bothered me again. After that conversation, I instinctively knew to cover my upper arms and thighs, where most of my bruises were.

Mrs. Bartkiewicz was different in so many ways. She

looked me square in the eyes and handed me back the letter. Taking it, I replied, "I promise."

•••

Dozens of tartan patterns stacked the shelves of the uniform store. Dark green, light purple. Navy blue and moss green. Cream and chocolate brown. Mustard yellow and black.

"And which school are you attending, young lady?" said the tailor who knelt at my feet, measuring my waist and leg length.

"Bishop Shaughnessy Academy." I held my arms out in front of the three-sided mirror.

"Ah. The new arts school."

"Yes, sir."

"Janine?" he said to a woman at the front desk.

Janine looked over her reading glasses at him. "Yes, dear."

"Another one for Bishop Shaughnessy."

Janine disappeared to a backroom and returned with a roll of the ugliest tartan I have ever seen. It was an off-putting combination of navy blue and bright red, accented with white stripes.

"This is it?" I had a difficult time hiding my disdain for the pattern. It got worse as the tailor draped the fabric onto me. I looked like a container of shortbread cookies.

"Stand up straight, Alma," said Mom, who sat on a folding chair beside me, her massive purse on her lap.

The tailor looked at my reflection and said, "Remember that this is the regulation length. Just above the knee." He put a pin into the fabric as a guide and pointed at it.

Janine was back behind the desk and added, "Back in my day, the nuns used to force us onto our knees, and if our kilt didn't grace the floor, we had to stretch our arms out and balance Bibles in both hands for the rest of class." She raised her eyebrows at me and went back to writing receipts.

At the end of the fitting, my mom approached Janine and put her purse on the counter. I knew what was coming.

"How much do I owe you?"

"For two kilts, three shirts and a cardigan, it'll be three hundred fifty."

Mom took out her wallet so that I could see the transaction.

"Will that be cash or credit?"

"Credit. I don't have that much cash on me."

"Of course."

Mom did not have the bills to count for dramatic effect, so she just whispered over and over again, "Three hundred fifty. Three hundred fifty," as she filled out the credit card slip and affixed her signature with a flourish of her pen.

•••

On my first day of school, I started my two-hour commute early in case one of the Scarborough buses failed me. Mom had already left for work, but I got a twenty-dollar bill taped to my lunch bag. The sticky note beside it read, *MONEY FOR TRANSIT TICKETS*.

Leah breastfed Jess on my bed while I got dressed in my brand-new uniform.

"Turn your kilt pin up," Leah said while Jess fussed at her mother's chest. The baby had gotten into the habit of slapping Leah's face if the flow wasn't strong enough for her and Leah was considering weaning.

"Why?"

"If you turn it down, it means you lost it."

"Lost what?"

Leah rolled her eyes and unlatched Jess. Switching to her other breast, she explained, "Lost your virginity, you loser. Unless there's something you're not telling me."

"Whoa. No. I haven't even had a boyfriend."

"I know. I was joking. As if you had a boyfriend."

I pierced the ugly fabric of my tartan with my kilt pin right side up to ensure everyone knew I was as virginal as untouched snow.

Leah and the baby waved from the kitchen window as I walked to the bus stop. She watched me with a look of longing in her eyes even as I turned the corner of our street. I wonder what was going on in her mind. Did she hate me for getting on with my life, for being able to live as a teenager while she had to face motherhood?

The bus stop was far away, a good ten-minute walk past nicer, more manicured, more lavish homes, housing people who were not likely to use public transit. Our neighbours were definitely the types to use their shiny cars to get around rather than risk a crowded Scarborough bus.

In the crisp autumn air and early morning sunlight, I stood with my fellow commuters and waited for the 54 to come. A nurse in scrubs. A mother with her stroller. An old man sat in the bus shelter eating an apple. We waited. And waited. And waited. Shifting from one leg to the other. Rubbing our arms from the cold. Watching the horizon for any sign. We waited.

Half an hour later, two buses arrived at the stop and I made the mistake of getting into the less crowded one. If I had gotten into the packed bus, then I would not have sat across from a middle-aged man who kept dropping his pen in order to look up my skirt. He did this over and over again, pretending to fumble then lingering with his eyes at the height of my knee. I crossed my legs tightly, but my discomfort made him grin all the more.

On the westbound train from Kennedy station there were no seats left, so I braced myself on one of the handle bars. A man sitting in the seat below me did a double take at the sight of my uniform and peered at me over the edge of his newspaper. Throwing all discretion aside, he ended up folding his newspaper and placing it on his lap so that he could get a full view of my body, his eyes scanning my knee socks all the way to the sway of my kilt. Where was his other hand? Was it under the newspaper? In his pants? The train hit the brakes abruptly at Coxwell station and he delighted in my thigh grazing his knee. "Carefuuuuul," he sang with a sly grin.

Leah had told me I could roll my kilt up to make it look like a miniskirt, but I didn't see the point. If this was how much unwanted attention I was going to get with it at my knee, I shuddered to think of how much I would garner with it mid-thigh.

The school was new, maybe too new. I was quite accustomed to St. Xavier being a crumbling ruin. It was strange to set foot in an institution with newly laid tiles and a fresh lick of paint. Bishop Shaughnessy was so new that if you looked closely, you could see certain corners where the drywall had yet to be set.

My drama teacher wasn't very impressed with me when the first question I asked was "So . . . where's the media lab?"

"You'll see soon enough," Mrs. Greenwood replied. "How about you go back to your group and continue brainstorming on your tableau series?"

I hated tableau. I didn't understand the point of it all. Why in god's name did we need to freeze in position, depicting the death of Christ or his birth? It drove me a bit batty how much artmaking revolved around Jesus and his life. I thought that being in a Catholic art school meant I would have to attend Mass in the main hall every now and then. I certainly didn't think my time there would be so god-focused.

Things got worse when I spent my afternoon in a class called Family Life. *Family Life* was a euphemism for sex ed, the Catholic assumption being that one does not have sex unless your intention is to make a family. For reasons still unclear to me, we were made to change out of our kilts into our gym uniforms. I wasn't sure why we had to wear shorts and a shirt when we spent our time in the gym sitting on crash mats. We were divided by gender, the boys in one corner and the girls in the other. While Mrs. Keenan taught the boys how to keep their junk clean, Mr. Gregor taught the girls various strategies on how to say no to sex. The pair of teachers thought it progressive to have a woman teach the boys and a man teach the girls. The effect, however, was comical. The boys ogled Mrs. Keenan in her shorts while she showed diagrams about pulling foreskin and clearing the penis head of smegma. Mr. Gregor, on the other hand, drove his point home by putting his hands on our shoulders while teaching us about the sanctity of our own bodies.

It was all worth it when, into my second month of school, I joined the AV club. Part of my duties involved delivering televisions and overhead projectors to teachers throughout the school. In return, I had access to the school's video cameras and editing suites. The club met every Wednesday after school, with very little structure. All Mr. Haynes expected us to do during club hours was sort through VHS tape supplies and do inventory checks. This meant that the rest of the geeks and I got to play and experiment to our hearts' content.

The editing suites were in high demand, especially since there were only two of them. We'd crowd around the two monitors, partly to wait our turn, partly to trade skills and ideas. Some guy a year ahead of me named Toby showed us all how to render the VHS tape into a digital format and splice the video.

"And all you do is drag and drop it right here, like this," Toby said, demonstrating to a handful of us encircling the desktop and nodding our heads. "Then watch this." Toby pressed the Play button and the last clip transitioned into a second clip with this animated streak across the screen.

"Whoa!" we all exclaimed. It was a swipe just like the transitions we saw in that television show *Home Improvement*. I thought of all the ways I could use this software, perhaps in the next short film I was creating.

One Wednesday, Toby and I were the only ones at AV club. He was already laying down a musical track over footage of a dance rehearsal. At my desktop, I was experimenting with the order of shots I took of a flower that was blooming in our garden at home. Toby looked over my shoulder, his ear close to mine. "That's some cool stuff you're doing there."

"Thanks." Nothing I had done in my life was ever called cool before. I waited for some punchline to indicate that he was joking. It never came.

I looked outside the window of the lab and realized that the autumn light was quickly fading. "I'd better get home."

"Home? Where is home?" Toby said while standing up and putting his jacket on. Was he leaving too?

"Scarborough. I live far away."

"No way! I live in East York. Wanna take the TTC together?"

"Um . . . sure?"

Toby and I talked and talked without a moment of silence. We talked non-stop as we transferred from the southbound train to the eastbound train.

"There are awesome Jamaican beef patties at Warden station. Want to get one?"

"But aren't you getting off at Victoria Park station?" I asked him. The darkness of the concrete tunnel opened up to the purple of the twilight sky. The subway swayed side to side through towering high-rises.

"Yeah, I know. I'll just double back."

We sat on a red plastic bench outside the bakery at Warden station and ate one patty each. We split a third one. He bought all three with his own money. There was a bit of pastry flake in his sandy-blond hair and I was tempted to brush it out.

"You're really cool," he said to me with a smile. "You're not at all like what everyone says you're like."

My cheeks grew hot. "What do you mean? What are people saying?"

"I don't know . . . I heard some things about you being a dyke or something."

I had no idea what a dyke was, but I imagined it wasn't good.

"You know . . . people were saying you're some kind of she-male."

She-male. Oh. *Dyke* was another word for a lesbo.

"Who? Like . . . everyone is saying this?" The image of my classmates at Linda Lowry's party flashed through my head. But instead of them laughing at me in that ridiculous pink dress, they were laughing at a disgusting creature. Half human. Half freak. She-male. I didn't want to be that. My heart sped up. What did I have to do to not be one?

"Well, not everybody is saying it. But I've heard it some places. In the cafeteria, maybe? I don't really remember." He ate the last of his crust and licked his fingers.

My brain scanned the situation quickly. If there was one

thing I learned living in my house, it was to make quick decisions in order to protect yourself. If I pretended to crush on him, surely everyone would think I was normal. Yes. That's all I had to do. *Be like a girl. Be like a girl,* I cheered myself on. I felt my hand reach out and brush the pastry flake out of Toby's hair. Not casually. Lovingly. Like in films where a character would finally make the first move. For maximum effect, I flashed him a warm smile. Surely a dyke or she-male wouldn't do that.

"I'd better get home." I stood up and dusted the crumbs off myself. "My mom is gonna kill me."

Toby went west. I went east. It didn't matter whether or not Toby was into me. What mattered was that he thought I was into him. I pictured him going back to his friends and clearing the air. He would tell everyone I made the move on him and all would be well. Relief.

My relief was short-lived once the 54 bus finally arrived in my neighbourhood, close to eight o'clock. The silhouettes of the tree limbs above my head created cracks in the lavender sky as I rushed home. I did what my mom had told me to do, reaching for my fork weapon in the front pocket of my bag and clenching it in my fist so that the prongs stuck out between my fingers. I speed-walked past the homes on my street, now lit up from within by the pulsating glow of television screens.

To the rhythm of my walking feet, I began singing a Janet Jackson song to myself that I had heard on the radio that morning. I didn't know all the words, but it helped to mumble the chorus over and over again to assuage the growing fear in my chest.

Was this what happened to you on that trail? Did he tap you on the shoulder and introduce himself? Did you try to outrun him?

My singing was interrupted when I heard someone whistling. The sweet, melodic tune sounded menacing in the growing darkness. I looked behind me and saw the silhouette of someone about two hundred feet away. Were they following me? I quickened my pace, checking every now and then to see if the figure was still there. My mind raced. I couldn't remember what we learned in that self-defence class when I was eleven. How many seconds did I have in a chokehold before I would pass out? Was I supposed to kick him in the groin or not? Where was my rape whistle? Where the hell did I put that thing? I looked behind me again and the figure was closer. The one thing I did remember was to shout right away and tell the perpetrator to back off.

Just as I was about to turn around, just as the words were about to escape my lips, the man looked at me and smiled. His tiny scrub-bud of a puppy sniffed at my feet and the man pulled at the leash.

"Filbert . . . no thank you. Sorry about that. He's just a pup." The man turned the corner and left.

Chapter 12

All the magazines in the waiting room are at least a year old. I flip through the sticky pages anyway. On the cover of *Cozy Home!* is the headline *25 ways to make your shoe closet stylish AND organized! Page 152.* Damn it. Someone ripped that page out. Who does that anymore? Who puts articles on their fridge to read later? Oh wait. I do. To be honest, I would have done it if someone hadn't beaten me to it.

"Mrs. Alvarez?" I approach the receptionist. "Before you head in to see the doctor, I need to record your weight." She points to the scale beside her desk and I reluctantly remove my shoes.

I want to remove all my clothing. Maybe the contents of my stomach too. Whatever it takes to get a smaller number. I had forgotten my gynecologist has her scale in the middle of the waiting room. Thank goodness no one else is around today. The receptionist fiddles with the weights on the scale until it balances. I can't bear to look because I know it's accurate, unlike my analogue one at home where I could shift left and right to make the needle retract. I manage to glance at the receptionist as she records the weight into my file. The way her eyebrows are raised, I know she is judging me, comparing my last weigh-in with today's. What an asshole.

"Okay. Head on into room four, please."

Inside room four, Dr. Atwal insists on conversing with me while she shoves the speculum into my vagina. It's probably something she learned in school, to keep chit-chatting during a pap smear for the sake of good bedside manner. I'd rather not. Like all times when I am experiencing discomfort, I would rather dissociate, go somewhere deep within myself. But this woman keeps bringing me back into the land of the living with her inane repartee about what happened during my weekend.

"Ooh. Sixty-nine. That's a big birthday. Did your mom have fun?"

"Sure."

Dr. Atwal cranks open the speculum and I feel cold air deep inside myself where no one should ever feel cold air. "I mean . . . of course she had fun. What with all of her family around."

"Not sure if she noticed. She has dementia." I squeeze my eyes shut at the sensation of something wiping me from within.

"Oh no!"

"Yeah. It's okay," I say dismissively. I hold my breath. A sharp sting.

"And how is your father about it all?"

"My dad passed away. I didn't really know him anyway." What's with all the personal questions? Does she want me to monologue? Tell her about his yearly phone calls, which ended altogether once he had children with his new wife?

"Gosh. No. I'm sorry."

I pretend to be casual even though I am surprised by the lump in my throat. "No worries. It happened a long time ago." Long enough that I truly can't remember his face at all. Only Ricardo Montalbán's.

"How old would he have been if he were still alive?" Is this woman making me do math while her gloved fingers are tinkering under my hood? Is this what's happening?

"I dunno . . . seventy-two? Seventy-three? As I said, I didn't really know him."

I feel a nudge on my knee and I open my eyes slightly to see Dr. Atwal between my legs, the light of a standing lamp making her face a silhouette. "Relax your legs open. The more you breathe, the easier this will be." Fuck this examination. Fuck this speculum. Whoever invented the speculum deserves to rot in hell.

Dr. Atwal finally de-gloves her hands and offers me a paper towel to wipe the lube from my crotch.

She wheels her chair to a corner of her office and begins typing on her laptop. A paper sheet exits the printer on the second shelf of the desk. She hands it to me.

"That's your req for a mammogram. You can even go today if you want. The lab is downstairs. There might be a bit of a wait, but you might get lucky. It's usually pretty empty early in the afternoon."

"Thanks."

"Are you examining your breasts regularly?"

"Kinda."

"Kinda?"

I want to snap at her and tell her I feel my boobs up while masturbating. Instead, I say with a smile what every public health poster says. "One week after my menstruation starts."

"Awesome."

In the lab downstairs, the radiation technologist tells me to step forward. I am naked from the waist up in front of this stranger who only looks at me from the tits down.

There is no dignity in this process.

She begins the torture of pressing my boobs into unnatural shapes for the mammogram. Turning my face away and closing my eyes, I can't help but think of that playdough toy that crushes clay into square tubes . . . or that compacter machine that demolishes cars in junkyards.

"Great. Thanks. We'll send the results to your referring doctor." The technologist leaves me in the room, still topless. It's like we had a quickie one-night stand. What a relief this torture is over. Although, I have to admit, it was nice to take a day off work.

Driving home, I languish in this small taste of what it will be like once this television series is wrapped. It's almost there. We're looking at about a week or so to go before I can show the producers what I have cut. I can't wait for this to be over.

Bracing myself against the flood of these memories has taken a toll on my body. I connect my phone to the car's Bluetooth stereo system and listen to my Spotify liked songs list. Mateo ridicules me all the time for my taste in music, but guess what? Mama is in the car alone and that means Soul II Soul is going on full blast! And you best believe it will be loud enough that my rear-view mirror will vibrate. I even roll down the windows, knowing there will be some other middle-aged people on the sidewalk who want to hear my old school tunes too. Millennials give me a confused look from the crosswalk, but who cares?

From the side of my eye, I catch an image of you in the passenger seat, singing along, and I slam on the brakes. A loud honk. I look to my side and the passenger seat is empty. Still shaken, I reach my hand out my window and wave as an apology to the vehicle behind me.

Holy shit. I really need to take some time off. No. I have to do better than take time off. I should treat Nira to a real vacation. Nira has always wanted to splurge on a luxury destination. She'd love that. Maybe I could surprise her, I think, rubbing my sweaty palms on my pant legs.

•••

When I pull into my driveway, I see Hong rushing down our stoop stairs with her head down.

I get out of the car as fast as I can. "Hey. Hong? Are you okay?"

Hong steals a look at me then looks back down to her

shoes, as if she was about to say something then changed her mind. "Yeah. I'm okay."

"You sure? You don't look okay."

Her eyes meet mine finally. The skin around her cheeks and lids is chafed red. "I . . . um . . . I left something in the mailbox for Mateo. Can you make sure he gets it?"

"What's going on?" She's starting to worry me.

"It's nothing."

"If there's something you want to tell me, I'm here." I look at the time on my phone. "Listen. Nobody's here right now. Would you like to speak to me alone?" I can't believe what I'm saying. "Is it Mateo?"

Hong nods yes and begins to cry. She wipes her face with the sleeve of her jean jacket. Of course it's Mateo.

"Hey. Hey." I look around to see if anyone is watching. Not that I care what people think, but I want to make sure Hong's privacy is honoured. "Come inside. I can make you some tea."

Opening the cupboard doors, I don't know why I told her I would make her tea. We ran out of tea a month ago. Both Nira and I have forgotten to buy it each time we've gone to the grocery store since. "Sorry. Do you want some hot chocolate?" It's a balmy thirty-five degrees Celsius outside. "Or some fizzy water? Or cookies?"

Hong sits at our kitchen island and leans her face into her hands. Her eyes are far away. I've seen that look before. No. I've had that look. I shake my head to refocus and be present.

To help her feel safer, I stay on the other side of the counter. Keep my distance. "So . . . what's going on?" There is a pregnant pause in which Hong's lips move slightly but nothing comes out. "Hong?"

Finally she blurts out, "Mateo won't let me break up with him."

"What do you mean 'won't let you'?" I can hear my own heartbeat.

"It's not that I haven't tried. I have. I have tried over and over again. I've said it a few different ways and . . . I don't know how to describe it. It's like . . . it's like he's not hearing me. At first I think he's heard me, then we're talking and he's insisting, then he's crying and . . . and . . . he's texting me asking me when he's going to see me next, and then he just shows up! All the time! He even broke into my locker to put flowers in there. I told him not to do that, but then he started leaving notes in my binder instead." Her volume is on maximum now, unleashed and unbridled. Face red. Tears streaming. "He's scaring me!"

My eyes widen. Mateo *scares* her. *Scares* her. My son, my child is *scaring* someone. "I'm so sorry, Hong."

Hong collapses her head onto the marble countertop, her back convulsing with every sob. I round the island until I am on the other side. I want to rub her back, but I should keep my distance. "Have you told him that it scares you?"

She looks up at me and shame clouds her expression. "I don't know how. If I say stuff like that . . . it may hurt his feelings even more and then he might do what he did last time and tell all my friends he's begging me to come back to him." Hong swivels her bar stool to face me. "I haven't slept. I'm having trouble eating. I keep skipping classes just so that I can avoid him, you know? But he's always *there*."

"That does sound scary."

"It is! I keep telling Mateo that I don't feel the same way he does anymore. I can't pretend. But he doesn't listen. I'm scared he might hurt himself if I finally cut him off."

"Wait, wait. What?" This seems a bit overdramatic. "Did he ever—"

"Yes."

My heart sinks. "The last time I broke up with him, he took the utility knife I had in my pencil case for art class and slashed his hand." She demonstrates, pretending to slice the thin skin between her thumb and pointer finger.

I look away and take a step back. This can't be happening. This can't be real. But then I remember the bandage on Mateo's hand. The spot of blood. I take a breath. Fuck. She's telling the truth. Why would I ever doubt Hong?

"Okay . . . um . . ." While looking out the window, running through all the possible actions I could take here, I recall Leah dismissing me and my story of Mr. Stolks's creepy handshake. *He didn't mean anything by it. That didn't happen.* But it did. It did happen.

I hear my voice say, "Would you like me to . . ." I can't believe I am saying this. ". . . talk to Mateo? Talk some sense into him?"

Hong's face is a mixture of discomfort and hope. "Maybe. Do you think that will help? Will he listen to you?"

He never listens to me. "I'm not sure. But it would probably help to hear from someone else that the relationship is over. It'll give him some perspective."

Hong thinks for a second, and just as she says, "Okay, yes," I hear a key in our front door. "Fuck!" Hong gets up from the bar stool. "Is that him?" The fear in her eyes breaks my heart. I shuffle her out to the back mud room.

"Mama?" I hear Mateo say as he closes the front door.

"Yup!" I call back, watching Hong run through our backyard and out of sight.

"You're here early."

"I had a mammogram."

"A what?"

"Never mind." No. Not never mind. I shake my hands out. I can do this. I can talk to him. I take a deep breath, but just as I am about to say something, Nira barges in, all smiles. I want to immediately pull her aside and tell her what happened with Hong. But she has news.

"Listen up, everyone!" she says as she swings her purse off her shoulder and onto the sofa. "You are looking at the next vice-principal of Ablenook Junior Public School!" We all squeal in delight, me a little quieter than everyone else. To appear as normal as possible, I feel my hands clapping for her. I even try to jump for joy.

"Thank you, everyone. I had a feeling, but I didn't want to assume and jinx it."

Hugging her close to me, I say, "Babes. Congrats. Holy shit. This is amazing."

Mateo embraces Nira as well. I'm trying my best not to stare at him.

After she does a little happy dance, she pauses. "I have to admit, I will miss teaching those little monsters at Kelmore, but this is life-changing." Nira holds our shoulders and smiles. "Shall we celebrate?"

"Hell yes!" I say in my most convincing voice.

We celebrate with a hefty order at the nearby roti place. I try my best not to eat the entire order. My nerves are getting the best of me. As much as I don't want to ruin the evening, there's no way I can let the situation with Mateo and Hong slide. I will have to talk to Nira at some point this evening.

After dinner, I clean up our takeout containers and head upstairs. Nira is in our ensuite washroom shaving her legs and humming to herself.

"Hon?" I say, leaning on the door frame.

Nira sits on the edge of our bathtub with one leg propped up. It's an unnatural position, one that flexes her chiselled calf muscles. She stops what she's doing and gives me an alluring look. "Yes, my love?"

"We need to talk."

"Do we?" she says coyly. After wiping the remaining shaving cream off her legs with a damp washcloth, Nira begins to approach me.

"Yes. It's important." I'm not sure if I should avert my eyes or make meaningful eye contact—something that signals this will be a difficult conversation.

She begins to loosen the tie of her short silk robe. "I think we should keep celebrating. On our bed."

Shit. Not now. Nira tucks her fingers into the collar of my shirt and I have to remove them and hold her hands. "Babes. It's about Mateo."

Nira holds her breath for a moment then realizes this is not a romantic opportunity. She sighs. "What now?"

"I'm sorry . . . it's just . . ."

"Whatever. Tell me what's happening." She sits on the edge of the tub and crosses her arms.

"Please don't be upset with me."

"I'm not upset. I'm frustrated."

"With me? Why?"

"I'm getting tired of you shirking all of my advances."

"That's not true."

"Isn't it? Think, Alma. When was the last time we fucked?" I take a little too long to consider this question. "Exactly. It was that long ago."

"I'm sorry. I didn't realize it's been a while."

"Jeez. That hurts even more now. You didn't realize? Like . . . don't you long for me? Are you not attracted to me anymore?"

"It's not that! It's . . ." How do I explain this? Do I tell her I'm triggered? Do I tell her the stupid show I'm working on is fucking with my mind and that I'm seeing visions of you? Do I remind her of the history my body holds? All these questions catch in my throat.

"Never mind, Alma. Just tell me what's happening with

Mateo. I don't have the patience to watch you pretend everything is fine with you when it's not."

We are silent for a while, looking at our feet.

"I saw Hong this afternoon. He doesn't seem to be getting the message that things are over between them, so she had to write him a letter. But the worst thing that she said was . . . she said she's scared of Mateo."

Nira's eyebrows knit in confusion. "Scared? How can she be scared of Mateo? He's tall, but he's skinny. Anyone can take him down. He's harmless."

"That's not the point—"

"And what message is she sending exactly? Is she clearly stating that things are over? How much do we know? It could be a case of mixed messages, push and pull. That kind of thing."

"I hardly think that—"

"I just don't buy it, is all. This sounds like teen drama, and we shouldn't get involved."

"Are you serious?!"

"I am. The more we coddle them, the less they'll learn how to deal with their own problems. They need to figure out how to communicate with each other, and it won't happen with us intervening."

"I think we do need to intervene here, Nira."

She is suddenly standing with her hands on her waist. "Babes. Do you remember when he was a child and how many times you intervened on the playground? Always playing referee when some other kid took his dump truck or Mateo took some other kid's jump rope? That was highly unnecessary. If we step back and let kids negotiate these things themselves, they will figure it out eventually."

I shut my eyes and take a breath. Of course. Yes. I remember now. This is another case of Helicopter Parent Alma to the rescue. That's what all this has been. This is silly. I'm silly. Nira is right. Nira is right? Yes. Nira is right.

I try to smile and make things lighter. "Who do you think you are? Some kind of vice-principal?"

Nira smiles weakly but keeps her eyes down and her chin stern. She pats my shoulder twice in a way that signifies the end of this conversation. As she leaves me in the bathroom, I can't help but feel ashamed. I'm ashamed of how unattractive she thinks she is because I haven't made a move on her in a while. At the same time, is it my job to help her feel attractive? This is a marriage. Isn't a marriage where we're supposed to find safety to be who we really are? And if what I am right now is untouchable because of all the memories flooding in around me, don't I have the right to say no to sex for as long as I want to?

She flops onto the bed and begins turning the pages of a magazine. The movement of her hands is sharp enough for me to know she's still pissed at me. I've failed her. Again. I've failed Mateo by not teaching him how to be good in this world. I've failed Hong with the harm Mateo has done to her. It's all my fault. That familiar heat rises from my chest to my cheeks.

I want to cry. Find someplace to hide and hurt myself the way I used to. I don't have a spot for that anymore, because I thought I'd left that kid far behind me, in that space between the dresser and the closet.

I head to the kitchen. I'm going to find something to eat. I'm not hungry, but I want to witness my adult hands grab at something of my own accord and eat it, eat it without my mother, without my sister, without my goddamn wife policing me. I make loud noises opening up the stepladder and reaching for the fun-food part of our cabinet. With my hand I can feel a box of Pop-Tarts. That carton of chocolate truffles. Chips. Yes. Chips. The ones I like too. Salt and vinegar. I will start with the chips and end with the brownies. Yeah. I'll start off with salty and crispy, then end with soft and sweet. All I need is something fizzy and fun. In the far corner I grab at the last can of cola. I don't even get off the ladder. I stand on the top step and rip open the bag of chips. If I open my mouth wide enough, I can cram more than a handful into it. The crisp texture quickly becomes mush in my mouth. I should have just fucked her. I should have given it to her. Let her do things to me. When will I ever learn? I'm a horrible wife. I deserve to die. The ball of masticated chips takes its time moving down my esophagus. Washing it down with a gulp of soda, I stuff my mouth with the brownie. I literally slam the brownie into my mouth using my palm. Maybe if I slam it hard enough, I'll choke and die. Nira will be better for it. Mateo will be better for it. Die. Die. I wanna die.

The mailbox. Hong left something inside there for Mateo. I just remembered. Fuck. Stepping down from the ladder, I almost lose my footing. I can barely feel my legs. *Put the junk food down, Alma,* I tell myself. The fresh air on the other side of the front door snaps me out of my downward spiral and I take a deep breath. My fingers feel for the inside of the mailbox and I find an envelope. It's a reused greeting card envelope, taped shut, with Mateo's name scribbled on the outside. Using my thumbs, I feel for the contents. Is it a necklace? What do I do with this now? Should I give it to Mateo? Should I tell him first what Hong told me? Should I do neither? Holy hell.

From my stoop, I can see the shadow of a parent pushing a stroller. It's obvious by the slow and steady steps they're taking that the parent is trying to get their baby to sleep. I remember those days. Things were so much simpler back then. Or maybe it's simpler than I think or simpler than I'm making it out to be. Perhaps Nira is right. I shouldn't intervene. I'll make sure Mateo gets the envelope. At least then I will have fulfilled one of the promises I made to Hong. For now, I head back inside and put it into a canister on the kitchen counter. It's one of a set of canisters that have become a catch-all for random things like old keys and spare batteries. In the emptiest one, with paper clips littering the bottom, I place Hong's envelope. I'll give it to Mateo as soon as I can. Yes. That's what I'll do.

Chapter 13

There was a lull in the attacks. Well . . . back then, we thought it was the end of them. Before the lull, there were a total of sixteen victims. All women and children. Eleven dead. Five survivors. Then it stopped. Poof.

When attacks started again a year later in another town an hour west of Toronto, the police didn't connect them with the Scarborough Stalker. Would it be weird to say that our community was relieved, even though the perpetrator hadn't yet been caught? Yeah. It was weird. But those were weird times. Even weirder was that your body was still missing and then the police arrested your boyfriend for your murder. It never felt right. It never made sense. And still, we rejoiced. Attacks had stopped in our area. An alleged killer was caught. We were safe again. Or so we thought.

•••

The camcorders at my new school took a while to get used to, but I liked how compact they were in comparison with the one Mrs. Bartkiewicz gave me. I had just learned all the basic steps for setting up my camera shot. I levelled my tripod on the beach sand in front of the Scarborough Bluffs. I did my white balance. I considered my composition and placed the waves of Lake Ontario to the left third of the frame, the cliffs to the right. After placing my backpack on the bottom of the tripod to weigh it down against the wind, I looked through the viewfinder at the sunset. My intention was to capture time-lapse video of the sun setting. Eventually, I would edit it together with other time-lapse shots and do a voice-over of poetry I had written. As creative as it was, in truth, it was all part of my ruse. After Toby had informed me of the rumours of my queerness, I thought that love poems, addressed specifically to a boy, would help quell everyone's curiosity. To give things more weight, I even made ambiguous references to Toby's glasses and dimples. The audio was already recorded. I just needed a few more shots to complete the project.

While I adjusted the focus on the camera, a girl blocked my view.

"Alma?" It was fucking Linda Lowry from St. Xavier. She was taller. Skinnier. Still pretty, although her hair had faded to a mousy brown. And wait . . . she was talking to me?

"Hey. Hi, Linda."

"Oh my god, it *is* you. I was over there with my friends and saw you and was like, 'Whaaaaat? Is that Alma?'" She carried her sneakers in her hands even though the air was crisp, crisp enough that I had my hands tucked into the sleeves of my sweater. "What are you doing? Shooting a movie?"

"Yeah."

"Still doing that, eh? So cool." Two teenaged boys in woven hoodies called her name and she waved at them. "In a minute." She turned to me and smiled. "So . . . is everyone at your school like you? All smart and artsy?"

I did a double take. Linda thought I was smart? "Um . . . yeah. It's fun to walk the halls and listen to all these musical prodigies in the studios practising the cello and stuff."

"Are you in touch with anyone from St. Xavier's still?"

I shook my head. There was an awkward silence for a moment and I could see Linda searching for something to say.

"Did you hear Mr. Fletcher died?"

"No way."

She laughed, delighting in having something to share. "Way. He hanged himself in his garage. Can you believe it?"

"Whoa."

"I know, right? And Beth got pregnant."

"Oh."

"Didn't your sister get pregnant too?"

"Yeah."

A gust of wind almost knocked my tripod down, but I managed to catch my camera before it fell. It was strange. Linda couldn't care less whether or not I was in the room back when we were in the same class. No—that's not entirely accurate. It's more like she took pleasure in ridiculing me in front of her friends. Now she was watching me right my camera in the sand with a longing I had never seen in her before. Like she was lonely.

"What high school did you end up going to?" I asked her.

"Sacred Trinity, but I hated that place." The wind whipped some of her greasy hair into her mouth and she used her finger to take it out. Linda looked away and added, casually, with her chin up, "I dropped out as soon as I could. I had better things to do." She shrugged her shoulders and I mirrored the movement as if I understood.

The boys called her name again.

"What's your pager number? Maybe I can text you and we can hang." Linda unclipped the device from her waist and looked at its screen. The digits shown made her grin and roll her eyes. She clipped it back onto her pants.

"I . . . I don't have a pager. Sorry."

"That's okay. I'll give you my number."

"Like . . . to call you on it?"

"No, silly. It's a pager. Not one of those mobile phones. All you gotta do is send me a numeric text and I'll drive over. When you're ready to hang, just text me 80085."

"What does that mean?"

"It's code for 'I'm here, come get me,'" Linda said over her shoulder before leaving the beach with the boys.

Later that night, I tried out the magic of this pager code system on the phone in the basement, which was the only phone we had with a numeric pad instead of a rotary dial. I pressed the numbers and hung up. Did I do that right? Within an hour, I heard honking outside. Whoa.

"Who is that?" Mom said, taking off her wet dish gloves and pushing the kitchen curtains to the side.

"Those are my friends. We're doing a project together," I said, putting on my jacket and shoes.

"Bundle up, it's still cold out there." I was surprised Mom didn't give me a hard time about leaving, but things had definitely changed since the attacks stopped. A year had passed since the last one, and a lightness was in the air. Children played carefree outside until dusk. The Wanted posters had long been taken down. People walked to and from the bus stop at a relaxed pace. We were the lucky ones, and I was glad for it. I wrapped a scarf around my neck and headed out into the night air.

Linda climbed out of a beat-up Honda Accord and opened the squeaky rear door. "Get in the back." Linda slid into the front seat. The smell of CK One cologne and cigarette smoke clung to the surface of the weathered nylon upholstery. She introduced me to her friends. Ian was driving and beside me was a guy named Parker. Parker didn't say anything. He just gave me a mini salute. I saluted back. The car sped off down my street. I felt for seat belts. There were none.

"Ian and Parker used to go to St. Xavier's too. But they were two years ahead of us. Now we all work at Wickle's Pickles."

"Well . . . *we* work at Wickle's Pickles," Ian said, pointing to himself and Parker. "You, Linda, just got fired." He and Parker laughed, and Linda did her best to laugh along.

"Wait. Isn't that the place that gives off that awful smell by the SRT station?" I asked.

"Yup. That's the one. It's going to take me a week to get

that smell off my hair. Glad I left. Fuck that place." From where I was sitting, I could see her face wilt in the side-view mirror. "Alma is at some fancy school now, making movies."

I shrunk, not wanting to make a big deal of myself. "Not really."

"Come on, Alma. When you're a director, can we all star in one of your films?"

"Sure." They all cheered.

Ian parked the car down a forested lane at the bottom of a hill. I could see in the dim light that there was a marsh ten feet in front of us. Beside us were several cars with foggy windows.

"Why are the windows all foggy?" I asked.

They all laughed. "Wouldn't you like to know?" chuckled Linda while she began rolling a joint.

"Welcome to Lovers' Lane, Alma," Ian said to me through his reflection in the rear-view mirror. He rolled the windows down a crack on both sides before sparking up the doobie. The smell of skunk. Ian took a drag then passed it to Linda, who passed it to me behind her.

"I dunno . . ."

"Here, I'll show you. See?" She showed me an expert pull, which she blew out of her mouth then inhaled through her nostrils. I tried. I coughed. They laughed, but not meanly. "Don't worry. Coughing is a good thing."

Linda suddenly banged the back of her seat and bounced up and down. "You know what we should do? We should egg one of our old teachers' houses."

"Eggs are expensive, man. What about TP? Hey, Parker. Your mom still has a shitload of toilet paper in your garage, right?" Parker held the smoke in his mouth and nodded, his eyes half-closed. "Then let's giv'er."

At Parker's house, a five-minute drive away, we snuck into the garage and grabbed about a dozen rolls of toilet paper. I couldn't believe this was happening. I had never been out with friends, ever. I had never had friends. And now I was part of a bona fide mission for mischief.

"Fuck. If Mr. Fletcher wasn't dead, I would have totally chosen his house," Linda said with her arm out the window as we cruised back into the neighbourhood. My eyes were getting dry and my lips were getting numb in the cold, but I was too stoned to tell her to close the windows. "How about Mrs. Jenkins? Remember that bitch who taught us band? But I think she lives in Pickering."

"Too far!" said Ian.

"Fine. Fine. Hey. What about Mrs. Bartkiewicz?"

"Yeah, that lesbo librarian?"

I sat up and tried to shake the cloud from my head as the three of them deliberated.

"Yeah. That bitch. Can you believe that she never excused my late fee for a book I borrowed back in grade four? Like . . . get over it, woman."

"You know where she lives?" asked Ian.

"Totally. Close to the Heron Park Community Centre."

Ian whipped the car around and the G-force nailed me back to my seat. "Let's hope we don't interrupt her and her carpet munching when we do this." Ian put his fingers into a V shape and licked between them.

"You're so gross, Ian." Linda slapped him playfully on the shoulder.

I didn't stop them. Not even as I watched the three of them park the car a block away and sneak up on Mrs. Bartkiewicz's house. Not even as they threw streams of toilet paper onto her driveway, onto her garden, onto her mailbox. Not even as Linda used her lipstick to draw the word *DYKE* onto her door. I stood there at the end of her lot and watched. I think . . . no . . . I know . . . I admit that I threw a roll myself. I did it. I wanted to. No one forced me. I did. Then the lights turned on inside the house. Then outside the house. The door opened. Mrs. Bartkiewicz emerged in her robe.

"What are you doing?! Get out of here!" Linda, Ian and Parker ran away, but I froze. "Alma?" she said as she spotted me. "Alma? Is that you? Did you do this . . . to me?"

Linda pulled my arm and I felt myself running, running for an eternity, until I was inside the car and it sped off into the darkness of the night.

• • •

"Hello. Would you like to try some sausage?" I said to a man who was passing by me in the Scarborough Town Centre food court.

He did a double take at the sight of my platter full of cut sausage rounds, each one artfully stabbed with a tooth-pick. "Hold on one second," he said into his brick phone. The orange light from the Links & Co. sign behind me created a soft glow on his otherwise pallid complexion.

It was my first job and, like many first jobs, it was dreadful. During my four-hour shift, I was expected to lure people to the restaurant by giving them samples of the sausages we grilled. This system was flawed because, seven times out of ten, people went on their merry way with their samples and never returned. These were premium sausages and it was obvious that the return on investment wasn't cutting it. Still, I did as my mean-spirited manager Dmitri told me to do.

"These ones are kiełbasa," I said, pointing to the rounds on the left of my platter. "And these ones are bratwurst. For $2.99 you get a sausage and salad with a choice of—"

"Thanks!" the guy said as he walked away, munching on the sample. He continued talking on his brick phone, the antenna pointing up from its top. "Yeah, I know. If we had sold it last month, we would have topped 200K, but look what happened, right?"

Thank goodness I wasn't paid on commission. Sure, I was only paid five dollars an hour, but it was enough for me to afford my new pager and buy myself clothes from stores other than Zellers. The money also kept me from asking for things from my mother and watching her usual martyr show each time she had to shell out cash for me. I took a deep breath and kept doing my job. "Hello. Would you like to try some sausage?"

An old man in a Hawaiian shirt stopped and examined the sausages as if they were scientific specimens. A small plastic bag was looped around his wrist, so he took it off and put it on the other wrist so that he could take a sample. Then he looked me up and down in my kilt. Dmitri insisted I wear my school uniform for this very reason. "Aren't you supposed to be in school?"

"It's the weekend, sir. These sausages are kiełbasa and these are—"

"Skipping school, eh? Running off behind the nuns' backs in that cute little skirt, eh?"

"I'm not skipping. I'm—"

He eyed my legs. "Look at your little socks." He pulled the sausage off the toothpick with his lips and gave me a wink. My skin crawled under my cardigan. With unsteady feet, he made his way to the counter, where my manager was waiting with a smile.

"What can I get you, sir?"

The old man looked back at me and grinned. "Whatever the young lady is selling."

To break up my day, Dmitri had me do other things, such as clean the murky floors with a filthy mop or do inventory. The worst part of the job was onion day. If my shift was on a Tuesday or Friday, I had the horrible task of shredding onions using Dmitri's ancient hand-cranked shredder. Its blades were no sharper than the edge of a spoon, which meant that when I placed an onion on one side and turned the crank, the machine squeezed the onion rather than chopping it, sending fumes into the air and into my eyes. On onion days, my eyes would be purple and stinging with tears.

I was expected to punch out at the end of my shift. The punch clock was at the end of a narrow hallway in the back of the restaurant. The phone was right beside it. Most days, Dmitri would be on the phone, talking to someone, leaning his hand on the opposite wall with the phone at his ear.

"No. No deal. You promised twenty pounds at ninety-nine cents, my friend. You think I have a bad memory or something?"

I'd tap the shoulder of his stained shirt. I'd tap. Tap again. "Excuse me," I'd say as clearly as I could. Still he wouldn't move. I would have to bend down and go under the arch of his arm in order to pass. I wasn't a human to him. I'm sure he'd move for a dog faster than he would move for me. I was just bait to him. Catholic schoolgirl bait.

What made it all worth it was leaving the food court and checking my pager. I always saved a quarter in my wallet for the pay phone around the corner of the mall, next to the shoe repair shop. Inputting my pass code, I would listen to the voice mail messages Toby left me.

"Hey! Meet me at Warden. I'll be there at four."

•••

I did. At Warden station, I explained to Toby my vision for my next short film, starring Elliot and Shamus from AV club. "Okay . . . then . . . right here is where I imagine some kind of dissolve into a shot of the hourglass." I scribbled my storyboard into another square. "But the hourglass is half-full instead of being almost empty."

"Ah! I get it. Time is moving backwards," Toby said before taking another bite of his beef patty.

"Exactly. So then it's a cue for the audience to know that the sequence of scenes we've seen before are all in reverse. Get it?" I tossed my patty's greasy paper bag into the garbage next to the red bench we were sitting on. *Our* red bench, which was in front of *our* favourite bakery at *our* subway station.

"Shouldn't those cues be moved closer to the beginning, then? Otherwise, the audience will be confused?"

"I dunno. Maybe. But part of me wants the audience to be confused. At least for the first two scenes. You know?"

"Your call. I like it."

"Really?"

"Totally. I think if you commit to it, then people will really enjoy the confusion. Nice." Toby wiped his cheeks with a thin paper napkin. His freckles had faded in the winter light. "Subject change: I'm taking my driver's test next week."

"Whoa."

"I know. My dad says he's going to post warning signs all over Toronto so that other motorists stay off the road. Are you gonna take yours?"

"Can't. I'm still too young."

"That's shitty. This is the last year before graduated licensing happens. I had to rush the process because I don't want to take three tests."

"Why three?"

"My dad says it's a cash grab. You take one test to get your learner's permit. Another test to be able to drive on your own and on the highway. Then another one to lose the stupid night driving restrictions. And you have to pay for each test."

"Crap," I said, even though there was no way I would ever have access to my mom's car. I shifted so that I faced him, and crossed my legs the way other girls did when they were interested in a boy.

"I know. But don't worry, I can help you when you're ready to practise. I'm pretty good at parallel parking. It's actually easier for me than regular parking." He bent down to reach into his backpack and pulled out a red piece of paper. "Did you see this?"

I knew what it was. It was one of the posters for the semi-formal dance happening on Valentine's Day. My heart fluttered with excitement. "Um . . . no. What's that?" I said as I innocently took the flyer from him. One of the visual art students had drawn a cheesy image of a boy and girl intertwined in a heart-shaped tree. Swirly bubble letters detailed the ticket price, date and time.

"Wanna go with me? As in . . . be my date?"

I embraced him tightly and squealed. It wasn't so much that I was happy he liked me, but I was elated that going with Toby to the dance meant that any rumours about me being a dyke must have fizzled out.

"Is that a yes?" he asked into my ear.

"Yes!" I answered with glee. I was going to kill it at this hetero thing. I was going to do as other girls did and laugh and giggle at everything Toby said. Dress up and be his arm candy. Dance with him in the middle of the dance floor, right underneath the disco ball.

I suddenly felt him kissing me. It wasn't so much a kiss as it was his lips swallowing mine. I tried my best not to recoil from the wet of his tongue and the smell of his breath. When he disengaged, I heard myself breathing as if I had surfaced from a deep dive into water. It happened too quickly for me to process its beginning and ending. The next thing I knew, Toby was walking me to my side of the platform, our fingers interlaced. I played along. This was what couples did.

...

My paycheque wasn't enough to cover my pager payments *and* a semi-formal dress, and Mom refused to shell out cash for a dress I was just going to wear for one night. She took it upon herself to call Tita Lorna for help. Always eager to appear charitable, Tita Lorna arrived at our home two nights later with a garment bag full of her daughter Belinda's hand-me-downs.

I wasn't really into dresses (I was starting to get into grunge fashion, as it helped hide my masculinity). However, a red dress in the pile caught my eye. It looked sort of like the dress Julia Roberts wore in *Pretty Woman* but with shiny satin.

I walked into the living room where Tita Lorna, Mom and Leah were waiting to see how it looked on me. Jess was busy scribbling in a colouring book. "Not this one. The cut is too low." Mom waved me back into my room. She'd been stern with me ever since I told her I was going to the dance with a boy. "Everyone will see your cleavage."

"Mom. She doesn't even have cleavage." Leah placed her arm on the side of the colouring book to keep Jess from marking the glass coffee table. "But that's beside the point. The dress isn't doing anything for you. You're not Julia Roberts."

"Jeez. Thanks," I said, rolling my eyes.

"It's true. Do you want me to be honest or what?"

I came out in another silk dress with a cowl neckline.

"I can see your underwear." Tita Lorna pointed at my panty line and snickered.

"That's because I'm ... wearing underwear."

"Lorna. Should she not wear underwear?"

"No, Mom. She needs to buy a thong so that you can't see the line."

"My Belinda has a seamless underwear."

"Can I buy new seamless underwear, then?"

"Sus! Another expense? You already have to buy new shoes. Now underwear?"

"This dress is free. Can I buy a thong, then?"

"You're not wearing a thong. Only those kinds of girls wear thongs."

"Mom!" Leah scoffed. "I wear thongs."

Mom's eyebrows lifted and she pursed her lips. "Next."

"Wait. I don't get it. What's wrong with people knowing you have underwear on?" This stumped the lot of them. "And then, if you wear a thong so that your underwear doesn't show, why is that considered slutty?"

"Oh my god, Alma. Try on the next one already. We don't have time for your big-ass life questions!" Leah peeked into the edge of Jess's diaper to see if she needed a change.

The last option was a simple blue spaghetti strap dress. It wasn't glamorous, but it fit pretty well and the A-line of the skirt hid my panty line. I did a small spin when I re-entered the living room.

"You forgot the top layer." Tita Lorna went into my bedroom and came back with a translucent lavender organza shift and evening gloves. I lifted my arms into the fabric and it went over the other dress so that my arms were covered in poufy sleeves and my chest was covered all the way to my collarbone. As soon as I put on the evening gloves, the only bare skin I had was my face and neck. Not only was it itchy, but it made me look like I was attending a Victorian high tea.

"Perfect," Mom said with a sharp nod of the head.

Leah grinned. "Wow. Mom's right. It's perfect." She tried her best to hold it in, then spat out a laugh into the bend of her elbow.

"Thanks, Ate Leah. Thanks a lot." I walked back into my bedroom to rip the dress off.

• • •

At my next shift at Links & Co. there was an extra pep in my step. I actually had something to look forward to: collecting my paycheque and buying a pair of shoes for the semi-formal. This was going to be the first time I would shop for anything by myself, without the puritanical input of my mother or demoralizing comments of my sister. I happily ducked Dmitri's arm tunnel to punch in. I mixed industrial-sized bowls full of coleslaw, elbow-deep, without complaint. I mopped the floors with a smile. I pushed sausage like it was my life calling.

"Would you like to try some sausage?" I said to a young Black girl who was a few years younger than me.

She shrugged and took a toothpick of bratwurst. Her eyes lit up.

"Tasty, right?"

The girl turned to look behind her and called out, "Mom! There's samples!"

"Samples of what?" The girl stepped aside to let her mother see my platter. It was Mrs. Bartkiewicz. We both froze.

"Can we have lunch now? Please?" said the girl.

With face red, Mrs. Bartkiewicz stuttered, "Um . . . sure . . . um . . . Is this where you want to eat, Emma?"

Emma turned to me. "Does it come with fries?"

Once I caught my breath, I recited the restaurant's special to the floor. "Uh . . . yeah. It does. For $2.99 you get a sausage and salad with a choice of fries or egg noodles."

A Black woman with arms full of shopping bags approached them. "Is this what we're doing now? We're eating?"

"Emma wants lunch."

"Okay, cool. Marta, I'm gonna grab us a table so I can set this all down."

Marta. Mrs. Bartkiewicz's name was Marta. It was weird hearing her first name. I had always assumed teachers had no first names. The woman pecked Mrs. Bartkiewicz on the cheek and sat down at a table close by.

"Here." Mrs. Bartkiewicz took out her wallet and handed Emma a ten-dollar bill. No drama. No martyr face. "Practise counting your change."

"Yes, Mom." Emma went to the counter and ordered from Dmitri.

Once I knew Mrs. Bartkiewicz had turned away from me, I watched her walk towards another restaurant in the food court. At the halfway point, she turned to her wife and said, "Vanessa? I think I'll get some beef stir-fry at the teriyaki place. Want me to order for you?"

"No, I'll get some poutine."

Mrs. Bartkiewicz never looked at me. In fact, she positioned her chair so that her back was to me. I stood there, unable to concentrate on my sausage samples. I stood there and observed her family eat a meal together. I had never seen a queer couple before. They paid no mind to the looks they were getting from passersby. They just ate and laughed. My jaw tightened watching them make eye contact with their daughter. The way Emma would say something and her two mothers would lean in and listen. That's the way Mrs. Bartkiewicz would listen to me in the library. It bothered me that she didn't shout at me the way my own mother would do. Instead, she ignored me, as if my betrayal meant nothing to her. She was obviously doing this on purpose. She was putting on a show to hurt me and make me feel small.

I rolled my eyes. Whatever. It wasn't my fault Mrs.

Bartkiewicz couldn't take a little joke. What's a little toilet paper? It's not like we spray-painted her door. Linda just used lipstick. And it was mostly Linda and her friends. Not me. I couldn't believe the bitch didn't even have the decency to say hello.

At the end of my shift, I crawled under the Dmitri arm tunnel to punch out. As I went shoe shopping at Le Château in search of something pointy and impractical, I have to admit that I hoped to run into Mrs. Bartkiewicz again. I even did a random stroll through the main veins of the mall, hoping to cross paths. If we ran into each other, Mrs. Bartkiewicz would be forced to introduce me to her wife. And then I could say something light and casual, like, "Listen. I just want to say, I'm super sorry that happened. We thought it was some random stranger's house, and boy was I embarrassed when you came out! Don't take it personally!" or something like that. But I never found them.

I shook it off. *Who cares what that lesbo librarian thinks of me?* I was going to the dance with a boy a year older than me. I had the dress. I had the shoes. Now all I had to do was act the part.

• • •

Mom pushed the lace curtains of our kitchen window aside to watch Toby park at the end of the driveway.

"When he comes inside, I will have a chat with him," my mother said sternly. "I don't want any interruptions."

"But we have to head to the dance and it—"

"No. Interruptions." Mom pointed to the hallway with her lips, which meant, in her unspoken language, that I was to stand over there and not get in the way. I could hear Leah trying to put Jess to sleep in her bedroom. In the kitchen, a pot of ox tongue stewed over the stove. Everything about my family was suddenly embarrassing and smelly.

Toby rang the doorbell and Mom solemnly opened the door.

"Hello, Mrs. Alvarez." His sandy-blond hair looked darker gelled back. Where did he get a powder-blue tux? He waved at me in the hallway. "Hey, Alma."

"Hey, Toby," I said apologetically.

Mom looked outside at the grey Buick. "Is this your car?" she asked, her voice alarmingly sharp.

"It's my father's."

"You have a licence?"

"Yup. I passed on my first try."

Mom nodded stoically then gestured with her arm for Toby to head to the living room. Just as Toby was about to go in, Mom said, "Uh-uh-uh," and pointed to Toby's shiny dress shoes. "Take your shoes off first."

"Sorry." Toby handed me a clear plastic container he was carrying. Inside it was a corsage. "That's for you," he said to me with a faint smile before untying his laces and removing his shoes.

Mom sat Toby on the couch and crossed her arms. "You see this?" She pointed to me. "This is my daughter. I don't want any funny business tonight."

"Yes, Mrs. Alvarez."

"What time will you be back?"

"The dance ends at eleven thirty and I will bring her straight home."

"Straight home. No funny business. No after-parties. No drugs. No drinking. No sex."

"Moooom!"

My mother threw me a look that made me cower, then she turned back to Toby. "Do we have an understanding?" She extended her hand to Toby and they shook on it, like I was a prize cow that had just changed owners.

"Okay, we have to go or else my dress is going to smell like ulam," I announced. "Let's go, Toby."

At the stoop, my goddamn sister came running out of the house with Jess hoisted on her hip and crying in nothing but a diaper. "Wait!" Leah said. "We have to take a picture!"

"Oh my god. I'm so sorry," I whispered to Toby.

Toby shrugged and put his arm around me. "It's totally cool."

Leah wound up the dial on her disposable camera and clicked the button. Her hands were still stained from the makeup job she did on my face. Toby and I smiled and posed.

"That's it. You're good to go. Have fun, you two!" My sister used her shirtless toddler's hand to wave goodbye to us as Toby backed out of the driveway. In a singsong voice she added, "Don't do what I did or else you get one of these!"

At the reception hall, Toby expertly parked the car and excitedly pointed at the clear plastic container in my lap. "You gonna put it on? Want me to do it or something?"

"Not yet. Hold on." I removed the organza layer, leaving the spaghetti-strapped gown underneath. I felt ten degrees cooler and much less itchy. I held out my arm. "I'm ready!"

"Whoa. You look hot!" Toby said as he stretched the corsage's elastic around my wrist. The orchid was the gaudy size of a baseball. Just as I was looking closely at the ornate sprays of baby's breath and palm leaves, Toby's lips were on me again. I froze. Once he was done, I was wet from my nostrils to my chin. I wanted to check if Leah's makeup job was ruined but didn't want to offend him.

"Did you notice I told your mom the dance ended at eleven thirty?"

"No. Why?"

"The dance ends at ten thirty. That way we can go somewhere afterwards."

"Where?" I asked. The smell of his spit drying on my face made me feel nauseous, but I smiled to cover it up.

"It's a surprise."

Our table at the dance was occupied by all the guys from AV club. Elliot and Shamus had their dates and then there was me and Toby. I had thought that Elliot and Shamus were bringing their girlfriends, but the looks of their listless dates, the way one slumped in her chair and the other looked at her watch inside her evening purse, made me think otherwise. Perhaps they were cousins or neighbours forced to be their plus-ones. Either way, they were certainly unwilling. I tried to make conversation when the meals were served.

"You wouldn't think the chicken would be moist enough. It's actually pretty good for a catered event, eh?" I said to the brunette with the high ponytail and ringlet bangs.

"Yeah. Sure," she replied with Elliot happily eating beside her. There was already a gravy stain on his lapel.

I looked across the table to the other one, with the Jennifer Lopez long layers. "Are you into filmmaking like Shamus?"

"No, not really," she said before turning around and resting her chin on the back of her chair to watch the dance floor.

Shamus paid no attention to his date's sullen posture. "You going to eat that?" he said, pointing to the full bread basket in front of me. I passed it to him and sighed.

When K-Ci & JoJo's hit ballad blasted over the speakers, the two girls snuck off to the washroom together to avoid slow dancing with their geeky counterparts.

"Wanna dance?" Toby asked me, his cummerbund gathering at his stomach.

I whispered into his ear, "Yes, please. Save me."

On the walk towards the dance floor, I felt eyes on me as Toby guided me through the various tables. I positioned my wrist in a way that everyone could see my flashy corsage, like a beacon telling everyone, *I'm not gay, people! Look at this thing. I'm not gay at all!*

The bass dropped in the song and I felt Toby's hands wrap around the bottom of my waist. I hoped he couldn't feel the seam of my underwear. He touched his forehead to mine and we swayed side to side.

"Can you believe Elliot's and Shamus's dates?" he said with a chuckle.

"I know. I'm embarrassed for them both. How will this night end?"

"That would make a good short film."

"It would. Maybe I can get them to star in it too."

We laughed. He put his hands lower, near the crack of my bum. Even though my back tightened, his hands remained. I let him. I didn't want to make a scene. Could people see him pawing at me? Were people going to laugh at me? Maybe this was a good thing. Maybe this would help people see me as someone's girlfriend. The heavy petting would make things real. I didn't know what else to do, so I rested my head on his chest and kept slow dancing.

When the event was over, Toby and I ran to the car through the February cold. Toby started the engine to defrost the windows. While the fan was on full blast, Toby's mouth was on mine again. I tried my best to turn my head side to side the way they did in the movies and pretend I was into it. I even tried to make whimpering noises, but I couldn't bring myself to close my eyes, afraid that if I did so, he would swallow me whole. All I could think of was the snow that got into my damp dress shoes and if the leather would survive walking through the salt and sleet.

Once the windows were defrosted, Toby began to drive.

"Where are we going?"

"You'll see."

The car drove down a hill that looked familiar to me.

Once I saw the faint shape of the marsh in the darkness, I knew where we were. We were in the same spot Linda and her crew had rought me to get high. Lovers' Lane.

"Surprise!"

"What are we doing here?"

"What do you think we're doing here? What do you think everyone is doing here?"

I looked. On either side of us, there were cars with steamy windows.

"Let's go to the back so that we have some room!" Toby was already out of the driver's seat and opening the back passenger side. I got out too, rubbing the goosebumps on my arms and blowing steam from my mouth. The reeds on the frozen marsh stood stiff against the periwinkle of the sky. I squinted and saw that there was one car with no steaming windows. Instead, a man sat in the shadow of his driver's seat, watching us.

I got into the back beside Toby. "Did you see that guy? There's a pervert just watching—"

Toby's mouth was on mine, mid-sentence, his hands pawing at my breasts. He squeezed them together. Pulled them apart. Pinched. "How's that? You like that?"

I wanted to say, "Like what exactly?" Instead, I said, "Yes. Yes." I wondered how much the pervert could see of us.

Toby began to string together phrases like the ones you hear in love scenes. "You smell so good." "I want you so bad." "You're so damn beautiful." Unlike watching a movie, I could not cover my eyes because I was in the scene and I was the girl.

So I did what girls were supposed to do and said a few cliché phrases of my own. "That feels so good." "There. Yes, there."

Out of breath, Toby lifted his cummerbund higher so that he could unzip his pants. He reached into the opening and pulled out his penis. I had never seen one before. It was pinker than I thought it would be. Smaller than I thought it would be. But it was definitely hard. He took my hand and wrapped it around the shaft. While my cold hands were relieved by the warmth of his skin, I must have made a face, because he said, "You're looking at it like it's an alien."

I wanted to say, "Um, yeah, because it looks like an alien. It looks just like E.T. when it wore that blanket on its head." Instead, I said, "No . . . it's, um . . ." I peered out the window again at the pervert in his car, who changed positions so that he was staring directly at me. Even in the darkness, I could see the intensity of his gaze. "It's the guy. He's in his car and watching us."

Toby turned around to confirm. "So?"

"It's creepy."

"Is it? Don't mind him. Keep going."

"Keep going with what?"

"With this, Alma."

"Maybe we should—"

"Fine. Fine." Toby zipped up and wiped his face of my remaining lipstick. When we were back in the front, Toby started the car and said petulantly, with no eye contact, "Did you have a nice time?"

"I did."

"Glad I bought you a ticket."

"Me too. Are you upset with me?"

"Listen. Are you gay or something?"

"What? What are you talking about?"

"Sometimes I have to wonder. Especially when you act like this," he said, pointing to the back seat.

"No. No. I love being with you, it's just . . . that man . . ."

"Sure. Whatever."

He drove me home in silence. As he backed out of the driveway, I waved at him with my dress all wrinkly.

Chapter 14

Can we please go over the hand signals again?" Nira looks in the mirror of her compact and applies another layer of lip stain. I don't know how she does this without painting all over her face, given our Uber driver is a bit heavy on the brakes.

"I know the hand signals already." I straighten my bow tie. It's a futile task. This clip-on was cheap and looks cheap.

"No, you don't. You never remember."

"Okay, fine. Show me."

Nira puts away her makeup and shifts her torso in the back seat of the car so that I have a full view of her demonstration. "This . . ." she says while tapping her chin with two fingers, "means one of my exes is in the room and we need to change direction and hide." Nira has many exes, none of whom she is on good terms with. At events like tonight's wrap party for that *Infamous* series I edited (am still editing), we change direction and hide often. "And this"—she tugs her earlobe—"means that I need you to rescue me from the person I'm talking to."

"Cool."

"You'll remember?"

"As you wish," I say a little too sharply. There is an edge to my voice, as there is an edge to my body. I haven't felt quite right since my conversation with Hong. I haven't felt right for a long time.

"Don't sass me, Alma. I don't like going to industry events and you know it."

"I don't like them either."

"Then why do we go in the first place?" The Uber driver almost turns right on a cyclist. We both brace ourselves on the headrests in front of us as the driver hits the brakes.

"I dunno. Because . . . capitalism? We have a mortgage. A kid's college tuition coming up. These parties are networking opportunities. That's how I get contracts, Nira."

"I don't know why the film industry can't use LinkedIn or Indeed like everyone else. Instead, we have to eat hoity-toity appetizers and oysters and laugh at bad jokes." She brushes lint off the shoulders of my suit. Out of spite, I search her sequined dress for something to adjust, but, as usual, she is picture perfect.

"You're gorgeous, my love."

"Don't try and sugar-coat this, Shortcake. After tonight's thing, I want you to take me out for late night tacos." She pinches my cheeks.

The Uber driver drops us off at a warehouse conversion in the hip west end of the city. I'm a bit surprised at how big this party is. Usually there isn't this much hubbub over True

Crime. However, since the series is hosted by celebrity Max Woodruff, it looks as if production has pulled out all the stops. At the coat check I can hear the bass of the DJ spinning some tunes. Lots of moody lighting inside. Evocative art hanging on the walls. It all seems a bit premature . . . well . . . it always feels premature to celebrate at a wrap party to those who work in post-production. People rarely understand the months of work that happens after the director calls cut on the final shot. Usually, I'm rushing out of my editing suite in jogging pants to change into something a bit more formal for these things.

"Please tell me you got drink tickets at the door?"

I hand the chits to Nira and she cheers. "Thank goodness. I'll get something for us to drink. What do you want from the bar?"

"Something fizzy."

"I'll be right back," Nira says. Only two steps in the direction of the bar, I see her make a face at someone across the room. Another woman in a flashy suit runs towards her with her arms outstretched. "Are you kidding me? Olwyn, is that you?" The two engage in a jumping embrace. Nira waves me over. "Alma. Come meet Olwyn." We shake hands. "What the hell are you doing here?"

Olwyn bends her hand down to display her rock of an engagement ring. "Guess who's going to be Mrs. Woodruff?!"

"You're lying!"

Olwyn points to Max Woodruff in one corner of the room, surrounded by the producers and holding court.

"Since when? Oh wait. I forgot, you moved to LA. Whoa.

How did this happen? Wait. Come with me to the bar and tell me all about it." Nira tells me over her shoulder, "Babes. We'll be back," then runs off with Olwyn. I'm kind of relieved. Even though it hurts a bit to be left alone in a crowd of people, I'm glad I don't have to babysit Nira's boredom. To me, it's work. To her, it's a nuisance. Also . . . I kind of want to sit here on this leather couch and mope.

I feel a tap on my back.

"Almaaaaa!" I turn around and see Eduardo, one of the producers, reaching out to hug me. I feel like a cactus plant right now. I don't want to be touched. I hug him anyway. "Great work on the pilot. I saw the rough cut last week. I knew we could count on you to get the job done."

"Thanks." I don't actually like my own cut. It's too simple, too by-the-book. I wish I could play with the grammar of it all to create a greater impact and convey the lax attitude the police force had when investigating the crimes, but really, I just want this job to be over.

Eduardo steps aside and gestures to an older man beside him. "Remember this guy? Ian Holbrook. He's the investigator who arrested the Scarborough Stalker." I do remember him. His thick neck. His smug grin.

We shake hands. His paws are meaty and sweaty. "How do you do?" he says to me. He eyes my masculine suit and my boyish haircut and gives me a speculative look.

"Hey."

Eduardo shouts over the loud music into Ian's ear. "Alma is the editor of the series."

"Editor? What does an editor do?" Ian shouts back, not to me but to Eduardo.

"She cuts and arranges all of the footage to tell the story. All of the news clips, interviews, crime scene photos, et cetera."

"Crime scene photos?" Ian says. "I reckon you got to see what I saw, then."

"Yes, sir."

"Gruesome stuff, eh?" He grins, as if he's proud to have hunted a mighty stag.

"Yup." I don't want to get into things with this dude. I can tell he wants me to ask him questions and I don't want to give him the satisfaction of sharing his war stories. I see Nira across the room. What was the signal for saving someone from a bad conversation? Was it a wink? Tapping on the head? I suddenly remember and tug my earlobe, but she's too far away to see me. So much for that. "Nice to meet you," I say curtly to Ian, and weave through the crowd to my wife.

By the time I am beside her, I notice something different about Nira's eyes, like they're heavy and sleepy. Is she stoned?

"My loooove!" Nira says as she wraps her arms around my neck. "Olwyn and I are having the best time catching up. Can you believe she's attended the Grammys twice now?" She and Olwyn giggle into each other like there is some joke I'm missing. Nira whispers into my ear. "Babes. I am soooo high. I think Olwyn's weed is laced with something. Is it obvious?"

It is. But I say, "No, no. I could hardly tell."

Olwyn tries to sip her glass of champagne and almost misses her mouth. "And what do you do, Alma?"

I'm kind of offended Nira hasn't brought me up in conversation yet. "I'm an editor. I edited the series. Well . . . I'm still editing it."

"Wow. This series?"

"Yeah. A lot of people think things end when the director calls cut on the last shot, but there's months of work before it gets released and—"

"Oh my god. Is that a chocolate fountain?" Nira points to the dessert buffet on the other side of the room. Next thing I know, the two of them are gone. Nice. Wasn't Nira supposed to get me a drink? I head to the bar and try my best to get the bartender's attention. Nothing works. Not waving. Not calling. This guy with his gelled-back hair is too busy chatting it up with a party of four women to pay me any mind. Might as well get comfortable. Thank goodness there's a stool available. I park my bum on it as if I'm a lonely person looking for a one-night stand instead of an attendee at a glitzy wrap party.

"Satay skewers? Stuffed heirloom tomatoes?" says a catering waitress with a platter full of small things on sticks. Her arm shakes as I consider my choices.

"Listen. Can I just get the whole bunch of these? I'm really hungry and the bartender isn't serving me."

"Knock yourself out. Take them all. My arm is killing me."

"Thanks," I say, taking bunches of skewers with my hands. Her kindness is a balm even though it's short-lived. Off she goes back into the crowd to work.

I sit, eat and watch the night go by. Although I'm supposed to network, I can't bring myself to hobnob with all these superficial people. It's one of the reasons I got into editing. I like being alone mostly, in the darkness of my suite. With this cloud that has been following me around, though, I would rather crawl under a rock.

Of course, it's expected to feel horrified if your kid is bullying someone. But the nature of Mateo's actions against Hong has me feeling like one of those bugs, like a cicada or something, when it moults. Like my shell is here, doing all the things I'm supposed to do as a wife and mother and worker, but I've misplaced my true self somewhere and have yet to find it. Even eating the appetizers isn't helping. I can barely taste the sauce on the satay. I'm just on autopilot.

I hate to admit it, but it's already been a few days since Hong asked me to deliver that envelope to Mateo. No. It's edging on a week. It's still sitting in that canister on the kitchen counter, and I can't bring myself to hand it to him. What the hell is wrong with me?

"Hey, handsome." I feel Nira come up behind me and she rubs her hands on my chest.

My mouth is still full, but I manage to reply, "Hey, beautiful. Having fun?"

"Yeah. Olwyn and Max have already left the party. They have to catch a plane to London tomorrow morning. How glamorous is that?"

"Pretty cool," I say flatly.

Her hands get more curious. She whispers/spits into my ear. "Babes. I don't know what was in this weed, but I'm feeling so . . . so . . . horny."

"Wow." I don't know how to get out of this. I got out of sex the last time. What if I say no again?

"Let's get out of here." Nira reaches into my jacket pocket and pulls out my phone. She begins tapping away.

"What are you doing?"

"Ordering an Uber. It's Friday. It may take forever. But let's go now!"

There's one more skewer left. I'm not hungry for it, but I wonder if eating it will buy me more time.

"Awesome! It says it'll be here in five minutes."

We get our jackets and Nira rushes outside to wait. I join her. She opens her coat and wraps me inside it, her breasts pressed against my chest. "I'm so wet right now. I don't even know if I can wait until we get home."

I look around, embarrassed. "Hon. We can't do this. My co-workers. People can see us."

"No one can see." She naughtily rubs at my crotch.

"Stop."

"I bet you're wet too."

"Stop."

She steps back and closes her jacket without me in it. "What is it now, Alma?"

"We can't do things like that here."

"Are you kidding me? There were three people snorting coke in the washroom. I saw one woman giving a guy a hand job under the table in the lounge. No one cares."

"I care. And you're high."

"Fine."

The Uber arrives and we silently slide into the back seat.

Later that night, Nira brushes her teeth. She does her best thinking when she brushes her teeth. The fogginess of her face has dissipated a bit and I'm glad for it. She's super annoying when under the influence. This includes when she's had anaesthesia for tooth surgery or operations. She wipes her mouth and looks at me sitting on the bed, pretending to read. I've been on the same page of this book for weeks now. My head is too full to truly understand its words.

"My love. I'm sorry I acted the way I did. I shouldn't have made a fuss, especially at an event like that. I was stoned. I'll never smoke that much again."

"That's not the problem." I put away my book on my nightstand, on top of all the other books I have yet to finish.

"What do you mean? I was high."

"Yes, I know you were high. This is a bigger problem, Nira."

"Come on. I rarely get drunk or stoned."

Fucking hell. Of course she's trying to sidestep this situation and blame her behaviour on weed. "That's not my point!" I take the blanket off my legs and sit up to face her. "Am I allowed to say no to you? Am I? Just tell me. If I'm not allowed to say no, then I'll just concede every time you're in the mood. I will. If that's what you want, I'll do it."

Nira looks surprised by the volume of my voice. Is she cowering? "Alma. Of course you can say no."

"Could have fooled me. Because if your behaviour has been any indication, it's my duty, it's my job, to have sex when you want it. Isn't that right?"

She looks down at the carpet then back at me. Nira has never had an easy time of apologizing. "You're right. My behaviour has definitely told you that. And that's wrong of me."

My indignation lets a rush of heat flood my body and I'm sobbing. I choke out the words, "I don't want to have sex right now. I don't want to be touched. I'm so . . . broken right now. Okay?"

Nira tries to sit next to me and I get up and pace the room. "Babes. Breathe."

"I AM BREATHING!"

"Okay. But slow your breathing down."

"STOP TELLING ME WHAT TO DO! Fuck, Nira! You're always bossing me around, lording over what I eat, what I say, how I dress! Fuck off already!"

I've gone too far, shouting at her like that, and Nira knows it. "Hey. Hey. Let's be honest, Alma. We both have issues with consent. Don't act all superior over there."

A pause. I screw my face up and look at her. "What the hell are you talking about?!"

Nira puts up her hand to show all her fingers. "Five times. Five times, Alma. That's how many times it took for you to convince me to go on a date."

I run through our history again in my head. The story we have told a million times to anyone who asked about our courtship. Pub night. Tipsy. Begging Nira. Her refusal. Her friends reluctantly telling me what they knew about Nira's schedule. Me outside her classroom. Nira's disturbed face each time she'd see me. Then. Then finally. Lucky number five.

What made this story different from stalking? Was it Nira accepting my invitation? The fact that we eventually fell in love? The memory of Hong exclaiming "He's always there!" flashes through my mind and my heart sinks.

Nira continues. "I'm not saying I regret being with you finally. I'm saying I'm angry you think you've never wronged someone. And I'm asking you to be compassionate with me. We're all learning, okay? I screwed up. I didn't respect your body and you didn't respect mine. But we're here. I'm here and I am sorry, okay? I will do better." She stops herself before she cries. I assume she'll walk out of the room, upset with my rage. She doesn't.

For the first time in a long while, my eyes feel like they are back in their sockets, and I look at my wife. Really look at her. I see the crow's feet on the sides of her eyes. The way she carries herself, that determined angle of her chin, is gone as she sits before me.

"May I?" I ask. She nods yes. Beside me, she feels like someone I've known for a lifetime and yet someone I am just getting to know. "I'm sorry I shouted at you. I'm sorry I didn't respect you when we first met."

"Thank you for saying that," Nira says solemnly, her tears making a jumbled mess of her diction. "I appreciate that so much. And I am really sorry I didn't respect you. I know what happened to you that time and I don't want to be like him. I never want to hurt you like he did. You never deserved that back then and you don't deserve that now."

Even in my forties, I hear my wife say that and I still have doubts. Didn't I deserve it? Did I do all I could? I cover my mouth and wail into my palms. I sob for some time. A long time. How long? I do not know. When I open my eyes, I see Nira reaching for a box of tissues and handing it to me. I wipe my face and blow my nose. I feel my body go into its foggy place again, but hearing Nira's voice keeps me tethered to the present. She does what she always does when I am in this state, but asks me first. "May I touch your feet?" I tearfully nod. She sits in front of me and presses her hands on my feet firmly until I am back in the here and now, until my breathing has slowed down and I can feel the fabric of my pyjamas on my legs.

Chapter 15

Our drama teacher, Mrs. Greenwood, came to class one morning with a thick stack of day-old newspapers. We were preparing for our mask performance at the Easter celebration the following week. I hated mask work. Not as much as I hated mime, but mask was a pretty close second. It was torture watching my fellow teenagers pretend to be old people while wearing old-people masks. The way they made their voices quiver made me want to scream. I just wanted to head back to the AV room and edit my film project.

"You've spent this month using the supplies in our Tickle Trunk. However, today, we will make our own masks!" Mrs. Greenwood exclaimed.

The drama nerds all squealed with delight. I rolled my eyes. The first step was to sit on the dirty carpet of the studio and cut all the newspapers into strips. I got to work, using dull craft scissors to slice through the front page of the *Toronto Star*. There were two photos side by side. Each image was a school photo of a teenaged girl, both of them reported missing in a town an hour west of Toronto. They both had uniforms like me.

"Ahhh! I don't have enough breath to inflate this thing," said Caroline, drama nerd number one as she blew into a balloon. Her blond hair was perfectly braided and pinned to make a halo around her perfect little face. "At drama camp last summer we did the same thing, but with plaster strips. Much stronger. Way more professional-looking. The teachers at Bishop Shaughnessy are such cheapskates."

I shrugged my shoulders.

Ellen, drama nerd number two, mixed the bowl of glue with a bit of water. "I agree. I wish we were at Newman Collegiate. They have the best programming."

"I heard that too." Caroline tried to tie a knot at the end of the balloon, gave up and handed it to me to give it a go. The nub was wet with her spit.

"But my parents wanted me to stay in a Catholic school, which sucks cuz I'm totally an atheist and they don't get it." Ellen dipped the strips of newspaper into the glue and started to cover the balloon.

Caroline joined in with the messy application of paper. "Me too. Although . . . I'm more of an agnostic."

Ellen looked around our classroom, her shiny coils tamed into two poufs on either side of her head. She leaned into our circle. "Did you hear about the Droopy Twins?" The Droopy Twins was the nickname for a set of twin sisters who were flautists in the grade eleven music program.

"No . . . what?" Caroline whispered back.

"I heard that they snuck out of their gym class to make out in the shower room."

"Whoa! No way!"

"Way! Sharn from visual arts told me. She was the one who walked in on them feeling each other up. She has chemistry with them as well, and supposedly they finger each other under the counters."

"Holy shit. That's wrong in all sorts of ways. Not only is that incestuous . . . it's totally lesbionic." Caroline suddenly looked at me and held up her hand. "No offence."

"What do you mean?" I asked, a heat growing in my throat.

Caroline looked at Ellen, then they both shrugged their shoulders. "Nothing," Caroline said as casually as she could. "Although . . . I mean . . . is it true?"

I pinched hard at the nub of another balloon, which was half-inflated in my hands. "Is what true?"

"About you being a lesbo," Caroline clarified.

A contrived friendly smile played on Ellen's face. "You can trust us. You can tell us anything."

Would the Droopy Twins agree?

I scoffed and blew into the balloon until it was twice the size of the last one. "Where did you hear that nonsense?"

"Around."

Caroline added, "Yeah. Around. Doreen from dance is the sister of Elliot from AV club and she told me you didn't want to fuck Toby because you're gay or something."

"That's stupid."

"I thought so too!" Caroline said before she and Ellen side-eyed each other.

I slapped strips of sticky newspaper onto the balloon in my hand until half the globe was covered. A strip of paper from the headline reading *MISSING* sat across the brow of my mask. Once Caroline and Ellen began chatting about signing up for the improvisation team, I quickly went to the girls' washroom to rinse my hands. Well . . . that's what I told Mrs. Greenwood. What I really wanted to do was run to the washroom and cry.

Inside the stall, I closed the lid of the toilet, sat down and hugged my knees to my chest.

"Is someone in here?" a person on the other side of the stall said, trying to open the door.

"It's taken," I said with the best normal voice I could muster.

The bell rang and the washroom suddenly became abuzz with activity. High-pitched laughter. Many pairs of feet walking back and forth under my stall. I had to talk to Toby. He had been avoiding me lately and wasn't at AV club at the same time I was this past week, which was weird.

Later that week, our drama class booked the auditorium for our tech rehearsal. Our performance involved a mask interpretation of the fourteen stations of the cross. It was hella hokey, with us in our silly handmade masks, illustrating Jesus's harrowing journey to his crucifixion. What made it even more painful was Mrs. Greenwood's obsession with Enya at the time. It was hardly a surprise that she figured out a way to include Enya's New Age music into our tableaux.

"One more time from Veronica wiping Jesus's face," Mrs. Greenwood said. "Cue the music, please."

My classmates all got into our positions. I assumed the posture of someone in the crowd, pointing at Jesus and condemning him to death. Thank goodness for the mask, because no one could see that I was actually looking at the exit to the theatre. I knew that Toby was one of the few technicians who handled the light board in the control room. If I was to run into him, today would definitely be the day.

"Hello? Anyone up there?" Mrs. Greenwood called up to the tech booth.

Toby stuck his head out the window. My heart stopped. "Yes, ma'am. Music, coming up." Toby disappeared into the depths of the booth. How long was he watching? He must have thought it was hilarious, me in a robe with rope ceinture. Oh wait. I had my mask on. Maybe he didn't know which one was me.

At the end of the rehearsal, I waited to approach him until my class shuffled out of the theatre. He had turned the house lights on and was twirling cables into neat piles by the lip of the stage.

"Hey, Toby."

He didn't make eye contact. "Hey."

"Did you know it was me? Behind the mask?"

"Sure."

"So stupid. I hate mask work." There was a long silence, which I broke by saying, "Are you still mad at me?"

He walked to the fly deck, took a pair of leather gloves

from his back pocket and began pulling one of the curtains up. "Maybe."

"Toby. I'm sorry, okay? I just didn't want to be watched. That dude was so creepy."

Returning his gloves to his back pocket, he finally said, "Is that all?"

"Is that all what?"

"It's not something else?"

"What? Being gay? I heard from people around school that you've been saying I'm gay."

"Whatever. I said that to one person in private."

"Word gets around, Toby."

"I have a right to express myself to friends. Express my concerns and all."

"Well, you have nothing to be concerned about. Okay? I'm not gay. Can you please stop saying that to people?"

He crossed his arms and shifted on his feet, his lips in a slight pout. "It wasn't me, then? It wasn't because you're not into me that you stopped?"

"No, Toby. I thought what was happening was . . . it was super hot. I did."

"You promise?"

I stepped forward and put my hand on his elbow. He softened to my touch. "I do. I promise."

Toby walked to the ladder, which led to the catwalk above the auditorium. When he looked back at me, he said, "Then prove it."

I laughed and followed him up the ladder. Sure. Whatever.

If facing my fear of heights was what it was going to take for Toby to believe I wasn't gay, I was all for it. The ladder was narrow and metal, surrounded by a cylinder cage for safety. I wasn't sure if I was more afraid of the height or the feeling of the cage closing in on me. I followed him all the way up to the top of the ladder, where he helped me onto the catwalk.

"Whoa!" Below me, the empty theatre seats looked like miniatures. Seeing the dust on the tops of the lights made my stomach queasy. "Okay. I did it. Let's go," I said, turning back towards the ladder.

"Not yet." Toby walked to the middle of the catwalk and put one hand on each side of the railings. "You said you'd prove it."

"I did?"

"Yeah, prove it to me." He unzipped his pants and pulled out his dick. "Suck it."

"What?"

"Suck it."

With legs shaking, I traversed the mesh metal catwalk until I was immediately facing him. I knelt. I did it. I did it, afraid of falling to my death. I did it, afraid another classmate was going to walk in on us. I did it. I completed the task.

After I was done, Toby's arm was around me again, but I could barely feel it over my shoulder. With eyes dead, I played along and tried my best to act casual. I was under complete control. We walked the hallways as a couple and everyone saw what I wanted them to see. I wanted this. Everything was going as planned.

"You're late!" Leah said to me as soon as I walked through the door later that day. She handed me Jess, who was covered in stickers and having a tantrum.

"Sorry, Ate."

"Whatever. She's already eaten her dinner. Her last dose of antibiotics is at seven. Don't forget." Leah stepped into her Doc Martens shoes and put her backpack over one of her shoulders. I had forgotten that she was starting night school today. "What's wrong with you?"

I shook my head out of my fog. "Nothing. Why?"

"You look like a mess. What's happening?" she asked, even though she was patting her jean jacket for her keys.

"I'm good."

Leah found her keys and gave one last kiss to Jess's chubby cheeks. "Be good for Tita Alma. Only one movie tonight. Okay?" Then she rushed out the door.

I took care of Jess in complete silence, thankful that I could stop pretending. That suited Jess just fine, as she was more irritable than usual due to her recurring ear infections. I gave her the last dose of pink liquid antibiotics, then sat her down to watch *The Little Mermaid*.

Leaning my head into my hand, I could still smell Toby on me. The only position in which I could sit on the couch and not be reminded of what I did was lying on my back and staring at the popcorn ceiling. My eyes got heavy. I woke up to Jess scribbling marker all over my face. Night had fallen. On the television, Ariel was getting her happily ever after.

"Hello?" Mom said as she walked through the door. She was out a lot lately, trying to do the executive dinner party circuit with the finance team. She called it "schmoozing."

"Hey," I said groggily.

"What happened to your face?" asked Mom, looking up from the mail she was shuffling in her hands.

"Um . . . Jess was playing makeup."

I began getting Jess ready for her bath by filling up the tub with soapy water and toys.

I could hear Mom in the kitchen shutting the microwave and pressing buttons. Beep. Beep. Beeeep. Hummmmm. These dinners often ended with my mom at home eating another meal, because the food was rarely enough. Stuffed peppers and chips and dip could hardly be called a meal to my Filipino mother. The smell of pork adobo wafted through the house as I was in the washroom, lowering Jess's naked body into the water and scrubbing her clean. Jess dunked a plastic cup into the water and tried to drink the suds. "Hey. No drinking. That's dirty."

"I nee go pee, Tita Amma," Jess said with her black wisps plastered to her forehead.

"Pee? You just got in here."

"I nee go pee now."

I sighed and wrestled her wet body onto the toilet. While she peed, I washed the marker off my face. "You done? Ready to go back into the bath?" Jess answered by wrapping her damp arms around my neck. I picked her up and put her back in the tub to splash about.

In the living room, Mom turned on the television while she ate her second dinner. "The mother of Suzanna Perth called police only an hour after the teen hadn't returned home," the voice of a news reporter said on the television. "Danah Desmond's parents, however, did not alert the police until she had been missing for a total of four days, explaining that it was not unusual for their daughter to hang with friends for days at a time."

Later, when I was cuddling up with Jess on Leah's bed and reading her a bedtime story, Leah walked in, smelling of cigarette smoke.

"Hey. Thanks, Alma." Leah took off her jean jacket and stuffed it into the bottom of her closet. She kissed Jess, who was already half-asleep, and put her child's floppy body over her shoulder.

"No problem." I got up to go. I was weary, to say the least.

"How was she?" Leah put Jess into her crib, which was jammed between the mattress and the windowsill. Jess rolled over, hugged her stuffed bunny and went to sleep.

"Great."

"You okay? Are you getting sick?"

"No."

"Boy trouble?" She smiled. My long pause made her suspicious. "Is it that Toby guy?" The way I shook my head made her even more suspicious. Leah pursed her lips. "Where's Mom?"

"Asleep."

"You sure?"

"Pretty sure."

Leah opened the door of her bedroom and peered down the empty hallway. "Meet me in your bedroom in five minutes," she said before sneaking out.

I did as she said and walked to my bedroom. In exactly five minutes, Leah entered with her arms full of junk food. Fudgee-Os. Doritos. Pocky. Two cans of cola. She shut the door quietly then plopped herself on my mattress.

"These aren't even opened yet. Mom will find out."

Leah rolled her eyes before ripping open the packages. "Mom's not going to find out."

I pulled the tab on the cola and took a sip. "What's the occasion?"

With her mouth half-full of orange chips, she replied, "I dunno. I like pigging out when I'm sad. It makes me feel better. You looked sad. So I brought this for us to share." I passed her the other can of cola and she washed down the orange chips with the fizzy black liquid. "Plus . . . I've given up looking like I did before the baby. Might as well live it up!"

I pulled the tray of cookies out of its pristine folding bag. Leah was right—the sight of a flawless lineup of fudge sandwiched by crisp biscuits was making me feel better already. I took one cookie and split it in half so that I could indulge in the soft, chocolatey centre.

"So, what's up with you? What has Toby done?"

"Nothing. I'm just confused. Or . . . things are confusing. That's all."

"Are you fucking yet?"

"Ate Leah!"

"Well? Are you?"

"Not yet." The image of Toby letting his uniform pants fall to his ankles flashed through my mind. One of the leather gloves that he used to pull the curtain fell from his pocket and descended to the theatre chairs below. I didn't want to fall the way that glove did. I shook that memory from my head.

"Okay. Well . . . boys can be confusing. And fucking pushy. They can't help it. Sure, girls get horny. But boys . . . boys . . . it's like their brain is in their dick, you know?" Leah took the clear plastic wrap off the box of Pocky and popped open the carton from the top. "It's scientifically proven that all of their blood from their body goes straight to their dicks and they don't think properly. So they say stupid things. Do stupid things. Does that explain it?" She playfully elbowed me.

Did it explain things? Maybe I was making this out to be bigger than it was. I had heard that when you lose your virginity, it hurts a bit. You could even bleed. Maybe it was like this for all sexual activity. It would feel weird until it didn't.

"At least you're getting some. Man. I don't even remember the last time I got laid. No one wants to screw around with a teen mom, Alma. Remember that. It's like I'm radioactive. All of them assume I want someone to care for me and my kid. And I'm like, 'Hello! I just want action, okay? I don't even want to introduce you to my kid, you loser. Can you just fuck my brains out and leave already?'" She brushed the crumbs off her shirt.

I sat up and looked at my sister. She was much older now. Since the baby, she had suddenly become an adult.

"Can you promise me you'll be careful with this Toby guy? I know in the moment all you want to do is screw around. It's so easy to forget what's important." Leah retied her ponytail. Did she cut her hair herself? "Not that I don't adore Jess . . . but you're living your life right now. At least you get to. What you have, the opportunity to achieve at school and in life . . . that's not in the cards for me, you know? Like . . . I was in that night school class and was surrounded by other teen moms trying their best to get their high school diploma. One of them had her boyfriend outside, taking care of the kid. He was knocking on the window every five minutes asking how to change a diaper or how much formula to put in the bottle. He was a kid himself. What did he know about being a dad? It was a goddamn nightmare." She vigorously rubbed her right eye, smearing mascara across her face. "Just put a condom on before doing it. Okay?"

"Okay."

Leah gathered all the snack wrappers and left.

•••

The next morning, I was on the subway heading to school. There were two delays on transit. One was on the bus into Kennedy station. A teenaged boy stormed the back door, trying to dodge paying the fare. The door got jammed open and we all had to exit the bus and wait for another one. The other delay happened in the subway, after Sherbourne station, just before I was to transfer to the northbound line. Over the PA system, the conductor mumbled something about us having to wait because of a stalled train ahead of us. Someone had committed suicide by jumping in front of an oncoming train.

In the darkened tunnel, no one was paying attention to the announcement, though. In my seat in the crowded train car, I was surrounded by people reading copies of the *Toronto Star* newspaper, their various fists holding up folded sheets and their heads hidden behind its spine. Like patterned tile, a face looked back at me from the front covers. It was the same face I saw on the side of the garbage truck, the same face I saw on the Wanted posters throughout my neighbourhood, the same face projected onto the screen when we were learning to protect ourselves from the Scarborough Stalker. Only this picture was his mug shot. Blue eyes. Brown hair. The headline read, *Dentist charged in Suzanna Perth and Danah Desmond murders and Scarborough Stalker cases.*

"I hope he rots in hell," said one woman to another in the seats beside me. While folding up her copy of the *Toronto Star* and putting it into her leather purse, she added, "Can you believe the cops got two tips that he may have been the Scarborough Stalker and they did nothing? If they had looked into it like they were supposed to, he wouldn't have moved to another town and killed more women and girls."

The other woman applied lip balm and said, "Did you see the wedding photos of him and his wife? The investigators think the wife was in on it."

"Jesus Christ."

"I know. People are sick in the head these days. Did you see the part in the article where the cops seized thousands of

VHS tapes? Not only were they depraved enough to kill, they were depraved enough to record themselves doing it."

"I did. It makes my stomach turn thinking of the investigators who will have to watch that footage from beginning to end."

"Not to mention the jury members."

"I can't even deal."

"Me neither. Well . . . at least we're all safe now."

The train finally started moving and the two women got up to exit, one of them leaving her copy of the *Toronto Star* on her seat. I took it into my hands. It was still warm. I read his name. Did I know he was your killer? No. Not at that time. No one did, except for your boyfriend, who knew he had been falsely imprisoned for your murder.

I arrived at school late because of the transit delays, but I felt this elated energy in my body, enough to make me fly from the subway station across the street to Bishop Shaughnessy in no time. I hadn't realized how much fear I was holding in my body, knowing the Scarborough Stalker was at large. Now that he was caught, as the lady said on the train, we were all safe.

"You're late," said Mrs. Greenwood in the wings of the theatre. The stage was already set up with an altar. One student stood on a ladder to decorate the walls of the front of house with images of bread, fish and doves. "Hurry up and get into your costume. The Easter assembly is about to start."

I headed backstage and found my drama classmates putting on makeup to go with their shapeless robes. I had never

seen people in the Bible wearing red lipstick and fake eyelashes, and weren't we going to wear masks?

Caroline did a double take when she saw me. "Thank god!
We thought you were a no-show."

"There was a delay on the train—"

"I'll catch you up while you're dressing," she said with a
hand gesture for me to hurry up. I found my robe and ceinture
on the clothing rack while she updated me on the change in
staging for the Pontius Pilate scene. "When Pontius Pilate
says, 'I am innocent of the blood of this just person,' and
washes his hands, Mrs. Greenwood wants us all to gasp and
put our hands up like this, like we're in shock or something."
She demonstrated. I nodded. "Can I see you do that?"

Who the fuck did Caroline think she was? Bob Fosse?
And the last time I checked, this was an Easter Mass, not a
Broadway performance of *Sweet Charity*. Nonetheless, I did
what she said just to shut her up, then got my costume on.

Once the auditorium was full of students, the house lights
dimmed. I thought of Toby up there in the tech booth. My boyfriend. The guy I fooled around with. Totally normal. I caught
sight of the catwalk just above the gleaming lights and my jaw
tightened. I shook my head free of any memories before putting my mask on. The Enya music started and I took my place
for the most ridiculous series of scenes depicting the death
and resurrection of Jesus. Between the scenes, our school choir
sang hymns accompanied by our award-winning orchestra. It
was so over the top. With the number of students performing
during the Mass, it was a miracle any students were left in the

audience to watch. But this Mass was special. Since this was the first Easter for our new Catholic arts school, our Mass was conducted by Cardinal LeFrancois and some bigwigs were present. Hence, Caroline's fervour in getting my shocked jazz hands move right. If there was anyone who was going to get her acting career jump-started, it was someone in the school board or archdiocese. Sure. Once we were done, we had to sit with the audience, still wearing our silly costumes, like we were these Biblical caricatures among students.

Cardinal LeFrancois took to the microphone in his scarlet choir dress for the sermon. His breath was heavy and his voice was raspy. "Easter weekend isn't about getting a long weekend to have fun with your friends. It's not about chocolate or the Easter bunny. It's about reflecting on sacrifice and faith." The look he gave us over his rippling jowls was one of disgust, as if he was looking into the centre of Sodom itself. "People often ask me, 'Cardinal, how did Mother Mary not doubt that her son would rise from the dead?' And my answer is sacrifice and faith. She knew, as soon as that angel came upon her many years before, telling her that she was to be the mother of God's only son, that she would have to sacrifice pleasure. Sacrifice the judgment of all around her, including her husband, Joseph, for being the handmaiden of God. And it was her undying faith that her sacrifice would lead to our salvation that helped her believe that Jesus would emerge from that tomb and open the gates of heaven." The cardinal adjusted the microphone stand, whose neck was wilting. "So my question to you this Easter is, what are you willing to sacrifice? Sure, you may have fasted during Lent. Given up chips or TV. But are you willing to sacrifice fornication?"

There was a snicker from the audience. By the time the adults turned their heads towards the sound, all the students had neutral faces.

To be hip, the cardinal added, "Are you willing to sacrifice making out? Chilling with your friends and snorting drugs?"

He droned on and on. I was still too distracted by the thought of Toby in the tech booth. I wondered if he was watching me from above, now that my mask was off.

"Saw you at Mass today," Toby said over lunch in the cafeteria. He always ordered poutine and orange soda.

"Sorry."

"Sorry for what?"

"That mask play was painful."

"It was. But just think: there are other Catholic schools out there with no arts students, where they have to endure Easter celebrations with only Bible readings and out-of-tune songs."

"Ah yes," I said, lifting my chicken burger to my mouth. "We have an orchestra too."

"An award-winning orchestra, Alma. Don't forget." We laughed and he held my hand across the table. "When can I see you this weekend?"

"It's Easter, so we may have guests."

"Saturday night, then?"

I forced a smile. "Sure."

• • •

Tita Lorna and Tito Benny were scheduled to come to our house for lunch on Easter Saturday. My strategy was to tell my mother I was heading out in the evening while company was over, to avoid her making a fuss. As usual, my aunt and uncle arrived mid-morning so that Tita Lorna and Mom could gossip in the kitchen while Tito Benny had his San Miguel beer–induced nap on our couch.

Mom pressed her lips together and touched cheeks with Tita Lorna. "Where's Belinda?"

"She's with her church friends. Youth group." Tita Lorna set down her signature pancit bihon on the kitchen counter before removing her jacket and handing it to me to hang. "That's my Belinda. Always social. Always celebrating Jesus."

"Maybe you should join the church group, Alma," Mom said as she began setting up the table for wrapping lumpia. She put spoons in the pork filling and in the bowl of flour paste. Tita Lorna took a seat at the table next to her and the two immediately got to work, wrapping the spring rolls and sealing them shut with the paste. "At least then I know you're not getting into trouble."

Tita Lorna paused for a moment and turned to look at me. "It's true. Belinda can be out all the time and I can trust her. They go to movies together. Listen to music. Visit each other's houses. No funny business." Tita Lorna added her wrapped lumpia to the growing pile of spring rolls.

I knew now would be a good time to ask Mom about going out that evening. It was a sweet spot where I knew she and Tita Lorna were about to gossip and wanted their privacy.

"Mom?" I said, my hands kneading together nervously.

"What is it, Alma?" Mom asked sharply.

"I have to go out tonight."

"Tonight? But it's Easter."

"The AV club has to complete a group project and tonight is the only night we can do it."

"Fine. Fine. Just be home by eleven. No later, ha?"

"Yes, Mom."

Tita Lorna suddenly stood, her hands still wet with raw pork meat. She pointed with her mouth at another plastic bag near the cake she bought at the store. "Alma. Take that and share with your sister and Jess."

Inside the bag were three boxes of chocolate bunnies. "Thanks, Tita." I touched cheeks with her.

"No problem. Enjoy!"

The two women began whispering the moment I left the room. I went outside to join Leah and deliver the goods. Jess was busy driving her plastic toy car on the driveway in a circle.

"Hey. Tita Lorna gave us gifts."

Leah took the plastic bag from me and pointed at Jess. "Look what she's doing. Can you believe it?" At a tree near the end of our lot, Jess got out of the car, picked up a twig from the ground and pretended it was a nozzle to refill the gas tank. "Look at her. She even has her hands on her hips, waiting for the tank to fill up. She's obviously copying her Lola."

"Hilarious. She's a mini person now."

"Tell me about it." Leah looked into the plastic bag and dove into the box labelled *Jess* first.

"Hey. That's for your daughter."

"Jess can't read. What she doesn't know won't hurt her," Leah said, breaking the bunny into pieces and shovelling the chocolate into her mouth. "Plus, I don't want her to be on a sugar high by tonight. You saw that cake Tita Lorna bought. There's only six of us and it's the size of a football field."

"Truuuue."

"Most importantly, I have a date tonight, and I need her to be asleep by no later than eight."

"With who?"

"Some guy I met at night school. The only guy in that classroom, basically."

"Cool."

"Not so cool. He's into drag racing. Remember that car crash that happened near Scarborough Town Centre last week?"

"Sorta."

"Ollie was involved in it. He didn't get hurt. Ollie and his friends like to take their race rockets to the top of McCowan and rev their engines. I have to admit, it's kinda hot. But also, he's in his mid-twenties, shouldn't he have a life? Ugh. Why do I always like the bad boys?" Leah licked the chocolate from her fingers then looked at me. "Speaking of boys. Did I hear you're going out tonight too?"

"Yeah."

"That Toby guy?"

Jess drove her toy car towards us and we stepped back to avoid her running over our toes.

"Uh-huh."

Leah reached into the back pocket of her khakis and gave me a handful of condoms.

"Whoa. What?"

"They have them at the door in a bowl at night class. Isn't that hilarious? A little late. Put them in your purse."

"I don't have a purse."

"Put them in your . . . I dunno . . . your jacket. Whatever. Just bring them. You never know."

"But if I bring them, we'll use them."

"So?"

"I want to save my . . . you know . . ."

"Oh god. Please. Your virginity? If you're already fooling around, you're halfway there. Best to be safe."

I distributed them among my four jean pockets so that the bulk wouldn't arouse suspicion in our mother.

Leah added, "Just tell Toby if he doesn't wrap it up, you'll have to wrap things up. If he really wants to fuck, he'll put it on. Trust me."

• • •

Toby arrived in his father's car at seven that night. Tita Lorna and Tito Benny were still at our house, now sitting on the sectional couch with my mom, watching an episode of *The Cosby Show*. I rushed past them and grabbed my jacket.

"Okay. I'm going now. Bye." They barely acknowledged me, still laughing at some scene playing on the screen.

I stepped into Toby's car. He leaned in for a kiss right away, then paused. "You smell like . . . bacon?"

I sat back in my seat, suddenly embarrassed. I smelled the collar of my jacket. "Uh . . . yeah. We fried some pork spring rolls today. Sorry."

A few minutes into the drive, I already knew where we were going. Back to the marsh. Back to the lovers' lane. I felt for the condom I brought in my pocket. Its wrapper was like those candies in the dentist's office, the ones in the bowls that no one touches. Instead of a caramel inside, it was a round ring sliding in some kind of liquid.

He parked. Since it was Easter weekend, I thought there would be hardly anyone there. I was wrong. The parking lot was packed under the light of a half moon.

"If it's a good day, I can get the signal from the Buffalo radio station," Toby said, fiddling with the tuner on the dashboard. Blue light hit his eyes. "Found it!"

"Energy Surge Radio 1010. Top twenty countdown. Number eight," said the radio voice, followed by the sounds of lasers. A slow jam by Boyz II Men played over the speakers.

"Let's go to the back seat." He took off his seat belt and climbed over ahead of me.

I thought for a second, then opened the passenger door with sweaty palms. I could do this. I was doing this. Totally normal. It's awkward until it isn't. It's like plucking your eyebrows. Or shaving your legs. Or putting on a bra. It'll just take practice.

I saw another vehicle right beside ours. An older man was inside it. He must have had the radio on too, because blue light from his dashboard painted over his sharp features and receding hairline. He unabashedly watched me walk to the back door and get in.

"There's another guy outside—" I said before Toby swallowed my mouth with his own lips. Slobber across my face. I tried to position myself so that my nose wasn't buried into his cheeks, suffocating me. Thankfully, he moved into the crease of my neck and I could breathe again. I looked up at the roof of the car and pretended to make moans of pleasure as his hands reached up my tee and squeezed at my breasts.

He unzipped his pants and I watched him. He chuckled and said, "What are you doing? Aren't you going to take yours off too?"

"My pants?"

"Yes."

"Wait. I have a condom." I frantically reached for my jacket, which Toby had flung into the hatchback trunk. Showing him the package, I said, "Let's put it on first."

"What? Where did you get that?"

"A friend."

"Uh-uh." Toby took the package from me. "This is the wrong size."

"There are sizes?"

He laughed. "Yeah. This is *way* too small for me."

"You didn't even try it on."

"Trust me. I know."

I tried the saying Leah had told me. "If you don't wrap it up, we'll have to wrap this up."

"Huh?"

"If you don't wear it, I don't want to do it."

He paused for a moment, scanning me. I held my breath. In a huff, he started taking his shirt off the headrest of the driver's seat and putting it back on. "I knew you were a dyke."

"What are you talking about? Just cuz I want to be safe?"

"I drive all the way out here to Scarborough to be with you, and all I get is attitude about condoms and creepy guys in cars next to us. You'll make up anything to get out of this. I don't know why I even try!"

"Toby, stop. That's not what I'm doing! I brought the condom. So we could have sex. Don't you want to?"

"I should've listened to Elliot and dumped your gay ass."

"Stop! I'm not gay. I'm not," I said, fear trembling my voice.

"Sure. Whatever." He looked at his own dick. "Look. It's floppy now. All this condom talk made me go soft."

I scrambled, trying my best to figure out how to right this wrong. "I can help with that," I said in as sultry a voice as I could make, wiping away a stray tear that was running down my cheek. I'm not sure if he bought my act. It didn't matter. He let me put my mouth on his penis anyway. Anything to make him shut up and stop threatening to leave me. I just wanted to hide, and the only place I could go was between his legs.

He grabbed my hair to push me down and I pulled away. "You're choking me." He grabbed my hair again and shoved my face down onto him. My eyes watered as I tried to keep myself from gagging. That's when I went into my foggy place. I left my body behind, the one that Toby slammed onto the seat and whose underwear he removed. I left my body behind in that car, beside the other car with the pervert watching, in that dark parking lot, to go off in my mind to somewhere light and easy.

In the cloud of my imagination, I saw Fred Astaire in top hat and tails reach his hand out to me, asking me to dance. Everything was black and white, including me. I was wearing a 1930s ball gown with ostrich feathers on my sleeves and on the bell of my dress. Fred whisked me around the room to the tune of some grand orchestral number. He foxtrotted me across marble floors, weaving through Corinthian columns until the end of the song.

When I came out of my fog, Toby was dressing himself. He spat into his sock to wipe a stain from the surface of the upholstery. I was still coming back into my body when he said fondly, "Hey. That was amazing." Even in the dark, I could see the shape of his wide smile. "It's late. Come on. We have to get going. My dad needs the car tonight."

I did as he said and dressed, zipping myself back together, piece by piece.

On the drive home, he rolled down his window to get rid of the condensation and instructed me to do the same. The casual way he tapped his fingers on the steering wheel made me wonder if I had imagined what happened. Really happened.

Toby did not pull into my driveway when he dropped me off, because he was in a rush. He did not kiss me good night either. Running my tongue over a cut on my lip, the taste of pennies, I weakly waved goodbye to him and watched his car speed off into the night.

•••

"Alma? Alma?" Mrs. Lessen repeated.

I looked around and found myself in my finite mathematics class. My classmates stared back at me. How long had she been waiting for me to reply?

"Sorry. Yes, miss?" I sat up in my chair to look more alert.

"Go on to the board and demonstrate the solution to this equation, please."

Getting up from my desk, I tripped on my backpack strap and had to hold on to the shoulder of Gabriella at the desk in front of me to keep myself from falling flat on my face. Quiet laughter among my peers. I righted myself and clumsily headed to the chalkboard. On the way there, I felt a soreness from last night's assault throb at my crotch and I had to file the pain in some drawer deep in the depths of my being.

"All right, Alma. In example 5D, can you show the class how we arrive at the quadratic mean, please."

The chalk piece I chose from the ledge was too long and it broke in my fingers. I took another piece and touched it to the black surface of the board. Quadratic mean?

"Alma?"

Holding the chalk piece in place, I just stared at my hand.

"If you are unsure of yourself, we can go step by step so that everyone can learn along with you."

My hand got tired and it started to slide down, leaving

a squiggle line of blue on the surface. The line looked like a carrot. A necklace. A length of rope.

"How about this, Alma. How about Derrick try his hand at it and you can watch?"

I dropped the chalk, took my backpack and wandered out of the classroom. Somewhere behind me, Mrs. Lessen called my name.

The office administrator handed me the receiver of her desk phone. On the other end, my mother hurriedly asked me why I was bothering her at work.

"I don't feel well."

"What do you mean you don't feel well, Alma?"

"Girl problems."

I handed the receiver back to the administrator and she let me sign myself out of school. Transit was easy coming back to Scarborough. No delays. Hardly any people. I didn't have a plan as to where I was going, or maybe I did. I just knew I wasn't going home.

On the final leg of my trip, I was on the 54 bus and I found myself ringing the bell to be let off at St. Xavier. Bypassing the school office, I entered my old school through a side door, walked past lines of shoes outside classrooms, past displays of construction paper art, past dusty trophies, and headed straight to the library. Would Mrs. Bartkiewicz be there? Would she hate me? Would she even talk to me?

The library was empty, but the door was open. I stood by the rotating bookshelf in the Canadian Classics section and did everything to keep myself from crying. I failed. I was alone. Even Mrs. Bartkiewicz couldn't help me. And why would she, after what I had done?

"Alma?" Mrs. Bartkiewicz called out. She had entered the library from another entrance, wheeling in a television and VHS machine. Did she catch me from falling? I think she did. Because the next thing I knew, I was on the mangled carpet, sobbing uncontrollably. And Mrs. Bartkiewicz was holding me upright as much as her petite frame could. Her arms enveloped me and I let myself be held. Looking down at the tangle of our collective limbs, I saw her ugly teacher shoes and was so damn thankful. What an embrace she gave me. Partly to keep me from collapsing on the ground and partly to show me she was there for me. The solid feel of her arms helped me soften into the mess I truly was.

Somehow, in between crying fits, I told her what had happened. How, I cannot recall in major detail. I do, however, remember her face as I told her. A quiet shock and seething anger brewed in her eyes. Tears welled up in the corners. I didn't realize until that moment how much I missed her listening to me.

Mrs. Bartkiewicz waited until my breathing had slowed down before getting up to close both doors to the library. She sat back down on the carpet beside me and gently said, "Alma. I believe you. What happened to you was wrong. I am so sorry it happened."

Hearing her say this, hearing her honour my truth, made me reach out for her once again. She went straight into my arms and held me close. Was she crying too?

"Listen. You hold the cards. Tell me, honestly, what do you need right now and what do you want me to do?"

"What choices are you talking about?"

"Well . . ." Mrs. Bartkiewicz sat back away from me and adjusted her stockings on her calves. "Do you want to report this?"

"To who? The police?"

"That's a possibility. Or to your mother?" I emphatically shook my head. "Okay. No one is forcing you to report. You don't have to if you don't want to. There are many reasons to report and many reasons not to. It's your choice. I didn't report my rape."

"You?"

Mrs. Bartkiewicz looked away from me and nodded yes. She nervously fiddled with her stockings again. "But this isn't about me. It's about you. If you change your mind and want to report later, I can help you with that too. For now, maybe the best thing to think about is your well-being. Um . . . are you hurt? Physically?"

I told her about the tenderness between my legs and the mysterious cut at my lip.

"Did he use a condom?"

Shamefully, I shook my head. "I'm sorry. No. He didn't. I asked him to." I started to cry again, but Mrs. Bartkiewicz waved her hand in front of me.

"Hey. That's all right. I understand. This is not your fault. None of this is your fault, okay, Alma? Do you understand that?"

"Sorta."

"Do you feel comfortable driving with me in my car?"

Mrs. Bartkiewicz left work early that day to take me to a nearby walk-in clinic to get the morning-after pill. On the drive there, she adjusted the radio dial to something jazzy and light. "I can't believe it's the nineties and we still have to get a prescription for the morning-after pill." She parked the car and looked at me. "One day, I hope we can just grab it off the shelves. One day."

The clinic was full to the brim, but Mrs. Bartkiewicz stayed with me, patiently reading through issues of *Canadian Gardener's Monthly* before we were called in. "Do you want me to come with you? For support?"

"Yes, please."

The receptionist guided us to a room. "The doctor will be with you in a moment." I sat on the crunchy paper of the examination table and Mrs. Bartkiewicz sat on the chair beside me.

To break the silence between us, I said, "Mrs. Bartkiewicz. I'm really sorry about what I did to your house."

Another few minutes of silence passed before she replied, "I'm not going to say what you did was acceptable, because it wasn't. But I will happily accept your apology." Mrs. Bartkiewicz's lips turned up in a slight smile. "I've missed you, Alma."

"Me too."

Thankfully, at that moment, the doctor walked in. The honesty of my conversation with Mrs. Bartkiewicz was almost too honest, too good to be true for me to trust it.

"Hello. My name is Dr. Friesen. What brings you here

today?" he said, looking at Mrs. Bartkiewicz and ignoring me, the person sitting on the examination table.

"My daughter needs the morning-after pill."

"Daughter?" both Dr. Friesen and I said at the same time. Although I said it quieter. I wasn't sure why she was calling me that, but I played along.

"Yes. Daughter."

Dr. Friesen sat on his rolling chair and took out his prescription pad. "And why do you need it?" he said to me with a discerning face.

"Why does anyone need the morning-after pill?" Mrs. Bartkiewicz interjected. "She had unprotected sex."

"I guess my question is, why was she having unprotected sex?" Dr. Friesen turned to me and leaned his elbow on the examination table. "You do know about condoms, don't you?" I shyly nodded. "Well, did you use one?"

"Doctor. There are reasons why she didn't use one and we needn't disclose them to you."

"Fine. Fine." He scribbled something illegible on his pad, ripped the paper from the adhesive strip and handed it to me with a roll of his eyes. "Here." He grabbed a pamphlet on safe sex options and gave it to me. "Lots of great ideas here for next time. The morning-after pill is for *emergencies*."

Mrs. Bartkiewicz stood up from her chair, her face determined and hard. "Doctor. This is an emergency."

She drove me to the pharmacy around the corner and paid for the prescription, a bottle of iced tea and a box of anti-nausea pills.

"What are those for?"

"Trust me. You'll need them."

In her car, I washed down both medications with a large swig of iced tea.

"Why did you call me your daughter in there?"

"Because otherwise I would have no business being in the room with you and advocating for you. Sorry. I hope you don't mind."

"I don't mind." In fact, I liked being someone's daughter. I knew I was someone's daughter already, but this was different. Someone was choosing me to be their daughter.

"Okay, let's think." Mrs. Bartkiewicz twirled her car keys in her hand. "It's your choice, Alma. Did you want me to drive you home? Or do you want to come have dinner with my family tonight? No pressure. I'm just wondering if you should be alone right now."

I felt my stomach turn as the medication started to do its thing.

•••

For some strange reason, I pictured Mrs. Bartkiewicz's home with toilet paper still on it. Of course, there wasn't any. However, the phantom guilt played over me. I wasn't yet used to someone forgiving me.

I used her phone to call my mother and make up an excuse that I was at a friend's house. Mom hurriedly told me to make sure I was a respectful guest before she rushed off for another meeting.

Vanessa came home with her arms full of dry-cleaning bags. "You would not believe the traffic! Some fuckface was on my ass from Bathurst all the way to Main Street." She looked at me, sitting at their kitchen table, confused. "Hi."

"Hi. I'm Alma."

"Oh, *you're* Alma. *The* Alma."

I looked to the side, confused. "Yes." *The* Alma? "Mrs. Bartkiewicz is changing the loads of laundry."

Vanessa put the dry cleaning on the table and headed down the hall to their laundry room. I could hear them whispering to each other. They both came down the hallway wearing formal smiles. "I'm glad you're staying for dinner," Vanessa said to me before opening the refrigerator and taking out a package of steak. "I hope you like stir-fry."

I nodded and held my stomach. The last thing I wanted to do was vomit in their house. I had already trashed it with toilet paper; I didn't want to burden them with my sick as well.

"Did you want to lie down on the couch? Or in Emma's room?" Mrs. Bartkiewicz asked. I chose the couch. She surprised me by handing me a blanket and one of the throw pillows. "Get comfy. Seriously. Lie down if you want to." She handed me the remote control. "The buttons on the top are for the television itself. The ones at the bottom are for our VHS machine. But we haven't figured out how to hook it up. I'll leave you be."

Vanessa went into the kitchen and began cooking. Mrs. Bartkiewicz joined her. I turned on the television but kept the latest episode of *Full House* at low volume to listen to the two update each other on their days.

"I have my suspicions about Rudy."

"How so?"

"I think he's a flight risk. I never thought he was a good fit for the job, and I was right."

"You always are."

Laughter. "Marta. Don't patronize me."

"I'm not patronizing you, Vanessa. I'm agreeing with you."

"Taste this sauce. Does it taste bland to you?"

"Just a little."

"Damn it."

"It's just a little."

"I was trying to literally cook with Chan and I don't think I got it."

"You will."

"Maybe never. I hate cooking."

Their chit-chatter was so soft, so agreeable and peaceful, that I fell asleep. I woke up to the sensation of someone taking the remote control from my hands by gently lifting my fingers.

"Sorry. I didn't mean to wake you." Emma took the remote control and sat down on the armchair beside me to start switching the channels. Her legs were longer now and she seemed about a foot taller than the first time we crossed paths.

Mrs. Bartkiewicz called from the kitchen. "Emma. Can you and Alma please set the table? You can show her where we keep things."

Emma cautiously side-eyed me the way young people do, always put in situations where we are suddenly supposed to interact with one another with no explanation. "The cutlery is in the credenza right here," she said, pointing at my general surroundings. "I'll get the plates and the placemats in the kitchen."

"Cool."

I didn't know what a credenza was, so I opened doors on a closed shelf unit in the corner, then the drawers on a wooden cabinet, until I saw the cutlery divider. The anti-nausea medication clouded my mind, making the simple task difficult.

I overheard Vanessa sighing in frustration in the kitchen. "Shit. Even the rice is screwed up."

Mrs. Bartkiewicz tasted a grain off her wife's finger. "How much water did you add?"

"As much as the package said to add! Sorry. I didn't mean to shout. This is just so frustrating."

"Can I help?" I asked.

The two women stopped what they were doing and looked at me.

"Sure. Take over. I am making a real mess of it all."

I looked under their sink, thinking I would find the rice container where it was in my house. I only found the garbage can.

"Whatcha looking for, Alma?"

"Where do you keep your rice bin?"

She shamefully presented me with a small bag. "You mean this?"

"Um . . . sure." Using muscle memory alone, I scooped out a cup, put it into a new saucepan, added water to wash off the starch, then added more water until it went to the crease of my middle finger. I placed the saucepan on the stove and set it to boil. "There. We should have rice in ten minutes, if you can wait."

"Heck yes, we can wait," Vanessa said with a laugh. "Anything to have properly cooked rice. Sorry, Alma. I am no chef and neither is Marta. We're more of a takeout kind of family, but I'm trying to learn."

"I can teach you. It's easy."

When the rice was done, I drew a cross on the surface with the ladle and set it down on the table on top of a trivet.

"Look at that! We should have you over more often," Vanessa said, marvelling at the fluffy grains.

I spooned some of the so-called stir-fry onto my plate. It looked like stew and it smelled like . . . well . . . it didn't smell like stir-fried anything.

"How is it?" Vanessa asked hopefully.

"It's great," I said, faking a happy face.

On the television, the afternoon programming gave way to a preview of the evening news. Footage of your killer's mug shot played on the screen. Vanessa pointed. "Can you believe he lived just a stone's throw from here? Unbelievable."

Mrs. Bartkiewicz quickly got up and turned the television off.

"Oh. You don't want to watch the news?" Vanessa asked.

"It's . . ." Mrs. Bartkiewicz looked awkwardly at me, then her wife. "It's not a good idea right now."

"What's not a good idea?"

"I'll explain later, hon."

Vanessa let it be. Mrs. Bartkiewicz sat back down and continued eating.

Emma stared at me from across the table. "Are you the one who papered our house?"

"Emma!" Mrs. Bartkiewicz said, with food in her mouth.

"Are you?"

A moment of silence. I pushed a bit of fibrous beef to the inside of my cheek to answer. "Yes."

"Emma Dorota Mason. We don't confront people like that, thank you very much. Not that it's your business, but Alma and I have discussed it all, she has apologized, and I have forgiven her."

Emma raised her eyebrows and continued to eat.

"You're part of the AV club at school, yes?" Vanessa chimed in, breaking the awkward silence.

"Yes. I want to make films." A twinge of regret coursed through my body, thinking about Toby. How would I ever go there again, knowing he would be there?

"If you're up for it—certainly not as glamorous as making films—do you think you can get the VHS machine hooked up? Emma and I want to tape tonight's episode of *A Different World* because we'll be at dance class together."

"Sure."

After dinner, I was told I didn't have to do the dishes because I was helping with their tech problems. Even so, Emma was made to assist me in my task. Another one of those adult manoeuvres to get young people to interact and suddenly become friends. She sat next to me on their parquet floor, sulking.

The back of their television and VHS machine was full of dust bunnies. I carefully wiped all surfaces and handed the dirty tissues to Emma, who listlessly threw them onto the floor in a pile.

Hugging one knee, she said, "I'm not adopted, you know."

"I didn't think you were adopted."

"Some people think I am because of my two moms."

"Okaaaay."

"People think all sorts of things because of my moms."

"They're pretty cool, I guess. What do you call them?"

"I call one of them . . . you know, Vanessa . . . I call her Mama and I call my other mother Mom." She touched her hair and added, "And obviously, I'm biologically Vanessa's kid."

"That's cool." I looked at the wiring and began organizing my connector cables.

"We don't usually have people over because of the whole lesbian thing. People are such jerks. Once people find out, they don't want their kids hanging out with me. And even if they do, it has to be outside of my house. But I heard of you before. Mom talked about you."

I connected the line in and line out and the television screen turned blue.

Emma scowled at me. "You know . . . I had to wash wet toilet paper off our bushes."

I looked down. "I'm really sorry."

Her face changed in an instant, as if all was forgotten. "That's okay."

"Did you want to try the remote?"

She got up and pressed a few buttons on the remote control, and sure enough the VHS machine worked. "Yay, Alma!"

Emma found a tape to use and I programmed the machine to record the show in their absence. "There's an episode of *Blossom* on there, but you can tape over it. I already watched it."

"When will *A Different World* be on?"

"Nine."

I set the timer. "Done."

"Mama! Mom! Alma did it."

Vanessa stopped drying the dishes and looked at us through the pass-through window to the kitchen. "That's awesome! I knew you could do it. I appreciate that."

Mrs. Bartkiewicz added her face in the window and said, "Okay, you two. Vanessa and Emma have to get to dance class. Alma, I can take you home from here."

"Do we have to go?" Emma sulked again. "Alma just got here."

In the car, I taught Emma how to make a sharp slingshot by hooking one end of a rubber band on the tip of her pinky finger, wrapping it around the pad of her thumb, then aiming with her index finger. She tried it out, aiming at the back of Mrs. Bartkiewicz's seat.

"Hey! I can feel that. Please point it elsewhere," Mrs. Bartkiewicz said, adjusting the rear-view mirror to give us both a dirty look.

Emma pointed the slingshot at me and I shielded myself. "No! Not me! Spare me!" I laughed. The elastic band landed on my lap, and I aimed it back at her. She giggled.

"Okay, Alma. Here we are."

I looked up and saw that we had pulled into my driveway. I could see flashes of light from the television in the living room. A feeling of dread filled my chest. After everything that had happened, the last thing I needed was to be around my family.

"Thanks so much for everything, guys," I said before I shouldered my backpack and stepped out of the car.

"Are you kidding me? Thank you for making rice and hooking up our television. You're welcome any time," said Vanessa with a sincere smile.

Mrs. Bartkiewicz got out of the driver's seat and met me on the other side of the car. "Set your alarm for when you have to take your next dose of the pill just in case the anti-nausea pills put you to sleep again."

"That's a good idea."

"May I give you a hug?"

I nodded and she held me again. She smelled like laundry detergent.

"You call me if you need anything, all right? Promise?"

"I promise, Mrs. Bartkiewicz."

"Call me Marta. I'm not your teacher anymore."

As their car drove off, I saw Emma wave at me through the rear window.

Chapter 16

I wake up to the sound of Nira snoring. We lie on the bed, facing each other, with our foreheads touching. How many times have we assumed this position since we first lay down together back in university? Back then, we used my lumpy student special futon, when we were both small enough to fit on it, but the sentiment was the same. It confirmed things. It confirmed that there was an "us." Over the last twenty-two years, we have done this, falling asleep after making love, falling asleep after talking all night. And, yes, after quarrelling. Now we are on a very expensive mattress in our very expensive home. Older. Wiser.

It doesn't feel quite right to kiss her yet. My skin still feels kind of prickly and untouchable, but the sensation is subsiding and I'm glad for it. I choose to link pinky fingers with her instead and Nira gently opens her eyes.

"Morning, Shortcake." Her breath smells stale. Mine probably stinks too. "Wow. You slept with me for once. Was I snoring less?"

"No. I just slept deeper."

"That's good to hear." She looks down at our intertwined digits and asks, "How are you feeling? How would you rate our conflict from yesterday?"

Oh yes. This is also a thing we do. We score each other on how well our arguments play out. It's become a bit of a hilarious game to see who can be the better partner. One of those weird quirks we have as a couple since we did marriage counselling a decade ago. Our therapist liked to grade everything. How would you rate this response? How would you rate the challenge level? It became a bit of a running joke. I smile.

"A solid nine point five."

"Really?"

"Absolutely. There were some raised voices, but no belittling. Lots of creative solutions."

"Tons of creative solutions. We were dynamite, weren't we?" Nira sits up a bit and rests her head in her hand.

"It was like watching Olympic athletes."

We laugh. Her eyes get soft and tender. "I love you, Alma."

"I love you too, Nira."

"I'm really sorry."

"Thank you."

"I'll do better."

"Now you're just trying to get to a ten."

Nira sits cross-legged on the bed. "You know what'll make it a ten? If I get us some croissants from the bakery. My treat. You can lie here and rest while I grab us some pastries and coffee."

"I would love that." I feel my body come into myself and the urge to be touched returns to me. "Can I kiss you?"

Nira's eyes get misty. I think I may have scared her last night. "I would love it if you would."

We kiss. Not too deeply, though. I can still smell our breath.

As she heads to the bathroom, my phone rings. The sound of Britney Spears's first number one hit. Who the heck calls this early on a Sunday? I look at the call display and roll my eyes. "Shut your face."

"*You* shut *your* face." Emma laughs. I can hear baby Wyatt babbling in the background.

"Why are you calling me so early?"

"Damn it. I didn't even look at the clock. Sorry. Now that I'm a mother, I think everyone is up at four. You sound rough."

"Nira and I partied last night."

"At your age?"

"Um, excuse me, miss, I'm only a few years older. You just wait for the perimenopause and we'll see who's laughing."

The sound of Emma putting down her phone then picking it up again. "Sorry. I had to change sides. I was breastfeeding. Anyway . . . I wanted to call you because I was wondering if you guys can come by and help us renovate Mom and Mama's living room next week."

"No way! They're renovating? Finally?"

"I know, right? You have no idea how much it took to get Mom to agree to things."

"I have a bit of an idea. I've been telling Marta to do it for years. Especially with that flooring?"

Baby Wyatt gurgles and Emma whispers something inaudible to him before saying, "Thankfully, now that Mom is retired, I was able to convince her to make it a project. They didn't agree to do the entire house, but the living room is a start."

"I'm not super handy . . ."

"You don't have to be. This is just the demo. All you need are some muscles and a hammer."

"Sure! We're in."

Nira peeks her head out of the washroom, still brushing her teeth. "Is that Emma?"

Of course, being the besties they are, Emma then shouts into my ear, "Is that Nira? Put her on the phone."

I walk the phone to Nira and she wipes her mouth with a hand towel before taking it from me. While the two chat, I get myself together for the day.

"I know. I'm excited too . . . It was a long shot, that's why I was surprised . . . No, you're right. You're right. I'm the right person for the job. Yeah . . . They're announcing it next week. Anyway . . . I gotta go and get us some pastries . . . Uh-huh. We'll be there for sure . . . Wouldn't miss it. Okay . . . Oh wait. Put Wyatt on for me. Hello?" She sits up, all perky, and her voice is suddenly whiny and melodic. "This is your Auntie Nira. Are you getting big? Are you giving Mummy a hard time? Are you? . . . Was he smiling? He was? Ha! I can't wait to see him. Okay. Gotta go. Bye."

Nira hangs up and her face shifts in a second, giving me a sarcastic look. "Is Emma even ready for the shitstorm that is parenting?" We both chuckle. "She asked me if I think putting

Wyatt to sleep to classical music will help build his intelli-
gence. Like . . . what? Woman. You just need to keep that baby
alive. Can you do that?!" She laughs so hard she has to hit her
pillow. "Are we old enough now to say things like 'Back in my
day . . .'? or 'Parents these days!'" Nira throws her hands up in
mock annoyance.

"I think so. We've earned it. Even though I know parents who are more experienced may think otherwise." As the
words come out of my mouth, the image of my own mother
flashes through my mind and I wonder what she would think.

•••

I remember, on the day of my college graduation, seeing
my mom and Marta share space for the first time. It was
nerve-racking leading up to the convocation ceremony.

"Mom. Where are you?" I screamed into my flip phone. It
wasn't so much that I was angry as I had to shout over what
sounded like high winds on the other end. I paced the length
of the classroom made into a dressing room, with all the other
graduates putting on their shiny blue gowns. Mine was practically sticking to my damp arms underneath, so I waved the
fabric like a flag to ensure my dress pants and shirt wouldn't
be stained with sweat after this was over.

She replied, "We're just around the corner."

No, she wasn't. She was still on the highway with her
windows down because the air conditioner broke on her
Oldsmobile. I kept telling her to trade that car in for a new
one. I kept telling her to please, for the love of god, hit the

road as soon as possible just in case there was traffic on the DVP. I badgered her, reminded her, nagged her, and still she was going to be late. And with a last name like Alvarez, it didn't give her a lot of wiggle room before I would be handed my diploma. Shutting my phone, I forced myself to accept that my family would be late or miss it altogether.

Self-pity would have overtaken me had I not looked across the room and seen my new girlfriend, Nira. She peered at her reflection, pinning her cap to her slick chignon. Once she was satisfied with her appearance, she turned around, saw me admiring her and flashed me the most dazzling smile.

"Hello, Shortcake." Nira kissed me on the lips in front of everyone, and I melted. This was the first out relationship I had ever had. Not to say there weren't any other women. Once I'd experienced my first queer sex during frosh week, I hopped from one dirty residence bed to another, trying to make up for lost time. Most of my freshman year was spent doing the walk of shame, still in my clothes from the pub night before, smelling of bodily fluids. But those dalliances were always on the down-low and short-lived. Nira, on the other hand, referred to me as her partner when introducing me to others. I did the same, feeling for the first time what it was like to be proud of your own identity.

"You ready for this?" Nira was referring to the ceremony as much as to the celebratory lunch where I would introduce Nira to my family. It was a big step.

Although I was nervous about it all, I kissed her ear and whispered, "I've been ready since I met you."

Nira squeezed my hand one last time before filing herself alphabetically in line with all the other graduates in the *D* section. I did the same at the front with all the other *A* names. We were led into the theatre's mezzanine. The orchestra down below was completely full of loving family members, holding camcorders and cameras at the ready. That is, except for the three seats I had reserved for my family. Bright-red upholstery. I bit my lips, trying to pretend none of this mattered. Then I saw something move. To the side of the empty seats, I could see Marta and Vanessa waving at me and giving me a thumbs-up. My heart leapt, remembering they were attending too. I was like all the other graduates. I was someone to somebody. I had family.

It was almost my turn. "Tanya Allen," said a voice on a microphone down below. The woman in front of me stepped onto the stage and accepted her diploma. She paused for a moment, smiling at her father at the lip of the stage, taking pictures.

"Alma Alvarez." I stepped onto the stage and heard something from the back of the theatre.

"Yay, Almaaaaa!" Everyone turned and saw my sister cheering as she rushed down the aisle with Jess on her hip. Mom wasn't far behind, apologetically waving to me and everyone around her. Walking the length of the stage, I could see my family plow themselves to their seats. I could barely see through my tears as I shook hands with all these academics onstage in funny regalia. Who were these people? It didn't matter. My family, chosen and blood, was there. I accepted my diploma and raised my arms in victory. Leah's and my mom's cheers mixed with Vanessa's and Marta's.

After the ceremony, Marta handed me an envelope. "Here. Emma sends her love from Korea." I found a photo inside of Emma and her English students holding up a sign reading *CONGRATULATIONS!*

"I love this. Look at how happy these kids are."

Mom approached us, hugging her huge purse. "Hello."

"Mom, this is Marta. Marta. This is my mother, Luz."

There was a moment when the two women looked at each other that felt like forever. Then, for reasons I am still trying to understand, my mother reached out her hand and said, "Thank you."

There was so much that was left unsaid in that thank you. But now, with the perspective time has given me, I think I know what that thank you meant. I always wondered why Mom never protested about me staying over at Marta's most evenings and weekends until I left for university. Mom was rarely kind to me, and this letting go of her child to be loved well by someone else was the kindest thing she ever did.

"Thank me?" Marta clutched her chest, overwhelmed with emotion. "Thank you for bringing *your* wonderful daughter into this world." Marta was artful in how she emphasized the word *your* so that Mom would not feel threatened. "You must be so proud. All your hard work as a single mom, finally paying off."

Vanessa joined our cluster, along with Leah and Jess. She draped an arm over me and said, "I heard this hotshot filmmaker is treating us to lunch."

It was true. I had saved enough cash from my joe job at a photo printing centre to host everyone. The plan was to then introduce Nira to my family. Graduating and coming out seemed like a good way to spend a day.

Mom's smile was pained and she held her purse tighter. Marta was right: My mom did work hard, against all odds. She did the best she could with what she had. She hurt me. She provided for me. She did not like me, but she loved me. All these things are true.

• • •

Now, as one of Mateo's mothers, it's time for me to do my best. I decide that I will hand Mateo the letter.

Nira has already left for work by the time Mateo comes down from his room.

"Hey, Mama." Mateo goes behind me to the refrigerator and grabs the milk.

Just as I'm about to ask him how he is, I realize he has his wireless earphones in. The lack of wires always confuses me. There have been times I've had whole conversations with him, not knowing he didn't hear a single word I said. He sits at the counter and begins eating his cereal.

My eyes go between the canister containing Hong's envelope and Mateo filling his bowl with Cheerios. He positions his phone upright and watches something that makes him laugh. I have to do it. I have to do it now. "Mateo?" I wave to get his attention. "Mateo!" His eyes meet mine finally. "This is for you."

I reach into the canister, take out the envelope and put it on the counter in front of him. He takes one of his earphones out and says, "What is this?"

"Hong dropped it off."

I watch him rip the envelope open and furiously scan the letter. A necklace falls from its folds onto the counter.

"Dropped it off when?"

My cheeks flush. "I don't remember."

"When? Think! When?" he shouts at me, and I flinch.

"I dunno . . . a few days. A week."

"A week?!"

"Don't shout at me," I say weakly.

"I can't believe this. Now I know why she hasn't been talking to me, why she hasn't returned any of my texts!"

I hold my hands up, hoping he will calm down. "Hang on, Mateo. From what I heard from Hong, she's already made it very clear to you—"

It has the opposite effect. He stands and steps towards me. I find myself stepping back. "Wait . . . what?! You talked to her? She talked to *you*? About *us*?"

I backpedal. "Not really . . . She just explained to me that—"

"Fuck!" he says while pacing the kitchen. The face he's making is scaring me. His eyes are fixed and wide. He's pulling his hair. "FUCK!"

"Mateo? Mateo!" I clap my hands, trying to summon the boy I know from this pacing lion. "I want you to think about this, okay? What does this say, if Hong has to come to me to tell me what's happening? Do you think that maybe—"

He steps towards me. I cannot step back any farther, as the pantry doors are at my back. I cower. How the hell did we get here? To this place, our relationship, how?!

He says, seething, "I think it means you need to butt out of my business! Get out of my fucking life!" He turns and slams the counter with his hands, and I recoil. *Me and my stupid questions*, Mom used to say.

Mateo moves to exit and I grab hold of his shirt. "Stop! You can't do that to—"

He frees himself from my grasp and storms out the door. Shocked and out of breath, I quickly consider my options. I decide to not chase him. I will wait until he cools down. Maybe after I come back from work, when Nira is with me, we will talk sense into him. *Yes*, I tell myself as I hold my head, still in disbelief. *That's what we'll do. All will be well.*

I get ready for work, try to get ready, despite my racing heart. Is that how he reacted each time Hong tried to break up with him? No wonder she was scared. Guilt from not intervening sooner fills the cavity of my chest.

I'm getting out of the shower when I hear the phone ring. I rush to the phone, thinking it's Mateo. It's not. It's his school.

I pick it up. "Hello?"

"Hello, is this Mrs. Alvarez?" asks the school secretary.

"Yes, this is."

"I have Mateo here in the office. You need to come to the school. He has been detained by the principal."

•••

I rush to Mateo's school. I turn off the radio, which was com-
peting too much with the ringing in my ear. Not until I park
in the lot do I realize that I am not wearing a bra. I roll my
eyes. Fuck me. Obviously, I was much too busy worrying
about my son's downward spiral into delinquency and forgot
how to dress myself. I do the buttons up on my blazer, the
blazer I wore to look like a responsible parent, hoping it will
help keep my boobs up.

"Please have a seat." Principal Ramkissoon invites me into
his office. It is as beige and unremarkable as his suit. I see that
Mateo is already there, sitting in one of two chairs facing the
principal's desk. Sullen and silent, he cocoons his fists in the
bottom of his T-shirt and does not make eye contact with me
as I sit beside him. "Thank you for coming in, Mrs. Alvarez.
Will Mr. Alvarez be joining us?"

"No. My *wife* is at school herself. She's a teacher."

"I see."

"What's going on?" I ask Mateo. His pressed lips quiver
but do not answer.

Principal Ramkissoon leans in, arms on his desk as he
explains. "This morning, Mateo interrupted Mrs. Julius's
Ancient History class, playing a guitar and singing a song."

"What?" I scoff and turn to Mateo, whose eyes refuse to
leave his feet. "Why would you do that?"

"It was addressed to fellow student Hong Nguyen. It was
a song dedicated to her. At the end of it, he went down
on one knee and asked her to this year's formal. When she
refused his offer, Mateo then took his guitar and smashed

it on the wall." My cheeks get hot as Principal Ramkissoon continues with a bit of a chuckle. "I know this is a case of lovesick teens, but we—"

"What the hell made you do that, Mateo?" My son refuses to look at me. I turn in my chair and try to steal his gaze. "Look at me and answer me!"

"Let's all calm down."

I pick up my bag. "Okay. Let's go." I tip Mateo's chair forward, forcing him to stand.

"But, Mrs. Alvarez . . . I wanted to discuss Mateo's disrespect for school property. The guitar was not in fact his but the band—"

"The guitar? Really? You're concerned about the guitar?!"

"Yes. While the wall was not damaged, the guitar was—"

"Principal. I need to parent my son and teach him to respect his ex-girlfriend. I can't do that in the presence of someone who cares more about school property than the safety of women."

"What are you—"

"Thank you, Principal Ramkissoon. Goodbye," I say, storming out of the office with my arm linked in Mateo's.

We walk past the receptionist into the hallway before Mateo disengages his arm from mine. "Let go of me!" His voice echoes off the endless rows of multicoloured lockers.

"What the fuck were you thinking?"

"She . . . she loves it when I sing songs to her." His voice cracks.

"Loved. *Loved.* Past tense. She is no longer your girlfriend.

Now let's go home." I exit the school and squint against the sunshine outside.

Mateo follows me outside in tears. He is no longer the monster I saw this morning. He whimpers like a small child. "Mama. She loves me. I know she loves me."

I hold his wet face in my hands and look directly into his eyes. "Mateo. This is not romantic. What you did embarrassed her. No—you scared her. You humiliated her and then you scared her."

"Humiliated?"

"Yes, Mateo. She has already broken up with you. She has ended things. It's done. And you did this . . . this thing . . . for what? What would it prove?"

"That I would fight for her. I would."

I remember what Nira said. Five times. How many times have we told that story and he has listened? How has this story, his story of creation, shaped his relationships? This is on us. We did this. We allowed him to be this way.

I step back. "There is no fighting it, Mateo. It's done. This isn't some movie where you can . . . I dunno . . . stand outside her window and scream her name or . . . chase after her before she gets on a plane. Movies might make them out to be romantic gestures, but this . . . singing and then smashing a guitar when you are told no, this is just fucking creepy." Mateo collapses on a parking barrier and sobs. In a gentler tone I add, "You can make a choice. Do you want to gather the little dignity you have and move on with your life? Or do you want to be a creep?"

"I need to make this right. I should apologize to Hong."

"No. No. You're not going to do that."

"Why not? I screwed up and I should tell her—"

"No. You will not speak to her. Got it? You will not interact with her. Like . . . at all. You've done enough."

He begins sobbing again. "But why? I can't . . . I can't live without her, Mama. Please. Please let me talk to her and make things right. I love her. I love her."

I pace a bit while he cries. I think of all the other times when I have bent for him, all the times I wilted to his wants. The satisfaction I once felt for making him happy, for appeasing him. But after the last while, after thinking of you, after thinking of your killer, and the killer of my innocence, I know that this is the moment when I can end this cycle. This is the moment when I become a parent.

I kneel down in front of him. "Look at me right now," I say in the firmest voice I can muster. It's a voice I do not recognize. Where does this voice come from? My feet? All I know is that it is low and final. "Too fucking bad."

Mateo's crying stops and he looks back at me. Perhaps he doesn't recognize my voice either.

"Hong broke up with you? Too fucking bad. It's done. You respect her wishes. When she said no, you believe her. She doesn't have to fight for her freedom. She said no. No means no. Too fucking bad. Now get in the goddamn car. I am driving you home."

Chapter 17

Mrs. Bartkiewicz—I mean Marta—greets us from the front porch. It always feels weird calling her Marta, even after all these years. These decades. What I really want to call her is Mom, but she refused the term a long time ago, telling me I already had a mother who was not perfect but deserved my respect. It hurt back then to hear it, but as always, Marta was right.

"How was the drive? I heard on the radio there was some kind of collision on the Danforth." This is what she does now that she's retired, listens to the radio while puttering about in her garden.

"It was fine. I think we got the tail end of it," explains Nira as she gets out of the car and stretches her legs.

Mateo gets out of the back seat, gives Marta a rushed kiss on the cheek and sulks his way into the house with his arms full of snacks we bought for the day. "What was that about? Why is he so grim?"

Nira sighs and gives Marta a hug. "Well . . . Alma has been

giving him some much-needed tough love and he's not happy about it. And he's especially upset that his two mothers are a team." Nira looks at me and nods, like *We got this*. I stand a little taller. We do. We got this.

"Oh, teenage stuff. I don't know anything about that," Marta says sarcastically. "Alma was a perfect little teen."

I roll my eyes. "Yes, yes. I know I was a handful, but not this much of a handful."

Nira and Marta enter the house, arm in arm. "All right, now. I want to hear all about these renovations."

"Gosh. I hardly understand the blueprints. It was all Emma's idea. Not mine."

Emma and Vanessa are in the kitchen, and as soon as they see us, they squeal.

"You're finally here!" says Emma as she unclips the baby carrier and hands Wyatt to me. "Please take him while I size this tool belt for Mama."

Wyatt is such a small package, with limbs still curled up like they were in the womb. He is that brand spanking new.

"Tool belt? Why do you need a tool belt, Vanessa?"

Vanessa adjusts the hard hat on her head to answer me. "You know me. I want to do this demolition in style!"

Nira cheers and kisses Vanessa on the cheek. "Yes! I love it. Do I get a tool belt too?"

Wyatt begins to fuss, so I start doing the two-step, side to side. "Okay, before we think of fashion, can we please talk about the plans for the renovation? What exactly are we doing today?"

Emma successfully adjusts the tool belt on Vanessa and shows me the "blueprints." Only they are not blueprints. It is a hastily drawn sketch on a scrap piece of boxboard. "Wait . . . what is this?"

"This is what we're doing."

"Did you actually measure things?"

Emma holds back a laugh. "Sorta."

"You can't just sorta measure things, Emma."

"We're not building a pyramid, Alma. We're just making things prettier." She points to various parts of the sketch done in indelible marker. "You know. Remove a wall here for sight-lines. Flooring. That's all. I watched enough HGTV. We can do this."

"Does this make you the foreman?" I say while making a face.

Frustrated with me, she says, "Give me back my son." She takes the wee baby and straps him back into the carrier. "Okay, everyone. It's time to choose your weapon. I'm gonna take the crowbar and focus on removing the parquet flooring. Alma and Nira? Can you focus on the wall between the kitchen and living room?"

"Like . . . take it down?" asks Nira.

"To the studs."

"All right. Sledgehammer it is," I say as I grab the tool from the floor. It's heavier than I thought it would be, but I pretend I can handle it.

"And Mateo. Where is he? MATEOOOOO!"

My son emerges from the washroom, still sulking. "Yes, Auntie Emma?"

"Take the hammer and focus on getting this built-in shelf removed. This will be where the bifolding doors are!"

We all ooooh and ahhhh Emma's plan.

"Did you hear that, Alma? Bifold doors!" says Nira to me, but I don't make eye contact so as not to commit to yet another project in our own home.

Emma continues, and taking charge really suits her. "Mama and Mom? Can I ask you to gather all the stuff that falls on the floor and put it outside in the bin? There's a wheelbarrow for you right here."

"Absolutely!" Vanessa says, all decked out in her tool belt and hard hat. She looks so darn cute. Although age hasn't truly hit her face, I see a gentle widening of her hips and a slowness in her gait. Marta, on the other hand, has aged exponentially since her stroke.

"Marta? You okay?" I ask, and suddenly everyone looks her way.

"I don't know why I'm getting so wistful about this. I just . . . I really do love it when everyone visits. But . . . I guess change is hard. That's all."

I drape my arm around Marta and realize that she is much shorter than me now and maybe a bit skinnier than the last time I saw her. "How about this? How about you write something on the wall before Nira and I demolish it?"

"Oh. Okay. I can do that." Marta looks around for something to write with.

"Wait! Look!" Vanessa reaches into her tool belt and pulls out one of those flat carpenter pencils. "See? I knew wearing this tool belt was a good idea." We all laugh. All of us except Marta.

Ceremoniously, Marta begins writing on the wall. *Thank you, dear home, for taking care of us. Now we are taking care of you.* Marta looks at Vanessa. "Anything else it should say, hon?"

Vanessa takes the pencil and traces her hand on the wall. We all follow suit with our own hands, and for baby Wyatt we trace his little foot.

"Mateo. Can you help us take one of those selfie things?" asks Vanessa.

Mateo places his cellphone on one of the soon-to-be-demolished shelves and puts a timer on the camera. We pose in front of the writing and tracings on the wall. Even Mateo poses.

"Okay. Are we ready?" I say with my sledgehammer over my shoulder.

"YES!" everyone answers back.

I swing the sledgehammer and it stabs a hole in the dry-wall. Cheers. We get to work. As Nira and I continue to take down the wall, I think of all the times we sat down for dinner together. It was here where we first heard that your killer was finally sentenced.

On that day, Emma and I were busy trying to figure out how to ride her new skateboard when Vanessa called us in.

"Emma! Alma! Come quick!" We ran into the house, past the wall dividing the kitchen from the living room. "Don't bother taking off your shoes. Just come!"

Emma and I still had our knee pads and sneakers on as we took our places, standing beside Vanessa. "What is it?"

"Ssshhh. Watch." Vanessa used the remote control to turn up the volume on the television.

On the screen was a reporter for the CBC who tried her best to keep her strawberry-blond hair from blowing into her face by tucking it behind her ears. Speaking into a large microphone, she addressed the camera. "Finally, after four agonizing months of reviewing painful testimony and gruesome video footage, the jury deliberated for a mere eight hours before declaring him guilty on all nine counts ..."

I looked at Vanessa, who framed her slack jaw with her hands. "Can you imagine what this reporter must have witnessed? The jury. The judge. Everyone. They all had to watch those videos. God."

The reporter's voice began to crack as she continued. "He has been sentenced to life in prison with no parole ..." She swallowed hard, fighting back tears. "Please forgive me. This has been a long journey for all of us ... especially the surviving family members of the victims."

Vanessa turned to us and opened her arms. Emma and I wrapped ourselves around her torso and we held each other tightly while Vanessa's body heaved and twitched in her silent cries. "All this time ... all this time I've been praying for this man to spare my family. How are we the lucky ones? God. Thank you for keeping my girls safe."

This is where that happened. Right here where I am standing and swinging this sledgehammer, to remove a wall, to let the light in. And right where Emma is chipping away at the floor is where Marta sat in her recliner chair and read us the newspaper article that announced that your boyfriend had been exonerated for your murder. Further evidence revealed that, despite your body never having been found, you were most likely yet another of the Scarborough Stalker's victims.

At that time, I was too busy feeding newborn Mateo to pay much attention. The news felt like an answer and a question, satisfying and dissatisfying all at once. No matter what mystery was solved, for your family your absence remained a wound that would never heal. No. I'm wrong about that. Why would I think such a thing? Of course there will be healing. I don't want to rob your family of that. I don't want to rob myself of that either. Haven't I healed? Sure, I get triggered every now and then, but am I broken? No. Hell no. That's what being a survivor means. I've survived. As much as Toby dismissed the boundaries of my body, this body has done some amazing things.

My body has rocked baby Mateo to sleep for a total of seven hours straight.

My body has marched at thirty-one Prides.

My body has tried rock climbing.

Ballroom dancing.

Yoga.

Hot yoga.

My body has made love out of choice.

Had one-night stands out of choice.

Masturbated.

Run through summer rain.

Walked through quiet snowfall.

Accepted awards.

Danced at weddings.

Danced at my own wedding.

Eaten pasta in Italy.

Eaten dumplings in Hong Kong.

Eaten kingfish in India.

Gotten lost in Guatemala.

Gotten found in Thailand.

Graduated.

Mourned my father's death.

Watched my mother lose her memory.

Taught English in Korea.

My body caught strange bugs.

My body expelled said strange bugs in horrifying ways.

It failed three driving tests.

It passed one.

Won every game of bowling.

Lost every game of air hockey.

Built Nira shelves from scratch.

Baked Nira and Mateo birthday cakes from scratch.

Learned to ride motorcycles.

Failed to use Rollerblades.

Paid off my student loan.

Paid off my wife's student loan.

Learned to dive into the water without plugging my nose.

My body did all these things. My body did all these things because it's my body and I can do whatever the fuck I want to do with it.

"There. I'm done. Can I eat now?" says Mateo while removing his dust mask.

I survey his progress. The entire ugly built-in shelving unit has been removed, and its parts lie at his feet in shards. He got it done so quickly. Damn youth and their energy. I can see from his face that he's proud of himself, even though he is still grumpy with me. I don't care how angry he is. That difficult conversation won't be the last we will have. It will be repeated again and again with both of his mothers. As Nira said, we are a team.

"Great job, Mateo. Come help me with this final section here." We get to work, side by side, removing the drywall then knocking the studs out. Once we are done, our entire family, our beautiful, clumsy, imperfect, makeshift, chosen family stands back and beholds this new room, starting from scratch.

"Whoa. Will you look at that!" Emma, who still wears baby Wyatt in her carrier, walks back and forth through where the wall once stood, as if defying physics.

Nira slides her safety glasses onto the top of her head and puts her hands on her hips. "Emma, I am so glad you suggested this for Mom and Mama. The light! It streams right through from the kitchen to the living room."

"This is going to be life-changing for our get-togethers," I add, slightly out of breath from all this sledgehammer swinging.

"We're actually going to get together in this space now," says Mateo. Is he smiling? Maybe he is.

Vanessa removes her hard hat and walks the space. "Do you think I can still have my kitchen island here?"

"Of course, Mama," says Emma.

"And will I still get my wine fridge? And bar? You know I can't cook, but I sure can mix a drink."

Emma laughs hard enough that Wyatt stirs from his sleep. "Ha! Of course, Mama. That too."

Vanessa goes behind Marta and wraps her arms around her waist. "Well, hon? What do you think?"

Marta's eyes are misty. Her eyes aren't moving about the room but to all the memories that are stored in its four corners. I worry that this may have been too much too soon. As Marta has gotten older, she has been less adventurous, and delights in the quiet simplicity of life.

She surprises us all. "I love it. This place is going to be fabulous," Marta finally says. "I don't know why we didn't do it sooner."

Epilogue

I ask your mother to please spell her name for me. I know how her name is spelled, of course. We just need to get her sound levels.

"P-A-U-L-A. Last name is R-U-I-Z."

"Good?" I say to Marvin, my sound recorder. He gives me a thumbs-up. Marvin begrudgingly accepted me using a VHS camcorder for this project so that I could reclaim the narrative of my youth by using technology of that era, but he refused to let me use outdated sound equipment. He told me he wouldn't work for me or come to my premiere if I disagreed.

Your mother presses her lips together as she watches the crew in action, putting the lights in the right place. I can tell she's nervous.

"While we're waiting, is there anything I can get you? Water? Or . . ."

"No, no. I'm fine." She anxiously runs the edge of her thumbnail on the palm of the opposite hand. Just above the beige armchair she is sitting on is your high school graduation picture. I realize I have never seen it before. It's not the same photo the police shared with the media. This one is one of those graduation pics you get in a package. Usually they're super cheesy, but you look simply stunning in it and it's no surprise your mom put this one closest to her favourite chair so she can admire this version of you for the rest of her days. You wear your cap and you hold your diploma in a way that allows you to show off your French manicure. In front of this blue backdrop, your focus is to the right of the frame, as if you see the future ahead of you. So much to look forward to.

When we begin, my first question to your mother is, "Can you tell me why you decided to speak with me for this film?"

A sharp inhale. "I am doing this now because I want to believe that I can count on you, Alma." Her directness catches me off guard. "You had come to me and told me that you wanted to do this film because Vickie deserved it. And I agreed. She did. But I want to remind you what you promised me. That this would be about her life. Not her death." I watch her point at me, driving the message home.

She's right. I had reached out to her through Tita Lorna and met her over coffee to discuss. It took some convincing, but since that conversation, your mother has been the film's greatest ally, having volunteered to write letters of support to funding juries. She even made the suggestion that it not be just about you but about the many others affected. We have since secured two other interviews with victim family members. So here I am sitting across from your mother, on day one of shooting our documentary. It's a documentary I believe in. I haven't believed in my work in a long time. But this is different.

"Tell me about Victoria. What kind of person was she?" I ask.

Your mother is still enough that I wonder if she has become a statue. Did I start off on the wrong foot? Maybe I should ask another question? Just as I am about to rephrase, your mother begins to speak, sparkles in her eyes.

"Vickie laughed a lot. She would laugh and laugh, and sometimes, when she didn't have enough air, she would snort. Like a pig! It made us all laugh too. At first I kept saying, 'Will you stop that? People will think you're weird or something.' But I realized . . . that's just how much laughter was inside of her.

"I told myself, don't forget her laugh! Don't do it. I was so scared it would leave me one day. Every year around the time of her birthday, I would play home movies just to hear that laugh. It wasn't a cute laugh, ha? It was like . . . you know. A witch's cackle? Like that.

"I think that's what made her so popular. She was always able to see the positive in everything. Even when she was a kid at summer camp. I told my husband not to send her to summer camp. We never did that when we were growing up in the Philippines, why do that to our kids? But he insisted. That's what Canadian parents do, so we did the same. Anyway . . . she was at summer camp and got a bad bee sting on her arm. When we went to see her . . . you know those camps, they have parent visit days when we see them halfway through the summer . . . she showed me the bite and was like, 'Look, Mom! I got big muscles now.' Ha! Can you imagine? She gets a bee sting and then she's going around to everyone showing it off. Who does that? She was so special.

"I remember when her little brother, Miko, was born, she was very, very sad. You know . . . she was the only child for a long time. Three years. Then boom. No more. She didn't even want to look at him. We kept trying to tell her, 'See, anak? Little Miko loves his Ate Vicks. Don't you love him?' and she wouldn't even look at him. Then, finally, someone from church told me this worked for her, because her son was also jealous of his sibling. She told me to put Miko in Vickie's arms. I thought that was dangerous. How do you have a toddler hold a baby? But my husband and I . . . we put the pillows all around her. We didn't tell her why we were putting pillows all around her. On her lap. Under her elbow. If we told her what our plan was, she would have run away, okay? So then . . . I took little Miko and put him on her lap. And her face just . . . like this . . . it lit up. I wish I had a camera. Because . . . you know . . . it's not like now when everyone has a smartphone with a camera. All of a sudden she was happy. All smiles. Then we couldn't get her away from her brother. In fact, I remember there was about a week when she insisted she was the mother of Miko.

"Seriously. I am not joking, ha? One of the things she loved most in the world was her brother, Miko. Even when Miko was older, she would attend every soccer practice, cheer him on. Sure, they would fight. But afterwards, of course, by and by, there they were in the back of our van. You know those Grand Caravans? We had one of those. Red. And the kids would be back there singing songs together.

"The other thing she loved was painting. She loved painting. Watercolour specifically. She tried oil in high school but almost vomited from the fumes, so she switched to watercolour. Suddenly her entire room was plastered with these beautiful paintings of different things. Like the Rouge Beach. The Bluffs. She enjoyed landscapes the most. Not portraits. Her favourite thing to paint was clouds. She showed me once. It was like magic. You think of the paper as the colour white. And you paint the sky in to create the edges of the clouds. I was surprised. I thought the white in clouds was made with white paint, but she explained that in watercolour, it's the reverse. You have to plan ahead, and even then you can't predict what will happen when the water evaporates.

"I will never forget my daughter and the way she would watch and wait for the water to dry. Each brush stroke was like a science experiment."

Your mother continues. She seems delighted to be able to talk about you for as long as she wants, with everyone in the crew listening with our full bodies, trying not to weep. I feel you near me, beside me, listening too.

Acknowledgements

Maraming salamat to everyone who made this book possible.

Much love and appreciation to Marilyn Biderman and Samantha Haywood for their determination.

To the many professionals who helped me make sense of this all, especially Rebecca and Erin. Thanks to you both, we are all slowly finding each other and learning to heal.

Thank you, Majda Drinnan, for your guidance into the world of film editing. You are a cool cat!

Thank you to my colleagues Jenny Heijun Wills and Alicia Elliott for your insights.

Thank you to Farrah Khan for working so hard at dismantling rape culture and sharing your thoughts about my manuscript.

Thank you to Nikola Steer and Kesta Graham for making much-needed connections.

To Jennifer Mothereffin Lambert: I'm so happy to have had three book babies with you. Thank you for your patient hand.

ACKNOWLEDGEMENTS

As always I have to thank my husband, Nazbah Tom, for being there to hold me when things got tough and to encourage me when I was brave enough to type.

Thank you to my ancestors for whispering into my ear. I am still listening.

To those lost and found: You were there at every moment. Thank you for writing and painting with me. I hope I did you proud.